IN REVERSE ORDER

BOBBY DAVISON

Acknowledgements:

A special thank you to Indi Butterworth for the excellent book cover design.

There were nine designs in total and between us we narrowed it down to the one used.

A clever design that depicts the title "In reverse order" shining onto the river Thames at night.

Indi is an art student based in Norwich, Norfolk and I look forward to working with her again on my future novels.

***

A special thank you to my wife Helen for all your help with the book.

Helen is my biggest critic, editor, proof reader, researcher and gave me a crash course in cockney slang, she is also the best wife a man could ever wish for.

To:

My wife Helen

Without you and your support none of this would have been possible

PROLOGUE:

2013

DI Pat McVeigh knew something had happened; he just couldn't quite remember what.

What he did know was that he kept drifting in and out of sleep, each time waking to the same scenario as if it was a never-ending cycle.

McVeigh was standing in a long brightly lit corridor. The walls were as white as white could be, like the brightness given off by fresh driven snow, the fluorescent lights were so bright it hurt his eyes, it was like looking into the sun itself.

At the far end of the corridor, which in his mind stretched for miles, the light that shone there was the brightest of all. It reminded him of a beacon of a light house that was off the coast of Wexford where he grew up as a child. Those happy, cherished days of his childhood, playing on the beach with friends, days that never seemed to end.

On each side of the corridor were many doors but none appeared to have handles.

Although he could not remember what had happened, he knew that it had to have been extremely bad. Why else would he be dressed in a hospital gown, pulled tight across his chest, ribbons flowing down the back and every inch of his body in agony at the slightest movement he made making him grimace with unbelievable pain.

McVeigh gradually inched along the channel towards the end of the corridor where the brightest light shone, but however far he thought he had got the light at the end didn't appear to be getting any closer as he stepped slowly forward with trepidation.

And then, every so often he heard that voice, the one he had been hearing on and off for what seemed an eternity. The voice was a West Indian or Jamaican accent and reminded McVeigh of a character in East-Enders, not that he watched it but Emily and the boys did and he had caught snippets. It was a deep and rasping voice but always with a hint of humour there.

"Yes sir, Mr McVeigh, you are going to get better soon and when you do old Winston here, he is going to be taking you to his Jamaican club in Hackney and we going to drink the place dry before we go home at five in the morning on the back of a milk float, where my wife will make us the biggest and best English breakfast in London, you see if we don't".

And then silence fell again, McVeigh was back in the brightly lit corridor and was still making no headway in conquering the thing that he now thought was harder than the top of Everest to reach. Then it all went dark again, blacker than black.

Again, in what seemed only a few minutes, but in reality, was days, McVeigh was back in the brightly lit corridor but still as far from reaching the lighthouse beacon as before.

And so, it went on time after time, switching between the corridor and complete darkness and still McVeigh could not remember what had happened, there was no recollection whatsoever, the only thing he could be sure of was that every part of his body was as unbearably painful as before.

He didn't know if it was an hallucination, but one time in the corridor he could see Emily and his twin boys, Jason and James, at the far end. He forced every last inch of his six foot two, fifteen stone body to stagger towards them, bumping off the walls each side of the corridor, ricocheting like a pin ball, calling their names and ignoring the excruciating pain as he tried to reach them. Then as quick as they had appeared, they were gone again and the darkness came once more, that blackness like no other, a coalmine, the bottom of a well, could this be hell itself?

McVeigh thought that he was dreaming, or was it real? Was his mind playing tricks on him? It was hard to comprehend what was real or not it was all so explicit.

Emily and the boys were playing in the sea whilst he sat on a sun lounger on the beach reading, another brilliant book by his favourite author, luxuriating in the peaceful surroundings on another glorious sun filled day. He looked up and all three were splashing about and having fun, he waved, all three smiling and laughing, waved back. He knew exactly where he was now, Coral Bay, Cyprus. They loved coming here for holidays.

The twins were now almost five years old, Jason the eldest by five minutes. Robert his eldest from his first marriage was thirteen and being a usual teenager, laying on a sun lounger beside him, his eyes glued to his phone, catching up on social media antics that teens seemed to do these days, barely a word or grunt coming from him.

They had been renting the same villa every year for six years now, the first year just Emily, Robert and himself but every year since all five of them. The villa was a short drive inland in a traditional Cypriot village called Tala, high in the hills with fabulous views.

It was everything you could wish for, the boys had their own bedrooms, there was a glorious sun filled patio terrace that they enjoyed a glass or two of wine on once the boys had disappeared to their devices.

If they were at the villa for the day, the boys would be well entertained with the lovely tiled pool and lunch would be enjoyed, fresh bread, cheeses, meats, olives etc for lunch. The villa was set high on a hill with the glorious vista of the sea beyond, you could clearly see the ship wreck that still sat a little out to sea just off the coast of Chloraka as it had done since March 1998. The tales that ship wreck could tell…

It seemed to McVeigh that when he was on holiday in Cyprus with his family it was the only two weeks of the year that he was completely happy and able to switch off from the outside world, the crimes, murders, horrendous scenes and people that he faced on a daily basis as a DI in the Metropolitan Police Force.

Then the reality or illusion stopped and McVeigh was awake, wide awake.

Emily, Jason and James stood at the end of his bed smiling. Despite his pain he could squint slightly and see Emily looking gorgeous as always in a white cotton summer dress delicately spotted with daisies and the boys dressed immaculately, white shirts and beige trousers and polished black shoes.

Emily always made sure that the boys were smartly dressed from the moment they were born. He briefly wondered why Robert wasn't there. The boy always seemed to have something to do as was the want of most teenager's, he guessed.

McVeigh tried to raise himself up off the hospital bed but the pain he felt with even the slightest movement, along with the tubes that appeared to be sticking in every crevice of his body hindered him and he slumped back down, exhausted, he felt that he had just run a marathon not just trying to raise his body up a few feet. The machines gently beeping rhythmically behind him. He tried to speak but no words came out. The effort of trying to raise himself had taken it out of him. He closed his eyes only for a second but when he opened them again Emily and the boys had gone.

Was this another dream? Had he imagined it? Then the door opened and a nurse came in. The nurse was male, a little stocky, short and black. His big smiling face stared down at McVeigh and then he rang the alarm bell beside the bed. "You are awake Mr McVeigh; praise the Lord I never thought this day would come. I have been praying for you every night. Allow me to introduce myself, I am Winston and I have been one of the nurses looking after you almost every day for the best part of ten months. Welcome back Mr McVeigh". McVeigh recognised the voice that reminded him of the EastEnders character then Winston offered one of his gleaming white toothed smiles.

McVeigh tried to speak and thankfully words did come out. "Where did Emily and the boys go? Where is Robert?" As he spoke the words barely a whisper, a husky whisper at that, thanks to the tube in his mouth that went deep down his throat so perhaps the auxiliary nurse called Winston hadn't heard him, either way he didn't offer a response.

CHAPTER ONE:

2013

Frank "Goose" Gosling pulled up outside the derelict warehouse in his 2013 sleek black Range Rover with its own personal number plate GOOSE 1.

He looked up at the ram-shackled building with its broken windows and graffiti strewn, broken bricked walls.

The Thames River lapped gently against the river bank a few feet away, its putrid smell overpowering to the nostril and debris bobbing uninvitingly.

His oldest, dearest and whom he thought was his most honest friend and the only person in the world that Goose fully trusted emerged from the warehouse and made his way over to him, Goose who had by now stepped from the gleaming car and leaning against the door had lit up one of his forty a day cigarettes'.

Joe Whyte approached his friend and respected boss.

The two had been friends for almost fifty years since meeting in Borstal as cell mates. Joe was in for manslaughter, Goose for GBH (grievous bodily harm), but unbeknown to the judge and jury he had also killed his father and Joe was in for murdering his despicable nonce of a brother.

As he approached the Range Rover, Joe couldn't help but notice how much Goose had aged over the last twelve hours, he looked every one of his sixty-five years and then some. Had it really only been twelve hours since they had last seen each other?

Goose drew deeply on his cigarette, he nodded towards the derelict building, "What the fuck made me invest in such a shit hole as this Joe?" Joe smiled broadly. He wasn't the most handsome of men and over the years he had been called "Bugger lugs", "Toby Jug" and more recently "Shrek" but surprisingly none of these to his face but his smile was his best feature and it could light up a room, partly due to the best dentistry London and sixty grand had to offer. "Money and the promise of the Olympics on prime building land?"

The two men looked across the stinking Thames and saw the Olympic stadium built for the London 2012 games far off in the distance. Goose drew deeply one last time on the cigarette and stamped the butt into the ground, "Yeh I got mugged off on that one too mate"

Joe laughed, "Yes but at least the councillor who promised you the world and gave you fuck all is now firmly part of the foundations of such a monumental building." Both men laughed, their problems momentarily forgotten.

Lighting another cigarette Goose nodded knowingly towards the warehouse, "They in there?" Joe lit one of his own cigarettes, despite the two men's closeness for years they didn't have the same taste in drink, cigarettes or certain woman. "Yep, they're there still not saying nothing, apart from the nephew, keeps ranting that he is telling the truth, poor fuckers pissed himself at least three times and fucking stinks like the Mithi river". "And him, the copper?" Goose asked, anger in his voice.

Joe looked at his best friend seeing and knowing the hurt, anger and aggravation this had caused etched into every line of his face. "It is true then Goose mate, it has been confirmed?"

Goose slammed his fist down on to the roof of the car, causing a huge dent, he'd have to deal with that later no doubt at the cost of an arm and a leg, "How the fuck will I ever live this down Joe? I am allegedly one of London's biggest known gangsters, people are afraid of me, petrified even and would suck my toes if I insisted on it and yet I allow a fucking undercover copper to breach my inner sanctum, our inner sanctum".

Joe was in two minds as to how he should best respond, but he and Goose had remained friends all these years purely because Goose always respected Joe's honesty. Joe could say things to him that if it had been anyone else would have been knee capped, beaten to a pulp or shot dead. Joe laughed "I told you so, does that help?" Goose grimaced thinking how on earth someone had had him over, a rare if unique situation.

From the day that Raymond Johnson had been allowed into the gang Joe had lost count of the times he had had conversations with Goose regarding the trustworthiness of Ray, Joe didn't like him from the outset, there was something about him that Joe could not quite put his finger on but there was something there that was untoward, that's for sure.

Goose slowly opened the door to the Range Rover and leaning across to the passenger seat, retrieved a manilla envelope, he handed it to his friend. "It's all in there, proof that the cunts a copper, but get this Joe, guess who he is working for?" and without waiting for an answer "McVeigh, fucking Pat McVeigh that's who!" Goose spat on the ground, as if he had swallowed poison not just because uttering the name McVeigh left bile in his throat, just the thought of him made him sick to his stomach, and that was not an everyday occurrence as far as Goose was concerned.

Joe took the envelope and opened it in silence. There were half a dozen pages of neatly typed information including plenty of evidential photos.

After a while Joe placed everything back in the envelope and slowly taking out his lighter from his jacket pocket, he set fire to it and threw it to the ground in disgust. Both men watched as it burnt, in silence.

It was Joe that eventually broke the silence. "Techno sure knows his stuff, don't he?"

Techno, real name Benjamin Walker-Brown, was a computer Wizz kid. There was not a server, email or telephone made that he couldn't hack in to and that he did in an extremely timely manner. Goose and other London gang Lords used him on a regular basis to get vital information and evidence. As a free-lance he was loyal to anyone who paid the money and the right amount to boot. But he would never play one gang off against the other and refused to divulge any information one gang leader wanted on another, for this reason, not only was he respected by some of the biggest criminals that London had to offer, his services were in high demand and did he know it when he made the demands for his payment, always paid into an offshore bank account that was growing very nicely, thank you.

Unbeknown to the other gang bosses though, Goose paid Techno a premium for his services so occasionally when he asked for it, Goose got inside information on rival gang members. In reality although he was freelance, when Goose said jump, Techno would ask, how high and for how much. It was no surprise therefore that when Goose was hammering on his door at two-thirty that morning Techno answered. He knew this was going to be a nice fat pay cheque by the hour and ferocity of the knock.

His latest pull, an eighteen-year-old flat chested northern girl called Lauren, a pretty little thing who had tits like fried eggs but nipples like coat hooks and who Techno had named Dyson for obvious reasons, was quite put out when she was hauled out of bed by Techno and virtually thrown out the door half-dressed and with forty quid to get a taxi home and the promise that he would call her, which he had no intention of doing. She was just another in a long line of conquests, girls, boys, girl with boy it didn't matter to him, whatever took his fancy at the time. She didn't question what was happening, just hoped he'd call her again.

The son of a father who was a successful barrister, and whose mother used to be a model before becoming a successful fashion designer, Techno had the up bringing that most children could only dream about. Private education, the best holidays all over the world, he could barely think of a country he had not visited with no expense spared, a monthly allowance the size of a small countries bank balance but then it all changed and he became the black sheep of the family overnight.

When Techno's mother died tragically and suddenly through a burst aneurysm on the brain in the prime of her life and his father took up with a whore half his age six months later, that was when all the problems started and the relationship with his father went downhill rapidly. How could anyone replace the mother that he had loved and in no time at all it seemed.

He was a Cambridge University drop out, without warning walking off campus one day without a by your leave when he realised that there was more money to be made hacking in to the computers of banks, businesses, foreign Governments and even once the Pentagon, just because he could. He had been studying Computer Sciences and was an A grade student, his professors had extremely high hopes for him in the elite business world, he was sure to get a first.

He once netted a quarter of a million pounds for an hour's work from the customers of a well-known high-street bank just by rounding down people's accounts to the nearest pound. Fleecing every customer for between one penny to ninety-nine pence and transferring the money into an off shore account in the name of a bogus charity. No doubt a few of the customers would check with the bank when they received their statements questioning the donation to a charity that they had never even heard of and certainly had no recollection of making, by which time it was too late. He certainly had his head screwed on when it came to making the bucks.

Along with the inheritance from his grandfather, which had sat in Trust growing nicely until last year, then following the sudden death of his mother, the money they had left him was enough to buy a penthouse apartment overlooking Tower Bridge outright. A beautiful Pied-a-terre, decorated to the highest level and all the furnishings tastefully sourced from the very best of unique establishments. And it was from there that he ran his little empire, it was also the reason that he was able to pick up so many one-night stands, the promise of waking up to one of the best views in London was a quality chat up line and generally worked a treat.

As Goose settled down and waited result's he had watched Techno doing his stuff in awe until dawn rose. The kid was certainly a genius at what he did, Goose could barely send a text unaided.

After only a few hours, by which time the two had shared a few lines of coke, nothing but the very best quality, Goose had all the information he needed.

Back outside the warehouse Goose lit yet another cigarette. "Come on mate let's go inside. Every copper in the country is looking for that bastard right now, and no doubt us too. This is probably the last place they'll come to as it's in the name of a bogus company and has no links back to me. My fucking phone hasn't stopped ringing and pinging the last two hours, I've had to turn it off, it was driving me mad. They're fucking raiding any place they can put my name to. I took a piss once in the loo at East Ham station, they are probably raiding that too. Let's get out of view, just in case a patrol boat comes up the river, those fuckers have eyes and ears everywhere".

As they moved towards the derelict warehouse Goose turned to his friend, "There's a suitcase in the boot of the motor, grab it for us can you mate?"

Goose walked purposefully into the warehouse. Inside was no better than the outside, worse even, and it had a vile stench. A combination of damp from the nearby Thames, pigeon droppings and piss. The latter thanks to the trussed up Asian lad and no doubt numerous junkies and tramps along the way.

Goose nodded to one of his henchmen, who was standing guard, Billy Roberts an employee of his for many years, ugly fat bastard that he was. He ignored the two victims tied to chairs with stinking, prickly old potato sacks covering their heads.

He made his way to the end of the warehouse where an office was on stilts, he slowly made his way up the rickety stairs, Joe a few feet behind.

Unlike the warehouse the office was clean and tidy and certainly secure. Goose often used this place for discreet meetings, it was out of the way and had no traceability back to him. As mentioned, it was clean and neatly presented, you would never have expected that walking through the filth below.

Wearily he sat down in an old leather office chair behind an oak desk. He pulled out one of the desk drawers and produced two cut glass crystal tumblers and a bottle of Glenmorangie whiskey, and a bottle of Morgan's rum. He poured two large measures, one rum and one whiskey, he knew that Joe hated whiskey. Joe had made his way to a similar old leather chair on the other side of the desk, he placed the suitcase on the desk which other than the two glasses, the whiskey and rum bottles and an ashtray was completely sparse bar a few scratches.

Goose lighting another cigarette, took a huge slug of his whiskey, whereas Joe sipped his rum.

"What I can't get my head round Joe, why didn't any of our coppers on the inside know what was going on? we fucking pay the leaches enough don't we?"

Joe studied his friend through the bottom of his nearly empty glass, he could tell this was really hurting him, eating away at him like a cancer, he for one was glad he wasn't Ray Johnson now.

"Who knows Goose, all I can say is that McVeigh is one devious prick, maybe he didn't divulge to anyone what was going on".

"Of course, you know who is to blame and needs a visit?"

With no answer forthcoming from Joe, Goose jumped in, "Fucking Lenny the Jew that's who, it was that slimy bastard that put that copper our way, and to think that I've had that sneaky little Jewish wanker round my gaff for dinner, best fucking steak together with all the trimmings, him and his thirty-year-old bimbo who grabbed a feel of my cock every time Lenny was in the pisser, which was every five minutes, filthy whore".

Goose downed the remainder of his glass and instantly poured another, he could sure down a few and he was on a mission that was evident.

Lenny the Jew was an old man of eighty years of age who was a small-time crook, pawn broker and Uncle to the East End locals. He had been in the UK from a teen when his mother and father had shipped him off once the second world war had started and he had left Poland before all the atrocities against the Jews had started. He had never seen his mother or father again, an agony he endured but he thought of them often and what their circumstances had been as he grew up in the haze of another country.

"It was obvious wasn't it, sneaky little bastard. Techno looked in on him for us last night, he was facing a stretch for selling stolen goods. Caught red handed. But then the charges were dropped and all evidence to his guilt disappeared around the time he came to us and said he had a good driver and body guard who was under used as he was stepping down, remember?"

Joe really didn't know what to say to his friend that would make any difference., he knew of old that Lenny was never to be trusted and was just small fry, creep that he was.

"What did you find at Raymond's place last night?" It was the first time that Goose had referred to Raymond by name that day.

Joe raised his eyes to the ceiling; Gooses' face spoke volumes and he poured yet another whiskey knowing deep down inside he was not going to like what Joe was about to tell him.

"I sent Jamie and Patrick, as you know Jamie was pretty stoned, but there was no one else available. Well according to Patrick, the land lady came out from the flat above Raymond's and wanted to know what they were doing. She had a sexy negligee on and was, according to Patrick, quite attractive and pretty busty, the negligee wasn't hiding much by all accounts. Being stoned Jamie got the horn and tried it on with her. Another neighbour saw the commotion and called old bill. Patrick said that he tried to get Jamie to leave but he point-blank refused said that the bird was cock teasing him and she was going to get what she deserved. Patrick got out just before old bill arrived".

Goose's face was red with rage, he downed his drink, "For fucks sake can this day get any worse, pair of fucking chancers?"

"Patrick watched on from a distance and saw Jamie get carted off" Joe could only say as he shrugged his shoulders.

"That cunt Jamie has become a liability and needs sorting out." Gosling barked

Joe shrugged his shoulders knowing that Goose was right but there were more important things on the agenda right now "I agree with you Goose, truly I do mate but I think we have enough to deal with right now don't you?"

Goose despite the anger he was feeling right now lent over and opened the suit case, when it was opened fully, he turned it round so Joe could see the contents. Joe took a large gulp of his drink before uttering "Fucking hell!"

Goose poured more drinks, as if they needed more at this stage.

"Joe, I think it's fair to say by close of play today I will be under lock and key, you too probably if we don't act fast, and all the rest of the gang if McVeigh has his way. If that bastard Johnson had anything decent on us, he would have passed the evidence to McVeigh and we would have been hauled in months ago. As it is, thanks to Jamie, we're not going to know now, are we? Needless to say, even if it's an unpaid parking fine I'm going be put on remand, McVeigh will see to that".

"What you saying Goose?"

"I am saying Joe, that I want someone free on the outside, that someone is you". Joe lit one of his own cigarettes and took a good glug of his drink. "The old bill will have me too Goose, there'll be no getting away from them, my face will be plastered all over the smoke".

"I know that Joe, but in the case is fifty grand cash and a credit card with another ten grand limit that is untraceable. Techno will liaise with you. There's a mobile phone, again untraceable. Techno will pay the phone contract and credit card off every month. He has access to one of the off shore accounts, he'll only take what needs to be taken and what he needs to be reimbursed for, he's assured me of that and other than you, I trust the kid".

Goose poured them both more drinks, just a smidge this time, they needed to keep their heads straight.

"In the case you will find an envelope, in that envelope is an address of a high-rise apartment on the Isle of Dogs, along with the keys, that is where you lay low, and I can call you if I need anything sorting, even banged up I'll have access to a mobile, I'm sure, if I can work out how to use the fucker. The flat cannot be traced back to us, I know you can't even boil an egg Joe so Techno is sorting a cleaner come cook, he'll sort out her wages, arrange for her to shop etc, you know the score, so do not leave anything on show in the flat that you'd want her to find. You'll also find an address and keys of an old disused MOT garage in Stoke Newington, it's a bit off the beaten track so pretty low key, in the mechanics pit you'll find enough fire arms and explosive that a small country could start a world war with. Give it a couple of days then take-out Lenny the Jew, also if that cunt Jamie gets bail take him out too, if he ends up on remand, find out where he is and get in touch with people on the inside to do it, they both need wasting".

"Do you think that's wise Goose, his old man works for us too?"

Goose lit a fag, "Peter's a good man, not anything like his son, he knows that he's reared a runt for a son, he will be upset of course, any father losing a child would be, but he knows deep down that his son is on a pathway to self-destruction and will not give us any aggro over it, in fact he'll be here shortly with your wheels".

Joe raised his eyes "My wheels?"

"Yes, as I said you need to keep a low profile, a painter and decorators van is on route, no logo but in the back is everything to make it look like you're a painter and decorator.

You'll go by the alias of Thomas Bailey, Techno will get you all the necessary paperwork to look like you're a legitimate business, headed paperwork, invoices, receipt book, business cards, vat number etc within the next day or two, all you've got to do is grow a beard and change your appearance, there's overalls and all that stuff too so you 're not easily spotted, also in the van taped under the driver's seat is a hand gun with ammo loaded and spare clips in case you need it".

Joe shook his head slowly "Fucking hell Goose, you've thought fast on your feet mate".

Goose threw his scotch back before lighting another cigarette, "Don't I always Joe me old son?" Joe laughed; it was a small respite from the seriousness of everything that happened the last half a day.

"A couple of things to finalise Joe", Goose was all serious again, "I know I said to keep low for a few days before sorting out things but I'm going to let the kid go, tail him and if he gets within a mile of a cop shop, put a bullet in his head. Also in the envelope are pictures of McVeigh's kids and an address of the school they go to; he has twin boys and an older son, who spends the majority of his time with his nan in the New Forest. You'll find a polaroid camera in the case, take pictures this afternoon of the twins and send them to McVeigh, a warning like. The polaroid automatically prints the time and date on the picture and you'll find his address in the envelope, his arse will be twitching in no time".

"That wise Goose? we never go after innocents, whatever the father is the kids shouldn't be brought into it".

Goose rose up from the chair, he was a big man, not as big as Joe but he looked a menacing figure nonetheless.

"For nearly fifty years we have been friends Joe Whyte, apart from once when I disrespected your family, we have never had an argument or serious disagreement, let's not fucking start another one today shall we? I am asking you to send a warning that is all, he needs to understand".

Joe rose up and any possibility of a potential argument dissolved immediately.

"You best get going me old China, I've lots to do before the filth feel my collar", Goose poured yet another drink for himself, slightly more than just wetting the bottom of the glass this time, and chuffed away at yet another cigarette, the packet was emptying fast that was for sure.

Joe zipped up the suitcase and giving his friend a hug, left. As he got to the office door he looked back and saw Goose cutting a couple of lines of cocaine. He never touched the stuff himself but if it got his best friend through this day who was he to complain.

As he left, his mind was working overtime as to what might be asked of him over the next few days, weeks even months and although he had freedom, which his good friend wouldn't have by the end of the day it seemed, it bothered him how far Goose was prepared to go in his private war with DI Pat McVeigh.

Joe got to the bottom of the stairs leading from the office just as Peter had reached them. Peter Bennet was a good man, a hard man who he had known for almost the same period of time that he had known Goose. He was quite short but stocky and had the face that could tell a thousand stories, the etched lines made sure of that.

"Fucking right state of affairs isn't it Joey boy?" Peter said handing Joe a set of van keys. "Your chariot awaits me old mate". Joe took the keys from his outstretched hand "Can say that again Pete".

"How is he?" Peter asked nodding upwards to the office with a slightly worried look on his face. "You know Goose mate" Joe summed it up briefly.

"Look Joe I am going to come right out with it, that son of mine has well and truly burnt his bridges, I know" Peter said rubbing his stubbly chin with one hand. Seeing no response from Joe he said, "Look I know the prick deserves to be taken out, truly I do, he has fucked up on a monumental scale, if fucking up was an Olympic sport he would have more gold medals than Mark Spitz, nonetheless, all I am asking is let me be the one to do it".

The look of amazement on Joe's face did not go unnoticed, here was a father who knew that his son, his very own flesh and blood was going to be taken out, the pain must be eating away at him, and yet here he was offering to do it himself.

Joe put one hand on Peter's shoulder, "let us see what happens hey Pete, come darkness tonight we may all be sharing a prison cell". Peter nodded, "I better go see what Goose is up to, you take care mate, and please, well just bear in mind what I have asked".

Joe looked at the man before him, he only wished that he could be half of the man that Peter was, he had nothing but the utmost respect for him.

Joe nodded towards Billy Roberts as he walked past. Then he stopped, put the suitcase down and walked to the taller of the two tied up figures. Standing in front of the trussed-up figure, he leant forward and whispered in his ear, then standing upright once more he brought his arm back and punched the figure full in the face through the potato sack. The blow was enough to knock the figure and the chair over and for it to skid about three feet along the floor.

Joe rubbed his bruised knuckle with his other hand, he spat at the figure on the floor and picking up the suitcase, he walked calmly from the warehouse "Be seeing you Billy".

CHAPTER TWO:

1964

Gerald "Bowie" Gosling sauntered with an arrogant swagger. He honestly thought that he commanded respect and that it didn't have to be earnt from anyone.

As a small time, pimp, debt collector, drug dealer and East End bully boy he thought that he was the bee's knees when it came to being a want to be gangster and a ladies' man, he would in truth, outside of his flat in Poplar which he shared with his long suffering wife Irene and son Frank, fuck anything with a pulse, whilst inside his flat he would beat anything with a pulse, he could turn like the tide, neither his wife nor son knew which Gerald coming home to expect, one day he would be all laughter and loving, the next he would walk in and punch his wife in the face because dinner wasn't ready or there wasn't hot water for his bath or just for the fucking hell of it.

Whichever Gerald was walking through the door obviously had visions of grandeur.

He was heading to East Ham to meet with his latest bit on the side, a barmaid that was all tits, dyed blonde hair and a mouth that sounded like the local fog horn, called Gillian. She had the sort of mouth that you would shove your cock in just to shut her up.

At eighteen she was right up his street, if he could get her dependant on drug's, she would be out selling her arse for him in no time, that was at least the plan, where as she thought that it was love, until a bigger better-known face came along at least. She'd been an easy pick up that was for sure but he'd soon let her go if she didn't perform to his demands.

Gerald had got the nick name Bowie due to his weapon of choice that was strapped in a sheath to his right leg. True to say that he used it more times than a Saturday boy at Billingsgate fish market.

Gerald was only five foot six but could handle himself when it came to a fight, he wasn't a looker but dressed himself well, in the early days back home, his wife and son would go hungry or cold because he had blown what little money they had on a pair of fashionable trousers from a lucrative tailor in the West End. Although he wasn't a looker there was something about him that could turn a lady's head.

It was Gillian's day off so he headed to her flat a short distance from the pub she worked in, she wasn't expecting him so it would be a nice surprise. By the time he was banging on her door, he had a raging hard on. She may have had a mouth on her but she was one incredible fuck.

On the third knock Gerald was becoming agitated, who the fuck did she think she was keeping him waiting. He was just about to kick the door in when it was opened by a man who Gerald instantly recognised. What surprised him most was the man had a towel wrapped round his waist and nothing else.

Billy Dobson was a well-known face, and was higher up the chain as far as faces go than Gerald, rumour had it he had even done a few jobs for the Kray twins a while back but had fallen out of favour for some unknown reason.

He was in his early twenties, a good-looking lad with the perfect physique and the sort of man that had woman throwing themselves at him.

"What you want Gosling? fuck off mate you are interrupting me little liaison with Gillian here". He grabbed at the front of the towel, "me ball bags need emptying mate and you are holding up proceedings so to speak."

Gerard's face was red with rage, what the fuck was Gillian playing at, no one made a fool of him, no one.

The bowie knife cut clean across Billy's throat before he even knew what was happening.

Gerald kicked him in the stomach and he stumbled backwards into the flat grasping at his throat with both hands as he hit the floor, blood pumping through his fingers.

Gerald walked in and closed the door behind him.

Stepping over the dying man and ignoring the rasping sound coming from his mouth Gerald went in search of Gillian.

He made his way to her familiar bedroom, the knife in his hand, still dripping with Billy's blood on to the worn, stained carpet that had seen better days.

Gerald still boiling with rage found Gillian naked on the bed. She grabbed at a sheet to cover herself as he kicked open the bedroom door with force.

She was petrified but also out of her skull, that was clear for anyone to see. Gerald noticed that she still had the tell-tale signs of recently snorted coke around her nostrils.

He grabbed her by the hair and hauled her from the stained bed to the floor, one hand covering her mouth to stop her screams from escalating all around the estate.

He was muttering obscenities into her ear, "You fucking whore, no one mugs off Gerald Gosling and gets away with it!"

He released the pressure on her mouth a little, just enough for her to breathe but not enough for her to holler and shout and manoeuvred her on to all fours.

"Please Gerald, he forced me, I didn't want it but he got me high, honestly, you're the only man for me, honest!"

Gerald punched her in the head "Shut the fuck up you lying whore!"

He moved her so she was on her knees with her arms resting on the bed and then he unzipped his trousers and thrust out his enormous erection.

As well as a good woman, violence also gave Gerald a raging hard on.

He forced himself in to her anally and thrust back and forward with all his might.

Gillian bit hard onto the duvet to stop her screaming out loud, the pain was excruciating, but she knew that to survive this, damage limitation was needed and just maybe she would get through this ordeal. Gerald could be persuaded that due to the drugs, she was manipulated into having sex with Billy.

Gerald ignoring the muffled screams of agony coming from Gillian just pushed her head in to the mattress and bed clothes further to stifle the noise.

As he came, he thrust the knife down with one hand into the back of her neck with such force that the knife penetrated through her throat and into the mattress. Gillian's whole body shuddered and shook, making Gerald's orgasm even more intense and satisfying.

He zipped himself up and pulled the knife out from the poor girl's lifeless body.

He made his way to the bathroom where he washed the knife, his hands, face and semi erect cock before walking calmly out of the flat, kicking an already dead Billy in the head as he left.

Today was going to have repercussions, Billy had a lot of friends, but Gerald was not bothered in the slightest. He had taken out an up-and-coming gangster and that in itself would earn him some respect from others, respect that he already commanded.

Two days passed and there was still no news on the street about the double murder in that squalid flat in East Ham which could only be a good thing as far as Gerald was concerned, obviously the bodies had not been discovered yet. Gillian had never been the most reliable employee so her boss at the pub would not think twice about her missing shifts and who cared about Billy's comings and goings?

After a few drinks in his favourite haunt in Stratford, Gerald had pulled himself a woman. A few drinks, a couple of snorts of coke and she was game for anything and he was back on a high.

Rosie Pearce, a part time brass that had seen better days, but she was just the tonic that Gerald needed right now.

She was about mid-thirties but her life that consisted of drink, drugs and walking the streets had taken its toll and she looked at least ten years older, not what you'd call a looker but she was game enough. She still had a slim figure but to look at her face it was hard to pin an age on her unless you knew.

She had gigantic boobs just as Gerald liked, her own too for a change and he had already had a quick feel and a knee trembler in the back alley of the White Horse.

With everything that had gone on the past forty-eight hours Gerald needed to unwind.

He wanted more sex, drugs and alcohol and Rosie was the one to give it to him, well the sex at least the other two were very easily sourced when in the know.

The pub had a lock-in between the afternoon and evening session and after several hours of drinking in the pub and snorting more lines of coke than he could remember, Gerald took Rosie outside once more and forcing her to her knees, she expertly took his cock in her mouth. Just what he needed.

After he shot his load in to her willing gob and she wiped her mouth Rosie smiled, "Randy little fucker today aren't you, Gerald?"

He zipped himself up and laughed out loudly, "too right darling and I'm not finished yet".

After another hour drinking, doubles every round, the pair sauntered to a fish and chip shop and got a large portion of fish and chips each, after all the drinking they needed something to soak up the alcohol.

"You know how to spoil a lady Gerald Gosling, buying me dinner too."

The pair, who for any passers-by looked like a normal couple as they sat in a local park and ate their supper, licking their lips and cleaning off their greasy hands on the newspaper wrapping.

After they had finished Gerald pulled Rosie none too discretely behind some bushes and when she was on all fours took her from behind, as if he'd give a shit about the state of her knees.

"Bloody hell Gerald, you are wearing me out mate" Rosie laughed as he finished off.

"I want more mate I want to go all night!" he laughed.

Rosie pulled up her knickers "I'm all for that mate but I don't want to be outside all night, and my knees are shot, where can we go?"

"Your place Rosie?"

"No sorry darling, me old man will be home from the twilight shift soon, what about a hotel?"

Gerald looked at her, she really was the breath of fresh air he needed right now.

"No hotel, most of them round here have more rats than guests, and the bed sheets could walk to the laundry room by themselves. And I'm not saying you are not worth it but the posher hotels charge an arm and a leg, even if they let the likes of you and me in, again no offence."

He looked deep in thought for a while and then said "Ok we will go to mine then."

Rosie raised an eyebrow as she looked at him, "Yours? But I thought you had a wife and kid at home."

Gerald laughed, "I do, she will have to like it or lump it. The flat is in my name and I pay the bills and she ain't actually giving me anything to stop me straying, so if she doesn't like it, she will have to fuck off wont she?"

Rosie laughed so hard that she thought she'd wet herself.

***

Frank "Goose" Gosling lay on his bed. He had been given the nickname "Goose" from his mates at school, it had stuck, he liked it so had decided that was what he would be called for years to come.

Goose at the age of fifteen looked and acted older, he was the tallest in his class by far, and looked at least twenty especially with his newly acquired stubble.

He was already taller than his father, the father that he hated with a vengeance, the father that he hoped and prayed every night would not come home and be found beaten or stabbed to death, found floating in the Thames or laying in a dingy alleyway somewhere choked on his own vomit.

Things with his father had not always been that way. Goose remembered how his father would sit him on his knee and relate stories of how he had worked for the Krays, how he had given them their first leg up in to the world of being renown East End gangsters, how they relied on him, he was their number one man.

In truth, his father's only fame to the Krays was to see them seated in a snug in a pub in the Old Kent Road through a serving hatch once but you have to impress your kid's, don't you?

He remembered the time his father took him to Southend for the day, they had gone to the fairground, plenty of rides to be had, roller coaster, dodgems etc then ate fish and chips and walked on the beach whilst Goose ate candy floss, all the while his mother lay in a hospital bed after his father had beaten her so severely the night before, she had to have her spleen removed.

The trip to the seaside and the fun they would have had been to bribe Goose to keep his mouth shut, as he had witnessed it all. His father knew that if the boy spoke to the police who had been sniffing round, such was the intensity of the beating, that his father could do a stretch inside, not a short one at that.

Goose also remembered the times his father had forced himself on his mother, shouting obscenities at her, because as his wife it was her duty to satisfy him whenever he felt the need. In reality it was nothing short of rape, but his father did not see it that way, or how his father would come home drunk or drugged up, or both on more than one occasion and would beat him for refusing to eat his dinner, or for staring at his father and a thousand other reasons, his father was a Jekyll and Hyde character alright who could turn in a split second over the most trivial of things.

He had lost count of the times his mother would end up in hospital, telling a nurse or doctor she had walked in to a door, or fallen down the stairs, or been hit by a car to explain the horrid injuries that his father had inflicted on her.

Goose had accepted the fact that one day, if his father escaped the beating or the stabbing out on the streets of the East End that he was long overdue, it would be Goose himself that would cause his father's demise, something that he promised his mother almost on a daily basis.

As he lay on his bed, restless and unable to sleep any further thoughts of his father were disrupted by the shouting coming from the living room. It sounded like his mother cursing and hollering like a banshee, the woman who once took a belt to his behind for daring to say "Jesus Christ" was now swearing and cursing like a two-bob brass who had been ripped off by a punter.

***

The black cab pulled up outside Gerald's flat in Crisp Street, Poplar. Gerald and Rosie virtually fell out of the cab.

The flat, quite tastefully furnished if out dated and a good size two bedrooms was above a bookmaker, Gerald owned both the flat and the bookmakers but the original owner still managed the shop for him.

He had acquired it four years before when the bookmaker, Jimmy Briggs, got into serious debt, a debt Gerald bought for a pittance but meaning that Jimmy was in to Gerald for a few grand. The saying that you never ever met a poor bookie didn't relate to Jimmy Briggs who was paying out more money than he was raking in due to some scams and fixed results that had gone wrong, with Gerald himself playing a part in his downfall.

The first thing Gerald did was to kick Jimmy out the flat and move his family in but he did let him stay on as manager of the shop, and paid him a decent wage too, but he scrutinised every penny in or out.

Jimmy was now living in a dingy bedsit in Canning Town, his wife and three kids long gone due to his excessive drinking and gambling. It was only the drink that got him through the day.

Rosie had thoroughly enjoyed her time with Gerald. She had seen him in the pub on many an occasion and knew his reputation, but to her today, he had been the perfect companion and one randy bastard and, you know what, treated her like a lady, well as good as.

She had enjoyed herself and the sex too if she was honest. Her old man was always complaining that he was either too tired or when he was up for the odd bit of how's your father, it would be over in minutes, and she would have to lay there frustrated listening to his snoring within a minute of his coming.

He never took her out for a drink or a meal, treated her much like a servant in their home expecting his clothes to be washed and ironed, food to be in the fridge and on the table in a timely manner.

A woman had need's, an itch to be scratched and Gerald had certainly scratched that itch today and then some. But she couldn't help feeling a little apprehension and nervousness as they headed to the flat, she only hoped that Gerald's wife was a deep sleeper because she could scream with pleasure like a banshee when a man hit the right spot and if this afternoon was anything to go by, Gerald was the man who was going to do just that.

The flat was clean Gerald's wife saw to that, it was spick and span and had the smell of bleach and furniture polish. The furniture was outdated and worn however and the carpet had seen better days, a little threadbare, but clean.

Gerald put on the electric fire, something that if his wife did, he would complain about the money it would cost to run and tell her he'd be deducting money off her measly housekeeping allowance.

He poured them both brandies into crystal glasses and they sat themselves together on the sofa.

He unzipped his trousers, for the God knows how many times that day, and pulled Rosie's head down to his lap. "Here you are girl get your laughing gear round that". Rosie didn't need to be asked twice. He was erect yet again.

Within minutes both were undressed, clothes strewn on the floor and Rosie was sat astride him on the sofa riding him hard, her enormous boobs bouncing up and down as he grabbed one and suckled on it, groping her arse with his other free hand.

Rosie was loving every second of it and her moans were getting louder and louder. Her orgasm was getting ever nearer and then as she climaxed with a scream, she slumped forward head-butting Gerald clean on the nose as she did so, blood gushed down on to his torso.

Gerald had only put on the glass table light which did not give out much light but he looked up and could make out his wife standing there in her flannel dressing gown holding a large frying pan, pain and sorrow etched on her face.

Feeling his nose, he realised he wasn't bleeding and then looking at Rosie he could see that the blood pouring on to his naked flesh was coming from a wound to the back of her head, the blood was spurting everywhere.

His wife was screaming obscenities and swearing like a two-bit prostitute. Not once in all the years that they had been together had he ever heard any blasphemous words come from her mouth but she certainly wasn't holding back now.

She would attend church every Sunday, taking Frank with her, yet here she was effing and blinding like a bus load of brasses on a day trip to Clacton.

"You fucking bastard Gerald Gosling, I have put up with some fucking shit from you over the years and now here you are bringing whores in to our home, with your boy not eight feet away sleeping in his room. You have sunk lower than a snake's belly tonight you fucking bastard. Is it not good enough that you've taken my spleen, now you want to rip my heart out too, you fucking piece of worthless shite!"

Spit was projecting out of her mouth as she ranted on, and her face was a bright red, like she was about to burst.

The next few minutes were a bit of a blur to all concerned. Gerald moved Rosie none too gently off him and she slumped on to the sofa, blood still spurting out of her head, he didn't know if she was alive or dead, he jumped up in an instant.

His fist smashed in to Irene's face before she had time to act, and then the blows kept coming at a ferocious speed. Gerald, using the pan as a weapon now, had knocked Irene to the floor and she had curled up in to a ball trying to protect her head with her arms to little avail, it was a scenario she had faced many times before.

Then suddenly the blows and the kicks stopped, someone had put the living room main light on.

Irene, when she dared moved, looked up. She saw her husband laying on the floor lifeless, she made out a figure through her blurred vision standing over her.

"It's ok Mum, he won't hurt us anymore", Goose, kneeling by his mother pulled her into his chest and comforted her.

He turned his head to look at his motionless father, he had stabbed him with such force the bowie knife had gone clean through his back and pierced his heart.

Goose's only disappointment was that it would have been quick and that his father would not have suffered, but the bastard deserved to suffer, deserved to die slowly and feel the suffering he had reigned on his wife and son for so many years.

A quote from a religious education lesson Goose had done at school the previous week came to mind and he smiled as thought of it "A man who lives by the sword, shall die by the sword". Never a truer quotation!

CHAPTER THREE:

DI Douglas Coulson left the squalid flat in East Ham and retched up what little food he had eaten that day.

At fifty years of age and more than thirty years on the force, he had seen enough dead bodies, enough gruesome crime scenes, squaller and deprivation to last a life time. But still, he couldn't help feeling nauseated by it every single time.

The discovery of a Miss Gillian Thompson and an unknown male was only made because a neighbour had made a complaint to the local authorities about the stench coming from inside of the young girls flat next door.

Gillian had been found still stooped over on all fours as Gerald had left her, rigor mortis had set in, she was naked and covered in horrendous purple and black bruises and dried congealed blood.

The unknown male was also in a state of undress laying in the hall way, his throat slit and a deep pool of blood beside him.

Coulson, shocked and sickened headed back to the station leaving forensics to gather their information to present their interpretation of what had happened in the flat to him later, he had great respect for the forensic boys and coroners alike, modern science was improving almost on a daily basis and a coroner could pin point a time of death almost to a quarter of an hour.

Coulson was still interviewing young Goose Gosling who had been brought in the day before on suspicion of the murder of his father and could well have done without more murders on his door step.

The lad's mother was in hospital and the word from the doctors who had attended to her was that even if she survived, she could be left brain dead, in a vegetive state such was the enormity of the beating she had taken, she had been conscious when she arrived at the hospital but then had an enormous bleed on the brain shortly after arriving and was now in a coma, this information Coulson had kept from the young, vulnerable lad.

The condition of the yet unnamed other woman found in the flat was improving, although she was still in and out of consciousness, doctors had informed him that she was improving hour by hour and the chances of her surviving the attack were now high.

Coulson knew Gerald Gosling well, he knew what he was, knew that he had beaten his wife to a pulp on more occasions than a prize fighter had opponents in a boxing ring. Certainly not someone you would cherish meeting in a dark alley on your way home, especially with a drink in him.

Frank Gosling, accompanied by a social worker had openly admitted to what had happened in the flat the previous night. His father was violently attacking his mother, he thought that he was going to kill her so he grabbed a knife and stabbed his father to protect her, however he didn't know about the other woman found in the flat and had only seen her on the sofa after it was all over.

He had in his own words, killed his father in self-defence, to prevent him from killing his poor mother. He stated to Coulson that he had witnessed far too many times the beatings that had been subjected to her at the hands of her drunken husband.

Due to the boys age, it was impossible to interview him in the way that you would do an adult. With an adult you could interrogate them, play good cop, bad cop, break them down with sleep, food and even toilet deprivation etc, especially if you knew for sure that they were guilty from the outset.

Just because young Frank had admitted killing his father, his guilt openly admitted, Coulson still had to ascertain all the facts, what happened to the unknown woman for a start. Where had she come from? What was she doing in the flat?

No sooner did Coulson think he was getting somewhere with Frank or Goose as he liked to be called, the fucking prim and proper, we must abide by the rules at all times social worker would call time on proceedings. Any fool could see this was wearing the young lad down, stopping and starting questioning, going over and over the same ground.

Forty-eight hours after the arrest of Frank Gosling, DI Coulson accompanied by the desk Sergeant on duty that night, an aging copper who was nearing retirement called Fred Fox who had many years on the job and was looking forward to hanging up his truncheon once and for all, went to Goose's holding cell.

After the Sergeant had unlocked the door Coulson motioned for him to go.

"You have got thirty minutes, that is it sir, I am already breaking the rules leaving you alone with him as it is" Fox said non to happily in his broad cockney accent.

Coulson smiled at him "believe me Fred, it is for the kids own good".

Once inside the cell Coulson closed the door and leant against it, lighting up a cigarette, he offered one to Goose who graciously shook his head, if his father had taught him one thing it was never to trust a copper, nothing came for free, not even a cigarette.

Coulson exhaled deeply after drawing on the cigarette.

"Some information has come to light Goose, about your Mum and Dad"

Gosling sat upright on the bed, "What information?"

"I should wait for the social worker to be present really"

Gosling shook his head savagely "No, fuck that jobs worth, just tell me, I need to know, this is torture".

"Ok, if you are sure" Coulson said as he crushed the cigarette out beneath his foot

"I have heard from the Doctor at the hospital treating your Mum, I'm really sorry to have to tell you this but it doesn't look like she is going to recover mate, the severity of this beating along with others in the past have finally taken their toll on the poor woman. If she doesn't die now then she will be left a cabbage, in a vegetive state needing twenty-four-hour care, three hundred and sixty-five days a year son, Goose, I'm really sorry that I had to break that news to you".

Coulson did not know what to do as young Frank Gosling put his head in his hands and wept.

Coulson eventually moved over to the young lad and put his hand on his shoulder "I am truly sorry Goose; believe me I am".

Goose pushed Coulson's arm away and wiped his nose on the back of his sleeve, "You said you had news about my dad, what's that?" he said calmly now, regretting that he'd shown this copper his emotions, it would be something that could be used against him, he was sure of that.

Coulson lit another cigarette and this time Goose did take one when offered.

"I don't know if you were aware, knowing your father I very much doubt it, but your father was having an affair with an eighteen-year-old barmaid, been going on about eight months by all accounts".

Goose was feeling a little dizzy from the cigarette but managed to shake his head.

"Before the attack on your mother, your father killed his bit on the side along with a young male, a well-known East End wide boy she was also seeing. They were found in the girls flat in East Ham, been dead a few days according to forensics. We have been able to take the bowie knife you used to kill your father and match it to the wounds of the diseased in the girls flat and we have witness statements putting your father leaving the scene around the estimated time of deaths".

Goose still a little light headed from the cigarette looked at Coulson.

"I'm glad he is dead, wish it had been sooner and I bet you are too, think of how much money the establishment has saved, now there won't have to be a murder trial".

Coulson looked at Goose, he was an intelligent lad that much was sure.

"Listen to me Goose and listen good, this is going to be a once in a lifetime offer, so do not blow it" Coulson looked at the lad, "The desk sergeant will be back in a few minutes so do not interrupt and make sure you take in what I have to say".

Goose looked at Coulson, despite him being a copper, filth in the eyes of most, he had taken a liking to him, a liking that over the coming years would not last. "Best give me another one of them fag's then mate and then you will have yourself a captive audience".

Coulson offered Goose another cigarette and then sat on the end of the bed with its hard mattress he was sure he would get piles, but it was better than standing for sure.

"We have had glowing reports from your teachers and you are apparently top of your class, a year or two in advance of the other pupils, you are an intelligent lad. So here is what is going to happen Goose if you stick rigidly to your knowledge of events, you are going to be charged with murder. Irrespective that he was putting your mother's life in danger, if you hadn't stabbed your father in the back, and let us say that you stabbed him in the chest instead, the judge and jury would look upon it as possible self-defence and the charge could be reduced to manslaughter. But your statement says otherwise, right?

We know that your mother hit the woman we have identified as Rosie Pearce, and luckily it looks like she is going to make a full recovery eventually with no permanent damage, that is until her husband gets hold of her" Coulson laughed at his own humour.

"Even if you retracted your statement, made up that it was taken from you under duress say, no one is going to believe that your mother hit this Rosie Pearce woman and killed your father whilst taking a beating that has left her near deaths door, and something that she will never recover from, no one is going to believe that you had no part in this, what a big strapping lad like you stood by while his poor mother was taking the beating of a lifetime or slept through it all. People are not stupid. You need to take some responsibility for what happened that night with as much damage limitation as possible".

All the while Coulson spoke Goose did as he was told and listened, with his brain working quietly in the background, ideas whizzing through his head like cogs of a machine, silently whirring round.

"Your father was a prize cunt mate and you could argue that he deserved what he got, and indeed not before time, whether that's saving the institution money on a trial or not".

Coulson took out his notebook from his jacket pocket, turned a page and read out loud.

"From your mother's hospital records we have established that she has been to either the emergency department or admitted to hospital forty-nine times in the past ten years all with un-creditable reasons from the marks she had on her body".

He replaced the notebook before continuing.

"Your father ruined your mother's life mate, do not let him ruin yours. I propose we rip up your previous statement and we create another one. You say to that bloody social worker you've changed your version of events when she gets back, you were not thinking straight, she fucking winds me right up by the way, like you say a jobs worth".

Goose nodded.

"Your mother will never ever be able to give her version of events, that Rosie bird was unconscious all the time and can't say what happened, and your father definitely can't explain what happened unless we employ a medium, so sadly you are the only creditable witness as to what happened in that flat, your explanation as to what happened also has to be believable in line with the forensics findings".

Coulson moved silently towards the door knowing that Fred Fox may well come back earlier than agreed, the sergeant certainly wouldn't want to fuck up his retirement and pension at this late stage of his career, and Coulson certainly didn't want any witnesses to what he was asking from young Goose.

"Here is what you are going to say. You find this Rosie and your father at it like rabbits, you hit her with the frying pan, through a mist of rage. To think that your father could bring another woman in to yours and your mother's home and have sex with her while your mother was asleep a few feet away. You grab a frying pan off the stove and bash the woman over the bonce. She falls forward and head butts your old man on the snout. Your mother comes in, your father starts blindly attacking her thinking it's her that hit Rosie, he is confused due to the dim light and after being head-butted by Rosie, you come in and pull your father off your mother, she scrabbles about and finds the knife and holds it in both hands whilst still laying on the floor trying to get up, your father fights back at you, you release your hold on him and push him away he stumbles and falls backwards landing on top of your mother and sadly the knife. Get my drift son? You will do time, for hitting the woman, possibly for your part in your father's death, you will be sent to a borstal and be out in three years maximum, what d'you say?"

When Goose realised that Coulson had finished what he had come to say he casually asked, "Why are you doing this, protecting me like this, what the hell is in it for you?"

"Because you are an intelligent lad Goose, as I have already stated you're already in advance of your years, physique, intelligence etc. and because by killing your father you've reduced my monthly income by a considerable amount".

Goose was taken aback, not understanding fully what Coulson was telling him.

Seeing the confusion etched on the young lad's face Coulson continued.

"Your father had his finger in more pies than you probably knew or gave him credit for. Gerald wanted to stay under the radar so to speak, in his opinion the higher up the chain you were there was always someone who wanted to take you down, he'd seen that for himself many times, to an outsider looking in he was nothing more than a bully boy, small time crook, pimp whatever you want to call him but he acquired a few businesses through debts owed. He specialised in it in fact, going after people that owed money and who had a decent business. His interest rates were so high the people that owed them didn't have a cat in hells chance of meeting the payments. Rather than lose a limb or worse being killed and buried in the Mud Chute in the middle of the Isle of Dogs, your father persuaded them that he could write off the debt if they signed over their club, pub, bookies whatever to him, and so, his Empire grew".

Coulson rubbed at his chin, contemplating the right words.

"I was on his payroll and he was on mine, in short, he scratched my back, and I scratched his, you get my drift?".

Goose could not believe what Coulson was saying "What my dad was a grass?"

Coulson laughed at the boy's naivety "Sure was, when required".

Goose was confused "Still doesn't explain, why you're helping me"

Coulson smiled "That my son is easy, I know where your dad keeps all the deeds to the property he has acquired over the years. Quite simply, with your dear old Mum in the state that she is in, you will be rightful heir to said properties. Now if you are banged up for murder, initially in borstal and then with the big boys in the Scrubs, you could get lost in the system, never get out or worse still, only get out in a box. Those boys in there like fresh meat, young meat".

Coulson was enjoying seeing the confusion on Goose's face.

"Ok, so let us say I agree and change my statement, do my three years, come out then what?"

Coulson smiled, "You play your cards right and you could become one of the biggest gangsters in the smoke. You have the intelligence and physique to be so much more than your father was, and however big you become I can tell by looking at you, that unlike your father you won't be perturbed by someone wanting a bit of prestige and taking you down. With his properties you'll also have a cracking head start in accumulating wealth, respect and notability from the outset".

"And you DI Coulson, I am sure that you are not doing this because you feel that I can be so much more than my father ever was, so what's in it for you?".

"You know me so well already Goose, while you are inside, I will make sure from a distance like, that all the clubs etc are taken care of, discreetly of course, I still have my career and pension to think about, but I will look after them until you are out. When you have rightful ownership, there is one club in particular that I am interested in, it's in Soho, a strip club, nothing more than a dive really it is called Bartholomeus. Your father stitched me up over that, by rights half of that club should be mine. You see I helped your father get it, he promised me half and sadly that did not materialise. Our relationship was never the same after that".

Goose looked to be hanging on every word that Coulson was saying, ideas already flooding thick and fast into his head, he would use his time inside wisely, planning the development of what was in short going to be his empire.

"So, DI Coulson, how did he stitch you up?"

"Danny Bartolomeu was a gambler of the highest order, some days he would lose up to fifty k on the dogs, horses or other sporting activities. He owed ten K to a local hood; your dad bought the debt for a small portion of that. No matter how extortionate the amount of interest your father put on the debt each week, Danny would always make the payments. Your father really wanted that club, it was a dive but had real potential to be the 'in place' of Soho".

"So, what happened?" Goose leant forward intrigued even more now.

"That is where I came in, the club was Danny's pride and joy, his only reason for getting up every morning. His wife had left him years before because of his gambling and sampling the wears the strippers had to offer. I raided the place, found perfectly placed drugs in the toilet, placed there by your father ten minutes before the raid. Danny was given an ultimatum, do a stretch, a long stretch, due to a kilo of coke being found and that the club would be shut down if he didn't agree to selling it to Gerald for a pittance".

49

Goose smiled and shook his head "Devious pair of fuckers you two, aren't you?"

Coulson laughed.

"Twenty-four hours later Danny signed over the club to your dad, who was then supposed to sign over half to me, he never did get to the solicitor though, always had an excuse. A few days after signing over the club, Danny Bartolomeu was found hanging from a rafter in a lock up he owned in Romford".

"Could I have another cigarette please DI Coulson?" Goose scratched his head, took the lit cigarette and drew deeply on it.

"So, you and me Dad were responsible for Bartholomeus death?"

"Steady on their kid, no one forced Danny to do what he did, other than himself. All I know is that club is my retirement pot, I was promised it, I did my bit and fair and square Bartholomeus was rightfully mine. When you get out and start building your business empire you will need people on the force to help you, a bent copper, the right bent copper can make things a lot easier for a criminal, evidence goes missing, statements get changed alibis appear out of the woodwork in their droves and so forth, I know who on the force is living beyond their means, there's certainly a few but I know who would be game, who are more likely to be persuaded to be of assistance. I will also help up to and after my retirement, anyway that is needed".

"You will help to get me bent coppers on my book's you mean, just like you?"

"Like I said from the outset, you are an intelligent lad Goose, I get the club you get my help to be as big a name in the East End right up there with Ronnie or Reggie Kray".

Goose laughed and stood up from the bed, his arse had no feeling in it and was freezing cold due to the mattress being like a slab of concrete. He looked menacingly down at Coulson who was still sat on the bed, with a worried look on his face.

"Or better, but just remember one thing DI Coulson, unlike my dad I am no grass, never will be, and no one, I repeat no one ever dictates or demands anything of me. My dad did that once too often and well, we all know how that story ended. You seem to be forgetting that you were only due half of that club and half is all you will get".

Coulson looked deep in to Goose's eyes and for the first time was afraid of what this young man could be in years to come. In his head he even contemplated briefly that he would use a dodgy solicitor, there were plenty of those to be had for a back hander and sign all of Gerald's businesses over in to his own name while Goose was inside. But something niggling inside him told him that if he did that, he would spend the rest of his life looking over his shoulder, waiting for Goose's hand to tap him on it.

He bravely decided to front the boy out, "Without me you won't find the title deeds to all the properties in Daddy's name, so think on boy, I want Bartholomeus in its entirety not a poxy fifty percent stake, you got that son?"

Coulson smiled smugly; he was pleased with himself but sadly he was also disillusioned. Goose stared back at him, hatred in his eyes thinking to himself that he would use this copper in front of him, then bring him down and take pleasure in doing it, slowly but surely, he would fuck him right over.

Coulson heard footsteps coming down the corridor. He moved his hand across his throat meaning to stop the conversation just as Fox unlocked the cell door "Time is up Sir"

Coulson winked at Goose "I think young Frank wants to see his social worker Sarge".

Waiting for his social worker and left alone in his cell Goose started to plan for the future. Not only the businesses that he would come out too, but also how Coulson would meet a slow torturous death once Goose had no further use of him.

CHAPTER FOUR:

Goose Gosling stormed in to his cell, he had a face like thunder, red eyes bulging. He slammed the door to his cell shut, ripped off his tie, threw his suit jacket on the floor and lay on his bunk facing the wall.

His friend and cell mate of six weeks Joe Whyte came in. They had been paired up and got on like a house on fire. "I heard you were back mate; how did you get on?"

Goose turned round and looked at him, the anger still clear to see on his face, "The judge was a complete and utter wanker mate with a capital W, and as for Coulson, he is a dead man walking mate, I can tell you that for fuck all".

Joe popped his arse down on the edge of his cell mates' bed with baited breath waiting, "What you get?"

Goose turned over to face the wall so that his friend could not see the tears brimming in his eyes.

"Six fucking years mate, six poxy bastard years, even with good behaviour I am going to end up in the Scrubs for at least two years, can you Adam and Eve them bastards?"

"Oh, come on mate, let me get you a cup of char, me old lady always used to say everything seemed better after a cup of tea."

Goose was still angry, he turned to face his friend "Yes sure thing… really did she say that after she found your brother dead after you had smashed his head in for fucking her six-year-old daughter, your sister, yeh I bet? And what did she say about your old man interfering with all three of her kids, fuck me, couldn't you all play scrabble, monopoly or normal games not incest a game all the family can play?"

It was Joes turn to be angry now, his fist connected with Goose's jaw, he hit him so hard he knocked Goose off the bed and he landed on the not too soft concrete floor. Although Joe was a year younger than Goose, he was bigger in size, a strapping lad and had been boxing at a club where he lived in Manchester from the age of six.

Goose had not seen the punch coming due to the speed it was aimed at, the look on his face showed that, not that he would have been able to do anything about it even if he had. Goose was going to be friends with this boy for years to come, that much was a given, whereas Goose was going to be the brains, Joe would be the brawn.

Joe gave out a hand to help Goose back to his feet, Joe looked at the boy he had true feelings for, unnatural feelings, and feelings he dared not disclose to him, he smiled and said "Alright mate, I will let you off this once, you were hurting and in shock, so I will let it go".

Goose looked up at his friend, "Fuck me if that is letting it go, I would not want to see what you would do if you were pissed off at me mate!"

The pair sat together on the bed and belly laughed, despite the jaw ache Goose was feeling. That day Goose knew that he had crossed a line with his friend, Joe despite being the younger of the two had taken him under his wing from day one, gave him the heads up on everyone, what you could and couldn't get away with and for that he would always be grateful.

Joe still being positive about everything "So why six years, not three as Coulson suggested, the filth even bought you the whistle and flute to wear in court today didn't he?"

Goose was rubbing his jaw; he knew that it wasn't broken but he would have a fuck off black and purple bruise in the morning and would struggle to eat comfortably for a few days.

"I suppose no one knew that bitch Rosie Pearce would drop down dead a week before me fucking trial, a bleed on the brain apparently. And although the judge couldn't for definite say it was the blow to the skull from the frying pan or the beating her old man gave her when she got out of hospital, he decided to lump me with the maximum sentence possible for my crime".

Joe looked at Goose and felt his pain, "Let me get you that tea, while I'm doing that you can hang that whistle up nicely, I will be needing to borrow it in a couple of weeks!"

Two weeks later it was Goose's turn to play sympathiser when Joe returned from his trial having been given a twelve-year sentence for the murder of his brother. Despite his defence saying that Joe's brother had been abusing his six-year-old sister and two of her friends, the judge during his summing up urged the jury that two wrongs did not make a right and that Joe should feel the full force of justice. Goose, just like Joe two weeks previously felt his friend's pain, "Who was the judge mate?" Joe tried to hide his tears and the anger he was feeling, eventually he managed to face his friend, "Harvey Emerson, right fucking ponce if ever I saw one" Goose jumped up from the bunk, excited now, "That is cos he is mate, bent as a nine bob note, few of the boys in here have had run ins with him, especially the ones….you know the rent boys, he has a reputation of liking boys and liking them young, leave it with me mate, I'll see Coulson, I feel an appeal coming up mate".

Both Goose and Joe lay in their respective bunks that night laughing that the whistle Coulson had supplied was jinxed.

***

Goose returned to his cell one afternoon after receiving a visit from Coulson, accompanied as always by his social worker, Joe was sad for his friend but then happy with what he then had to tell him about an appeal that Coulson was arranging on behalf of Joe.

Goose's mother had passed away peacefully in her sleep the day before having never regained consciousness shortly after being admitted to hospital following the attack by Goose's father.

Goose had shown no emotion when he was told, which surprised the social worker, he was well used to keeping his emotions bottled up and well and truly suppressed from authority. When the social worker was getting them all a cup of tea and a chocolate bar for Goose, Coulson confided to him that all was going well and he would come out to thriving businesses and a healthy bank balance.

Goose Gosling looked at Coulson and leaning forward whispered, "I fucking better had mate or you won't be long for this earth if I don't". It was the second time that Coulson had felt afraid of this young man before him, he could see the intention in his steely eyes, in a little under two weeks he was to be transferred to the Scrubs, there it would either make or break him, if it made him, something in Coulson's head was telling him Goose Gosling would be even more dangerous than he was now.

Goose used the visit as an opportunity to tell Coulson that Judge Emerson had stitched his cell mate up good and proper, he had to be quick before the social worker got back so talked fast. "Look into him for me, you know he is in to boys, what you got on him? If it is nothing you had better make sure you get something, you want the club you better work hard and fast, me mate is going to get an appeal and Emerson will be funding it".

Then the jobs worth of a social worker returned and Goose changed back to the sweet innocent boy that the social worker thought that he was. How you could pull the wool over their eyes, and they were supposed to be trained professionals, yeah right.

***

Goose was transferred to the Scrub's the day after his eighteenth birthday. Joe had arranged with a friendly old screw to bring in a birthday cake the day before. The laughter from the day before was soon forgotten the following morning as Goose gathered his worldly possessions together for what they were worth, Joe could tell despite his friends not giving a fuck attitude that deep down inside he was scared, being the King Rooster with boys your own age was a different ball game than being thrown in with serious hard nut lifer's.

Joe's appeal had been successful and he was being released within six months. Emerson had played hard ball at first refusing to be part of the conspiracy, but a few perfectly placed photos of him with young boys in compromising positions obtained by Coulson eventually persuaded him to change his mind and fund the appeal. He also stated on record that he had been too hard on Joe when summing up at the original trial which could have influenced the jury, and that he felt that Joe's crime was manslaughter not murder, Joe got four years so with time already served on the original charge and with good behaviour Joe was counting down the days to his freedom. The words in Coulson's ears had paid off.

The first two weeks of Goose Goslings time in the Scrubs were uneventful. He had kept his head down and stayed out of the way of the serious hard nut prison bully boys whom he'd already had the heads up on.

Initially he had been placed in a cell of his own, to help him acclimatise to prison life but then one morning as he entered his second week, he was moved in to a cell with a lifer called Dennis Briggs.

Dennis was in for murdering his wife and her lover, he had caught her cheating on him with his best friend of all people. He'd walked in on them in a compromising position and there was no getting away from how long this little affair had been going on for, allegedly unbeknown to the poor old guy.

At nearly eighty Dennis was harmless enough, frail but not a wicked bone in his body. He made Goose laugh by telling him that he was more concerned at losing a dear friend than his wife of over 40 years.

Dennis would spend time with Goose and as they walked around the wing the old boy would advise him of who was who, and more importantly who to stay away from.

Goose liked his cell mate, to him he was the Granddad that he never known, the likelihood however, was that Dennis would die in prison and that thought for some strange reason made Goose sad.

Dennis was on a hospital visit one morning, he had developed age related rheumatoid arthritis and was being treated for it, he rarely complained but you could catch that look of being in agony on his face with certain movements.

Goose lay on his bunk minding his own business and was preparing to have a Tommy Tank whilst looking at one of his cell mate's secretly stashed porn mags.

He had come across an eighteen-year-old model called Imelda, big tits and a shaved fanny and was imagining her giving him head when the door to the cell burst open and a hard nut, the bully of the wing Terry Jackson burst in.

Terry Jackson was serving three life sentences for wiping out a family of brothers who had beat him up a week before because he owed them a monkey from a card game, he killed them all with a machete when they least expected it a few days after the beating. Story went, two of the three brothers were beheaded and the third bled to death after Jackson had cut both his arms off. Clearly not a man to mess with.

Goose jumped down from the bunk, he was embarrassed that he had been caught reading a porn mag and having a secret wank and still had the showings of a semi more than anything else.

Jackson stood and laughed, dropping his trousers he looked at Goose and said "Suck this boy, now". Averting his gaze from Jacksons hard on Goose looked beyond Jackson to the door and could see that Jackson had two heavies keeping watch at the cell door.

When Dennis returned to his cell from the hospital, he could not believe the amount of blood there was, claret was spattered all up the walls and floor of the cell, screws and an assigned cleaning up team of inmates were mopping out the cell. One inmate a young lad called Benny Godfrey doing three years for burglary looked at Dennis, "Your mate Gosling went berserk mate, Terry Jackson wanted him to suck his wood by all accounts, Jackson is currently in surgery having his knob sown back on, his two heavies are in hospital, Gosling beat them to a pulp, it is touch and go if they pull through".

A friendly screw, Tommy Dawson, told Godfrey to shut the fuck up and get on with the cleaning, he looked at Dennis, "Ignore him Dennis, Chinese whispers and all that, although I will be very surprised if Terry ever gets it up again, go all right at the hospital, did it?" Dennis surveyed the scene it was like a blood bath you would see in a horror movie, he ignored the original question, "Where is Goose? Mr Dawson". Tommy Dawson smiled "He is in solitary as per regulations, but I expect him to be let out tomorrow, after all these fuckers brought it on themselves, it was self-defence, Jackson has had this coming for years, providing none of them die, the governor will see it as just that, now go and get yourself a cuppa whilst we finish up here". Dennis nodded, he liked Goose Gosling, knew that he was someone you wanted on your side, Jackson had fucked up big time but he had now ensured that Gosling would see out his sentence in peace, no matter how many tough nuts there were in here they would all think twice about getting on the wrong side of a certain Mr Frank "Goose" Gosling.

***

Six years later Dennis Briggs passed away peacefully in his sleep, still in prison, still in the same cell he used to share with Goose.

After Frank's release Dennis was allowed to have the cell to himself with every perk available.

Every week a screw would bring him a bottle of single malt and two hundred of his favourite cigarettes all arranged for by Goose.

After his death Goose Gosling made sure that his friend and old cell mate was given the funeral that he deserved, it was the send-off of all send offs. A typical East End funeral with horse drawn carriage, the works.

CHAPTER FIVE:

1969

Goose Gosling waited for the screw to undo the huge black gate of the Scrubs where he had entered less than two years ago.

He had been released early on good behaviour, the Jackson incident was long forgotten and Goose had not faced any charges.

The gate swung open slowly and he strolled casually through with a cheery wave to the guards as he went.

The beautiful sun was shining down on him warming his bones and his heart, his first day of freedom started now.

He headed across the car-park and saw a Jaguar with its lights flashing, he walked with a spring in his step towards it.

His friend Joe Whyte emerged out of the passenger seat and ran towards him, the two men hugged and Joe took the two bin liners that contained Goose's sad excuse of possessions off him. Coulson got out from the driver's side and waved a greeting, it was a half-hearted wave, Goose knew that Coulson had done a good job looking after his businesses but if he thought that Goose was going to sign Bartholomeus over to him on the back of that he was in for a shock, he wasn't getting his hands on that for sure.

Goose had many eyes and ears on the outside while he was doing his time, Bartholomeus was a top earner, one of the best businesses in the portfolio so if Coulson thought that he was going to get his hands on a lucrative earner like that, he was more of a fool than Goose gave him credit for.

The Jaguar was gleaming and only a few months old; Goose knew it was because of the money that Coulson had creamed off his earnings (if he could call it that), was the reason he could own such a prestige and flashy vehicle; well, he was in for a short sharp lesson in life. No one was going to take from Goose Gosling and reap the benefits for too long. Goose, through Joe, had put an insider in to Bartholomeus, a buxom, good looking barmaid called Janice Lee, she had noted what was taken in the till and what was banked and put through the books, quick guestimate Coulson had taken over fifty grand in the years Goose had been away, slimy bastard and that was just the one business, others reported very similar figures.

Joe had been out of borstal for just over two years, Goose had ordered Coulson to set Joe up in his own flat, no expense spared, he was to have all he wished for within reason.

The judge, Harvey Emerson, had committed suicide shortly after Joe had his successful appeal, again from reputable sources Goose had learnt that Coulson had used his head and was blackmailing the judge with the photos he had found of Emerson with young boys. The judge simply could not take the stress and anxiety caused by the knowledge that Coulson had him over a barrel and even meeting his blackmail demands, Coulson could blow the whistle on him any time that he wanted, Emerson knew for sure that he wouldn't hesitate to do that.

As Goose approached Coulson, Goose smiled wildly and held out his hand. Coulson took the hand warily and shook it as vigorously as he dared, little did Coulson know that before the end of the day, depending on how things went, may well be the day that he took his last breath.

The three got into the Jaguar, Coulson driving and Joe and Goose in the back, Coulson leaned over his seat, "Where to boys?" he asked cheerily, Goose leant forward "Bartholomeus of course DI Coulson, the main hub of our Emporium, we have business to attend to do we not?" Goose looked at Joe and winked. Coulson felt a lot easier now, was today the day he got what was rightfully his he smiled to himself, foolishly that is what he hoped.

Once in the office at the back of Bartholomeus Goose, Joe and Coulson set about getting down to business.

Coulson had made the grave mistake of sitting in the chair behind the desk. "Excuse me DI Coulson, no offence but I think that you will find that chair is mine" Coulson smiled, it hid the fear that he was feeling. "Wait up their Goose we had a deal did we not, I look after the businesses in your absence, even get Joe here off the hook for murder and in return I get the club, I mean come on Goose don't mug me off son, if it wasn't for me, you wouldn't even know about this place or the other businesses".

The tension was broken by a young barmaid walking in with a tray of cut-glass tumblers, a bottle of whiskey and a bottle of rum. Goose noticed that she was pretty, not beautiful but a looker nonetheless, she had big tits that were fighting to get out of her low-cut blouse, a slim figure and a fuckable mouth, by the end of the day she would be in his bed no doubt about that.

After she left, Goose watched her as her tight arse wriggled from side to side, she glanced back over her shoulder and smiled at him, a connection between them had been made. Coulson walked over to the safe in the corner, he was sweating, he was fearful of the hunk of the man Goose had become, but he wanted what was his, what he was rightfully owed.

He withdrew paperwork from the safe and placed them in front of Goose, "These are the title deeds to all of the businesses that your father owned, they now belong to you, there are eleven in total, make that ten when you sign over Bartholomeus to me, I have already had the paperwork drawn up, we had a deal Goose, you owe me as you know". Coulson was putting on a brave face but deep down inside he was shitting himself, he sincerely hoped they hadn't noticed the slight shake in his hand as the papers were placed on the desk.

Goose looked at Coulson, Goose had to give him his due, he looked like a rabbit in the headlights and was sweating like a paedophile in Mothercare but Coulson was sticking to his guns, despite his growing fear he did not want to let go of what Goose's father had promised him.

Goose took a steady gulp of his superior quality whiskey, the dark liquid burning his throat, it was only the second drop of alcohol he had ever touched in his life, he liked the warmth, the smoothness and taste of the drink though and knew that he would soon get used to it.

Goose ordered Coulson to sit, which he did immediately beside Joe, then Goose just sat and stared at him for what seemed an eternity, unbeknown to Coulson it was because the taste of the whiskey was still burning the back of his throat and he was afraid to speak in case no words came out. Eventually Goose spoke, he was talking calmly with no sense of the anger that was pent up inside him which is what Coulson made him feel like after mugging him off for thousands yet still sitting there demanding the club, the audacity of the creep.

"DI Coulson you have had all that you are getting from me, the club is mine, will remain mine. I have it on good authority that you have stolen from me DI Coulson, fifty grand from the club alone God knows what from the other businesses. Now I am grateful that you put the squeeze on Judge Emerson to get my dear friend Joe here out on appeal, we are grateful aren't we Joe?" Joe nodded then got up and walked to the office door to lock it, Coulson was sweating even more now, the beads of sweat could be seen on his forehead and upper lip, he was petrified and thought that his heart would give out at any second. Goose stared hard at the man before him, "We are also grateful that without you keeping an eye on the businesses and knowing about the title deeds that we wouldn't be here today, if you didn't know my dear old father so well, so here is what is going to happen Coulson so listen good; we are going to make you a once in a lifetime offer".

Coulson sat stock still not knowing who to look at, Joe was behind him and Goose in front of him, a fear like he had never known before was setting his heart rate racing and his blood pressure had gone through the roof, he could feel his blood pulsating through his veins. When Coulson saw Joe approach him with cheese wire between two wooden handles in his hands, Coulson begged Goose to tell him what the once in a lifetime offer was as he shamelessly pissed himself.

Goose laughed like he had never laughed before, tears even streaming down his face such was the belly laugh, he and Joe were in hysterics at this pitiful excuse of a man before them.

Once both Goose and Joe had calmed down Goose soon composed himself and became all serious again, he poured the three of them a drink, Joe only drank rum but he and Coulson took whiskey straight, he took a large gulp of the fiery fluid. "Here is what is going to happen Coulson, we will overlook the small matter of you creaming money off the top of your earnings, what you were due for kindly running things in my absence, as we shall overlook the sparkly new Jaguar you have parked outside, the rather comfortable three-bedroom house in Battersea and the two-bedroom rose covered thatched cottage in Cornwall, which I believe are all in your wife's name and paid for outright, I have my sources and I know this information is correct, so please don't insult me further and deny it".

Coulson clutched his glass tumbler so hard that he thought that it would shatter at any minute, he began to sweat profusely once more it was running down the side of his face, he simply nodded his head. He had mugged Goose Gosling off, he knew that, but he only hoped and prayed that he could put things right but was it too late? How stupid was he to think that by arranging a bust at the club for Goose's father to gain ownership that gave him rights to demand ownership for himself? He would gladly give everything he had up and live in a filthy squat just as long as he was still breathing at the end of the day.

Goose looked deeply into Coulson's eyes, one day he would take great pleasure in wiping him off the face of the earth, despite his treachery he still had use of him now, Goose would use him to get what he wanted then, when he was of no further use, he would rid the world of this poor excuse of a man, Coulson. He would take him out himself, people will learn good and proper that no fucker mugged off Goose Gosling and lived to tell the tale, prison had taught him new tricks, given him a new belief in himself so the world had better wake up and smell the coffee.

"Ok DI Coulson, Joe and I will be making headlines in the next coming months, years. We have big ambitions see, we are going to be the new boys on the block, we will make the Krays look like Sooty and Sweep in comparison". Joe laughed out loud, he liked that. "We are going to rule London and the East End with an iron rod mate, this time next year no fucker will be able to fart in the smoke without our permission.

We want an in on everything from prostitution, protection, drugs, illegal gambling, debt collection the fucking whole shebang". Coulson knew what was coming next, it didn't take an idiot to work out that Gosling would want bent coppers on the books to achieve his growing empire, like he himself had suggested all those years ago.

"Now DI Coulson, this is where you come in, you owe me and big, don't fucking ever forget that, I want you to recruit on the inside, I need coppers in every nick within a one-hundred-mile radius on my books, you once said you know how to fish out the coppers that live above and beyond their means so now is your fucking chance to prove it."

Coulson sighed a breath of relief, while he was of use to Gosling, he would remain alive for now at least. He drank his drink and offered it out for a refill, Goose duly obliged although he couldn't believe the bare-faced cheek of the man, he fought the demons inside his head that wanted to physically drag Coulson over the sturdy wooden desk and knock seven piles of shite out of him. Even more so when Coulson arrogantly asked, "Ok Goose what's in it for me?"

Keeping his temper in check but storing this information away for a later day, Gosling gave a false smile and through gritted teeth. "Every devout recruit who becomes of use to us you get a monkey, or to a northern twat like you that don't understand us southerners, that is five hundred smackers for every single recruit." Joe jumped up and mockingly shouted "Oy I'm a northern twat, mind your manners!" both Joe and Goose laughed again, it was only Coulson who couldn't see the funny side of anything right now, he was too busy working out in his head how much he could earn before his well-earned retirement in two years' time, little did he realise at that moment that he would never live to see it.

Coulson was dismissed by Goose. "Down your drink Coulson then get out, you fucking stink of piss me old mate." Joe was taking a swig of his rum and he spat it out in hysterics, Goose just sat stony faced, as Coulson neared the door Goose yelled at him "and do what I've asked Coulson you useless cunt, I want results by the end of the week, hear me?" Coulson shook himself down with relief and gave a brief shudder when he stood on the pavement outside the club by his Jag, London air wasn't the cleanest to breathe but to him it was like standing in a meadow in the middle of the countryside, he lit a cigarette and sighed a huge sigh of relieve, he looked up to the sky and thanked God for sparing him, he ignored the passers-by that were smirking and sniggering at the dark patch on the crotch of his trousers that he was barely aware of.

When Goose and Joe were alone, they drunk a toast to freedom, comradery and their new ventures. Goose was relaxed and as for Joe, he was just glad to be back in the company of his friend. Goose had been good to him, the fully furnished and ideally situated apartment in Fulham was just one of the perks that he had received and he knew that if it wasn't for Goose, he would still be inside.

The two chatted amiably about the future, the riches that they were about to reap then Joe looked seriously at his friend, "The flat is ready, the decorators finished up last week, it's been fully renovated as you asked, top of the range new kitchen, bathroom suite, complete new furniture and soft furnishings, it was Mandy that picked all the furniture, fittings and colour scheme, she has a right eye for it, too good to be working the bar in this joint if you ask me."

Goose raised an eyebrow "Mandy?"

Joe grinned "Yes, the girl that brought in the drinks earlier, Mandy Dobbs, we employed her a few weeks ago, got rid of the old hag that was behind the bar, her face was turning the punters drinks sour mate, she and Janice make a good team."

Goose laughed out loud, then he became all serious once again focussing on his mate "So you and this Mandy are an item then mate?"

It was Joe's turn to laugh, "No mate, no chance, not my type, but I'm sure she is yours!" as soon as he had said it Joe wondered why he felt the need to lie to his friend.

Goose was relieved at his friend's answer, there would be no way he would step on his best mate's toes over a woman, he had too much respect for him and valued his friendship too much to allow any woman to come between them, he didn't need shit like that.

He downed his drink in one, he had not eaten since the gruel he had been served in the nick that morning, he was beginning to feel light headed, "You don't mind if I have a go at her then mate?" Joe tried to hide his disappointment, he secretly had feelings for Mandy but by the time she had started working at the club Joe was already in a relationship with Janice, and he may be many things but unlike most men he treated woman with respect, so he bravely smiled, "Course not mate, she likes you already I could tell that by the way she gave you a backwards glance earlier" then he went silent before asking, "you sure you want to go back there Goose, to the flat in Poplar, its where it all happened mate, are you sure there won't be too many bad memories lurking about?"

Goose got up and placed a hand on his friend's shoulder, in truth they were like brothers not just mates and business partners "It's me home mate, the only one I've ever known, if anything it will bring me closer to me mother, God rest her soul, and besides it sounds like it's a right plush place now it's all been done up, I would be stupid not to, come on let's get going I am starving could eat a horse, hooves an all, and you're paying."

CHAPTER SIX:

Mandy Dobbs was twenty-one years of age. She left her hometown of Blackpool at the earliest opportunity to seek fame and fortune in the big city that was London. She had originally hoped to land a role in the West End.

She was a talented dancer and even better singer, voice of an angel they said, sadly one set back after another occurred, rejection after rejection for roles that she knew she was capable of performing and then she found herself working the bar of a seedy strip club in Soho, hardly what she had aspired to. It was here that her fortunes were to change however when Goose Gosling came into her life.

The first night of his release from prison was spent with him in his bed where they both lost their virginity to one another, since that first night she had only been back to her own seedy flat once in the six weeks they had been together and that was to collect her few belongings and give notice on her flat.

Within three months the pair were married at the Registry Office in Poplar, with Joe and Janice from the club as witnesses, when the ring was put on her finger and a warm arm slipped around her waist from Goose, Mandy Dobbs knew that life would never be the same again. As the wife of an up-and-coming gangster, she knew that despite him telling her fifty times a day that he loved her and truly he did, she would be one of his possessions, he would rule her life and despite the love she felt for this man it scared her, she only hoped that he was true to his word and that he would give her the world on a stick and never give her any reason to think that he was being unfaithful to her, which would be easier said than done with the circles that he was now moving in and the places he was frequenting.

Within three years of being married Goose and Mandy were parents to a boy of two and a girl of six months, Frank "Goose" Junior was the spitting image of his father, born at ten pound six ounces, he had almost killed his mother at child birth after a long and difficult labour, the birth of Betty May the girl was more straight forward arriving two weeks early she was petite like her mother and pretty as a picture.

Goose adored his children, doted on them even. He and Joe commanded the streets of London these days, they were a force to be reckoned with but Goose always made sure to spend quality time with his family and remembering to bring home little treats for the kids and a bottle of quality wine for his beloved Mandy.

Before the birth of Goose junior, Mandy had persuaded Goose that they should move, she loved the flat but with the limited space and with the vast amount of money that Goose was bringing home she thought a better and bigger place would be more fitting in their circumstances.

After a few weeks of being married, Goose had given Mandy her own slot singing at Bartholomeus three days a week, she performed under her real name Amanda and people came from all around to see her, she had even landed a role, albeit small, in a West End musical but the birth and near-death experience of having Frank Junior put paid to that sadly as she had really loved it, enjoying the applause and gratitude from the clients in the club.

Mandy was a talented artist and designer as well as a dancer and singer, she had an eye for detail and quality, she had persuaded Goose to set her up in business as an interior designer which she ran from their home in St John's Wood. The business took off quickly, partly due to Goose who gently persuaded some celebrities and politicians who he met through parties, charity events and art gallery events to use her services. Goose was the man to be seen with in London these days, it was a reasonable request said without malice, but in a tone where the recipient of the request was reluctant to say no to him.

For all her success, Mandy still feared for the future, what if Goose left her for a younger woman? What if he did a long stretch at Her Majesties pleasure? Goose paid for everything, the house was bought outright, but fair play to him, he had insisted in putting it in joint names, she had two cars, a MG Convertible and a more traditional family car, a Ford Cortina more suitable for taking the children to their various activities and school, Goose had put them both in her name. She also knew the code for the safe which held everything from cash, jewellery, stocks, bonds, title deeds to various businesses, properties and nine times out of ten, guns. She knew that if worst come to worse, she would be financially stable yet she still opened a personal bank account without Goose's knowledge and was putting money away when and where she could from her singing days at the club and the new business venture just in case. If anything happened to Goose was one thing, if she ever felt the need to take the kids and leave him was another matter entirely.

***

Goose woke, the sunlight was coming through the curtains, he looked across the bed and saw the naked girl lying beside him. The first pangs of guilt hit him; they always did.

Mandy was a brilliant mother, lover and business woman but things were sadly going downhill rapidly between them. The girl beside him stirred, the sun shone on her naked body as she lay on her back, she was no more than eighteen, a girl he had picked up in one of the exclusive clubs he frequented, beautiful slim legs, massive tits, just as he liked. She stirred and leant in to him, her head on his chest and her arm draped across his wash board stomach. Goose could not believe how easy it was to get a girl into bed, they just wanted to be seen out with a known crook, hardman, gangster, criminal mastermind whatever he was called in a woman's mind, prestige in their world counted for everything. By close of play today she would have bragged to everyone she knew that she had fucked Frank "Goose" Gosling.

Goose had been cheating on Mandy from virtually day one, even on his stag do he had fucked a woman, whose name he couldn't remember the next day or barely at the time of shagging her, on an overnight trip to Southend, a croupier from a casino they had all finished the night in.

Goose moved the girl none too smoothly off him, he couldn't remember her name, not that it mattered and why bother remembering names, she had been a good shag but the chances of it happening again with her was less than nil, that is what he did, fuck them once, remind them that they were just a means to scratch an itch, keep your mouth shut and move on to the next one once the guilt he felt for Mandy had worn off, which seemed to be taking less and less time.

Goose jumped up and started to dress, it was time to go home and face the music, Mandy was like a bull-dog with a wasp in its mouth when he stayed out all night, he would say that he was either in a poker game, or was on business that he couldn't go into, they would argue, she would throw things at him then by the afternoon she would be laying on her back, legs wide open, begging him to forgive her outburst and to fuck her rigid. It was the game they played, argue, fuck and make up time after time.

***

Goose and Joe were in the Red Lion pub in Stratford, they'd made sure they weren't seen going in and had parked up round the back in a side road. They were there to sort out a new supplier of heroin, or 'the brown' as it was commonly called these days.

Goose and Joe had fingers in so many pies these days it was hard to keep track of the money coming in every day, and it was in its thousands.

Drugs was by far the biggest earner, next to buying up debts for a pittance and persuading the person who owed the debt that it was in their interest to settle the debt quickly, which most did, just like his father used to do.

Prostitution was a close third in reaping in the money. Along with Bartholomeus they now owned a dozen clubs throughout the city and a casino, these were the legitimate businesses, the businesses that could be used to explain their ever-increasing wealth if the need arose. Bartholomeus was the in place to be in Soho, it made a small fortune on a daily basis, the casino which was just round the corner from Bartholomeus was a close second, the other clubs were not massive earners, but enough money was coming in, Goose referred to the revenue from these clubs as pocket money. Thanks to Coulson they had a hundred or more bent coppers on the books who they called on when needed which didn't seem to be too frequent thankfully. Coulson, much to Goose's dismay, had dropped down dead of a massive heart attack two weeks before his retirement and before Goose had the pleasure of extracting revenge.

He had summoned Coulson to a meet at a deserted warehouse in Stratford. Coulson had appeared on time, even Goose could see that he did not look his normal self. The man had piled on weight, was a heavy smoker and drinker and when he stood before Goose, was sweating and shaking profusely as he'd remembered him doing that day he came out of the Scrubs.

It had been Goose's initial intention to torture Coulson slowly, making him suffer for ripping him off all those years ago but Coulson had other ideas. He begged Goose for a glass of water as he frantically pulled off his tie and undid his shirt collar. He slumped in to a chair pleading with Goose to call an ambulance. Goose calmly poured himself a drink and for forty minutes watched Coulson suffer in agony, his pleading that he was having a heart attack falling on deaf ears. It was not the revenge death that Goose had in mind but he took some great form of pleasure in watching Coulson die slowly and in apparent agony, gasping for breath and clutching at his left arm and heart.

CHAPTER SEVEN:

Goose and Joe sat slowly sipping their drinks waiting for Jimmy Stirling, a Jamaican drug supplier, to show. They were early for a change so the two wiled away the time chewing the fat. "I tell you Joe, she is becoming a nightmare, and as for the kids, fuck me the little bastards are spoilt rotten, everything they ask for they get, and she has shipped the little fuckers off to boarding school in Gloucester, costing me three grand a term each for fucks sake!" Goose gulped at his pint; he did not drink shorts during the day, it helped in him keeping a clear head. Joe smiled, he knew Mandy would change, they always did in his opinion, but he knew that she was a good mother and wife. If she knew half of what Goose had been up to over the year's she would have fucked off long ago. But he had heard a rumour that Mandy was seeing a well to do banker, he wanted it clarifying before he said anything and was having her tailed by a private investigator on the quiet, costing a tidy penny it had to be said. If she was up to no good, Goose would kill her, he wanted to make sure first. If she, was it would be no more than Goose deserved but he would have to get Mandy away from him, she could tell Goose everything if cornered and he would not want that?

Three months previously Joe had arrived at Gooses house on a sunny Sunday afternoon unannounced. He had heard from his sister that his mother was ill in hospital, on her death bed in fact and he had to go to Manchester to be with her as the dutiful son.

Mandy had answered the door, although it was the middle of the afternoon, she still had a negligee and silk robe on that left nothing to the imagination in the right light, he could clearly see the outline of her perfect figure.

She was well bladdered that much he could tell as she invited him in. She led him in to the living room, the room was filled with modern classy furniture elegantly designed to Mandy's high standard, the carpet must have been three inches thick alone, the drapes in the Victorian lounge were floor to ceiling and of the highest quality, fully lined and a quality chintz, modern paintings, that looked like a three-year-old had splashed paint on a canvass adorned the walls.

Once Joe was seated Mandy handed him a drink, despite him telling her he didn't want one, he had a long drive ahead of him. She pouted her lips seductively, "Oh Joe don't let a lady drink alone." She moved across the living room floor and he could see a silhouette of her fulsome breasts as the light shone through the window, Goose had disclosed to him a few months before that they had been surgically enhanced and it was clear to see, a good job had been done, after two kids Mandy had insisted on it apparently.

Mandy poured herself another unneeded drink and sat beside Joe on the cream leather sofa, she moved her legs up onto the sofa and her robe parted showing beautiful slim legs. Joe had to stop himself from pulling her towards him, he had the occasional tommy tank thinking of Mandy, that said he also had the odd tommy thinking of Goose too, in reality he should have been more concerned for the welfare of his mother, not that he had seen or spoken to her since his release from prison but at the end of the day, she was his mother and he should be there for her.

"So, you want to see Goose, well when you find him, please remind him that he has a wife at home, I haven't seen the bastard for two days, said he was going up north on some sort of business, lying bastard."

Joe lied for his friend, knowing that Mandy would see right through it, "Ah yeah, bollocks I forgot Mandy he was going to meet some new suppliers in Newcastle, anyway when he gets back tell him I've had to go to see me dying mother in Manchester will you love?" Joe tried to get up but Mandy forced him back down, "Oh no you don't Joe Whyte, you are a lying bastard like he is, now I want the truth, is he cheating on me?" Joe felt himself blushing, but he was also getting aroused, he was seeing Mandy in a different light, literally, she was one fuckable bird, despite two kids, he was seeing her beauty as if for the first time. Joe took a large gulp of his JD and coke, his drink of choice these days, he didn't really know what to say, he found himself being placed in an unwanted position and could also feel a stirring in the nether regions. "Look Mandy love, I don't know right, if he is, he wouldn't tell me, he wouldn't put me in that position, he knows how much you both mean to me." Mandy looked scornfully at Joe, "I want to believe you Joe, really, I do but I think you're still lying, let's say I believe you, but in the past week I have found a packet of condoms with two missing in his suit pocket along with several pieces of paper with lady's names and phone numbers on, who incidentally when I call and they answer they mysteriously quickly hang up!"

Mandy was close to tears, she downed her scotch and got up and staggered across to the drink's cabinet bumping into the arm chair as she did so, she quickly poured another drink before returning and flopping down on the sofa. The sudden movement caused her left breast to emerge from her negligee top, Joe felt himself getting hard as he stared at the pink nipple and tanned fleshed breast. Mandy ignored the fact that her tit had broken free and was on show, she was angrier that a man she regarded as a friend was sitting there telling her bare faced lies. After she had made sure that she had his full attention she pushed the breast back inside her negligee. "Joe please stop mugging me off, has he gone up North? Is

he having an affair? please Joe, I need to know!" She was now crying, brought on by the

drink as much as anything and being upset about Goose's whereabouts, Joe felt a pang of

guilt, more so by being aroused than lying. "Calm down Mandy love, please, I don't like

seeing you upset" She pushed away the hand that he placed on her shoulder. "Don't like

seeing me upset, then tell me the truth you bastard" she yelled at him now.

Joe downed his drink and helped himself to another, he came back to the sofa and placed

his hand back on Mandy's shoulder, this time she did not push it away but looked deeply

into his eyes. "Please Joe, I won't ever tell him the information came from you, honest, on

me kid's lives." Joe looked at her then, he felt that he owed her this much if nothing else,

"Ok Mandy, I didn't know he was going up North, if indeed that is where he has gone, and

I know he has been seeing some woman, I don't know her name, all I know is that they met

at a charity event and she is an up-and-coming actress, she had a minor role in Coronation

Street apparently."

Mandy composed herself now, the crying stopped and she seemed almost relieved that the

truth was out, she leant in and kissed Joe on the cheek, "Thank you" she whispered softly,

then the pair looked at each other for several seconds and Mandy leaned in again, this time

kissing Joe fully on the lips, her tongue inside his mouth, her breast had fallen from her

negligee once more, only this time she made no attempt to put it back. "Where are the

kids?" Joe asked, his head was spinning and his cock was hard, Mandy was still kissing

him with more passion this time, herself getting more and more aroused, she had a tingling

between her legs, she felt now as Goose had made her feel in the early days. "They're at

my mothers, don't worry about them, they are not due back until morning." She unzipped

81

the flies on his trousers and placed her hand inside on his erect penis. Fear and excitement were battling against each other inside Joe's head, what if Goose returned at this moment, excitement won, he allowed Mandy to take his cock deep in her mouth and the pleasure was all his.

Joe pulled on his trousers and shirt, he looked down at Mandy laying on the sofa, "You know what we've just done Mandy? we've just signed our own death warrants that's what, if Goose ever finds out about this, we will both end up in a shallow grave in Epping Forest, fuck me!!"

Mandy lay on the sofa completely naked, her legs still wide open, the sun through the window reflecting off the sweat on her body "I just did" she smiled with one finger seductively in her mouth.

***

Mandy having replaced her negligee and robe stood by the front room window as Goose's car pulled up on the driveway. Joe had left only five minutes beforehand, she stood arms folded and watched her husband get out of the car, a bunch of flowers in his arms, she could still feel the semen from Joe running down her legs, she smiled to herself, "An actress is she, well so am I and tonight I am going to give an Oscar winning performance!" she laughed out loud, then turning round she saw the damp patch on the sofa from her love making with Joe and laughed even louder, she was still laughing when Goose walked in.

***

" You fucking listening to me or what Joseph, you've been spaced out for ten minutes mate" Joe's mind had wondered to the afternoon he had spent with Mandy but now he was back in the Red Lion listening to Goose with still no sign of the dealer. "She wants us to move to Wimbledon, I don't like tennis and I'm not a fucking Womble, what the fuck would I want to move to Wimbledon for, and I tell you something else Joe, she has become all posh and fucking lardy dah overnight, if I was to walk in and say I had just mown down thirty fucking coppers with a machine gun, the first thing she would say is, no need to swear!" Joe almost choked on his pint as he roared with laughter.

One man who had sat at the bar looking at the two men laughing like school boys shouted over, "Keep the fucking noise down, some of us have come in for a quiet drink", he was obviously from out of town and had no idea who he was shouting at until the landlord put a hand on his shoulder pulled him forward slightly and whispered in his ear. The colour drained from the drinker's face and he quickly had the landlord pour two pints and take them over as he waved an apology "Sorry I didn't mean anything by it" as he settled his bill and speedily left the pub.

Two hours later after the meeting with Jimmy, Goose and Joe left the pub and headed to a bed and breakfast gaff down the road. Joe stood outside as Goose knocked on the door, Barbara Wilcox had run the Stratford Road bed and breakfast for thirty years, she was a big woman whose only pleasure in life since her husband had run off with a younger woman twenty years earlier was pies, jellied eels, sherry and the occasional game of bingo. She stood on the doorstep her folded arms across her large chest, then she looked closely at the man on the door step and seeing it was Frank "Goose" Gosling her attitude changed immediately and she was all smiles and politeness offering him in for a cup of tea. Once inside Goose smiled, "I will forgo the tea Mrs Wilcox, but thank you for your kind offer, I believe you have a David Matthews staying with you." Barbara Wilcox was all smiles and laughter and kept touching the bun in her hair, "Mr Matthews? oh yes one of my regulars, do you want me to get him for you?" Goose smiled, "No that will be ok Mrs Wilcox, I have a bit of business to discuss with him, just tell me what room he is in if you'd be so kind." After receiving the information required Goose handed the landlady an envelope. "In there Mrs Wilcox you will find there is ten grand, yours to do with as you wish, in return all I want is for you to never say that I was here, are we clear?" Barbara Wilcox thought all her Christmases had come at once, Frank Gosling was as handsome in the flesh as the pictures of him she had seen and here he was giving her a wedge like she had never ever seen before in her life.

Barbara Wilcox sat in her favourite arm chair drinking sherry and running her hands through the contents of the envelope over and over again, tomorrow she would be down the High Street getting travel brochures as soon as they opened, she fancied a cruise, she tried to block out the terrible screams coming from the room above.

Ten minutes later Gosling was behind the wheel of his car driving away from Stratford, David Matthews the punter in the Red Lion had paid the ultimate price for insulting him, Goose was buzzing, the drink and the adrenalin he always got after a kill, plus the couple of lines he had snorted in the gents of the Red Lion before they had left the pub had helped. He looked at Joe as if he had two heads when his mate shouted for him to watch out, he turned back to face the road just as the car ploughed into the woman and child on the zebra crossing.

Goose got home a few hours later, he and Joe had worked tirelessly to make sure the hit and run didn't come back to bite them. The coke he had snorted had long worn off; the first thing he would do is cut another couple of lines. He walked in shouting "Mandy, Mandy where are you?" He searched the house, he needed an alibi, Mandy was going to have to tell the old bill he had been there all afternoon. When he went in the living room, he saw the envelope on the writing bureau, an antique Mandy had found in a shop in Shepherds Bush and had insisted on paying well over the odds for, it looked out of place with all the other modern furniture in the room, but she had insisted on having it. He opened the envelope, withdrew the letter inside, not believing what he was reading,

"My darling Frank, I am sorry to say that I am leaving you, I am taking the kids out of boarding school and going somewhere you will never find us, I know all about your cheating and womanising, you have cheated on me more than once.

The kids and I deserve better than this Goose, I only sent them to boarding school because they were listening to our constant arguing every day when you could be bothered to come home at all that is and you had stopped having anything to do with them, they will be better off without a father, especially one like you. M x

Ps I have emptied the safe, thanks for the leg up in starting my new life, do not try and find me, I have gathered some evidence on what you have been up to over the years that I will gladly give to the old bill if you do, and you will go away for life.

Give my love to Joe, I wish you could be more like him, he is a truly caring, sensitive man. You would do well to learn from him and be more like him x"

Goose screwed the note up in his hand his face red with rage. What evidence? Was all he could think of. He immediately phoned Joe, it went directly to voice mail, he left a message asking Joe to go to the kids boarding school and pick them up immediately. He poured himself a large scotch and cut two more hefty lines of coke, his heart felt like it would burst out of his chest any moment such was his rage and adrenalin. Quickly snorting the coke, he then downed the scotch in one, it was then he felt his knees buckle and he fell to the floor clutching his chest, banging his head on the corner of the writing bureau as he fell, he now knew what Coulson was feeling all those years ago.

The police who came to interview him three hours later about his car being involved in a hit and run found him lying on the living room floor gasping for breath, he would later be diagnosed as having the first of the three heart attacks he would have in his lifetime; he would never ever see Mandy or his children again despite all the private investigators he employed and the thousands he spent looking for her. Many found her but by the time he got a plane to Portugal, Spain, Dominican Republic and half a dozen other places she had already fled, one time he had missed her by only fifteen minutes. Little did he know that on each occasion she had been found he had told his best friend and closest confidant Joe where he was heading off to in such a hurry and Joe had contacted Mandy to forewarn her.

CHAPTER EIGHT:

Joe was in the shower letting the soothing hot water flood over him. What a fucking day it had been, if it wasn't bad enough that Goose had insisted on getting revenge on the travelling salesman, which as Joe had told him was a retribution that was way over the top for such a flippant comment, Goose then ploughed into the woman and child. All this because he was high on coke, booze and adrenalin. Then came all the rushing round to put a plan in place for someone to take the wrap, with the money Goose had given to the landlady and the money for the guy taking the wrap it would end up costing them over a hundred k for one afternoon of Goose's stupidity. Yes, they could afford it, to them it was just loose change, but lately Goose was getting out of control, it was beginning to grate on Joe, the coke and the woman were ruling and ruining his friend's life.

Joe sat on his sofa wrapped in a towel and listened to the voice mail, fuck him he thought, he would tell him that by the time he had got to the school the kids had already been picked up by Mandy, he certainly had no intention of driving to Gloucester at this hour in the day. The door intercom buzzed, he went to answer it half expecting Goose to be on the other end, he was surprised to hear Mandy's voice; "Joe, it's Mandy, I need your help."

Joe, now in t-shirt and jogging bottoms handed Mandy a scotch on the rocks, she was clearly upset he just didn't know why. After she had downed the drink in one and offered her glass for a refill, only then did she begin to explain why.

"I've left him Joe, left the cheating bastard, I've had enough, but I fucked up Joe fucked up big time, can I stay here for the night?" Joe put a comforting hand on Mandy's knee, "Course you can darling, Goose rarely comes here, but how have you fucked up?" Mandy leaned in to Joe, nestled her head on his shoulder, he could smell the strawberry shampoo and conditioner she used and her Chanel perfume, he felt himself getting aroused again. "How have you fucked up love?" he repeated trying to distract himself from his growing hardness.

"Mum has picked the kids up, they are on the way to Spain as we speak, the kids had passports from a school trip to France last year, I bloody never had one did I, never been abroad in me bleeding life, cut a long story short, it won't be ready to pick up until tomorrow."

Despite sensing her sorrow, Joe let out a small laugh, she playfully punched him, then their eyes met and the inevitable happened, she leant in and kissed him passionately.

Joe and Mandy lay in bed, her head on his hairy chest, she ran her fingers through the hair, she looked up at him, the love making had been fantastic, how it once was with Goose, better even, "Joe can I ask you something?" He looked down and kissed the top of her head, this was wrong, he had betrayed Goose again, but he just couldn't help himself, Goose had his Charlie as a drug, Joe's drug was Mandy. "Course you can love, ask away" Mandy leant both arms on Joe's chest and propped herself up to look directly in his eyes, "Are you bi-sexual?"

The question took Joe by surprise. "I don't understand, what makes you think that?" Joe started to feel awkard as to where the conversation was going, but somehow was not upset by Mandy asking him directly. She returned her head to rest on his chest, "Oh I don't know, I've seen the way you look at Goose sometimes, and we have been at plenty of parties together and I have seen you when a handsome man walks by, you can't take your eyes off them."

Joe did not rant and rave and go on the defensive as Mandy had expected he would, instead he wrapped his arms protectively round her, "Truth is I don't know Mandy, I've slept with woman lots of them, I find myself being attracted to certain men, but have never taken it further."

Mandy did not pursue the topic further instead she slipped down Joes body until her head was in his groin where she expertly took him in her mouth and went to work on him until he came.

Joe was up early the next morning making breakfast for them both, his mobile rang, he expected it to be Goose, instead it was Goose's solicitor, Joe listened in disbelief. Mandy came in to the kitchen wrapped only in a towel and wrapped her arms around his waist from behind, she placed her head with its wet hair on his shoulder. When he had hung up, she turned him round, "What's wrong Joe?" He looked down at her, she had just showered and even without make-up she was still beautiful. He took both her hands in his "Its Goose, he's had a heart attack."

Mandy sat on the sofa sobbing uncontrollably, Joe was doing his best to comfort her, "What can I do Joe" she murmured through her tears, "I can't go to him, he will kill me, even if he isn't able to himself, he will get someone to do it, maybe even you?" Joe grunted "That will never happen, stick to your plan, I'll go to the hospital find out what's going on, you stay here, don't let anyone in, where is your car by the way?" Mandy wiped away her tears, "I sold it, Goose asked where it was two days ago, I told him it was being serviced, I have a hire car, its downstairs in the car park." Joe got up and went to change, a few

minutes later he was ready to head out the door looking his usual dapper self. He leant

down and kissed Mandy fully on the lips, he noticed the full tumbler of whiskey she had

poured herself, deep down he knew then that she would not be going anywhere today

"Won't be long, I'll get the tube it will be better than getting stuck in the rush hour traffic,

as soon as I get back with news you can head off to the passport office, that is if you lay off

the sauce love."

An hour later Joe walked in to the private room Goose had at the hospital. Although an

NHS hospital Goose and his money had secured a private room, somewhere that he could

suffer in silence.

Joe looked at his friend and boss laying in the hospital bed, a man that looked vulnerable

and hurting, in more ways than one. Several tubes were coming out of parts of his body

and he was linked up to a heart monitor and blood pressure machine the machinery bleeped

periodically. His face was ashen and drawn and his eyes didn't flicker when Joe stared

down at him.

The room smelt of bleach and hospital, that distinctive smell that only hospitals gave off.

Goose lay still and silent, he had fallen asleep. Joe accidentally walked in to a trolly placed

at the end of the bed, Goose woke with a start. It took a few seconds for Goose to realise

where he was and then the pain hit him again, not the pain from the heart attack but the

pain from the heartache that Mandy had caused him. Seeing his friend at the end of the

bed, he smiled and manoeuvred himself in to a more comfortable position in the bed.

"Alright Joe, me old mate, you took your time getting here didn't you" he faked a smile. Joe could see the hurt in his friend's face, hurt that he had in some way attributed too.

"My mobile was out of charge mate, I was on the road to and from Gloucester, then when I eventually got home, I crashed out on the settee mate, first I knew you were in here was when Mickey phoned this morning"

Joe sat himself down on an uncomfortable plastic chair beside the bed, he felt uncomfortable lying to his oldest friend, but he couldn't actually tell him he hadn't been to Gloucester in his life and that he was at home fucking his friend's wife.

"How are you, Goose?" Goose either didn't hear the question or simply chose to ignore it, "Did you get the kids? please tell me you got the kids, that's why you have not been to see me earlier right?"

Joe averted his gaze from Goose and stared down at the floor knowing the further pain his answer would cause, that and the fact that he was going to have to lie to his friend about even going to the school, he cleared his throat which was dry, that always happened when he was about to lie, "No sorry mate by the time I had got there Mandy's mum had already collected them" only then dare Joe look at his friend directly.

The machines started beeping erratically, Goose's heart rate and blood pressure had obviously gone through the roof at hearing the news. Two nurses came running in to the room and Joe was asked to wait outside in the corridor while they tended to Goose. Five minutes later the nurses came back out and said that he could go back in but to be careful what he said to their patient, he was stable for now but anymore upset would result in a visitor ban.

Goose stared back at Joe as he took the seat he had sat in previously; he was calmer now but still hurting and angry, "Get everyone we have looking for that bitch Joe, I have already ordered a hit on her I want her dead mate, some of the boys have already been in to see me I have put the word out that she is to be taken out. I don't give a fuck how that happens either, they can fuck her with a baseball bat for all I care, then smash her over the head with it when they have finished, I just want my kids back. Where the fuck is she if that witch of a mother-in-law of mine has picked the kids up?"

Joe stood and put his hand on his best friend's shoulder, he had listened to his friend, although a part of him felt sorry for him, Goose had in all honesty brought this on himself. His womanising, drug taking and ignoring his children by being away from the marital home for days at a time had all attributed to Mandy leaving him, who could blame her? The fact he and Mandy had shared each other's bodies was not an attributing factor in the marriages demise, or at least Joe tried to convince himself it wasn't.

Joe looked at Goose, he had decided that he would lie through his teeth if it meant Mandy could get away safely "You sure mate? I mean what has she actually done, you two have history and two beautiful kids, you always said that she was the love of your life, remember that?"

Goose turned his head away from his friend, "No going back now Joe, she has threatened me with old bill, she hit me with the fact that she is holding some form of evidence to send me down, maybe even you too, she has made her bed, but she is not going to live long enough to lie it, we just need to find the devious bitch and fast!"

Joe looked down at Goose, the anguish was etched on his face "She is in Portugal mate"

Goose sat upright "What? How the fuck do you know that mate?" Joe moved uncomfortably in the chair, partly because the chair in itself was not the most comfortable to sit in but also the seed had been planted now, the lie had started and he was now going to have to manufacture a story that could be believed.

"She phoned me last night", as soon as Joe had uttered the words he realised the flaw, he had told Goose his mobile was dead so quickly added "On the land line, there was a message on the answer machine, all she said was she was leaving you, taking the boys and going to the Algarve."

Goose seemed to believe what he said, he never questioned it at any rate. A few moments of silence passed between the two then Goose simply uttered the words," Pass that info on to the boys will you Joe, now if you don't mind mate, I am tired, you have got businesses to take care of in my absence, best you get to it."

Joe knew Goose was taken aback by his lie, and when Goose was like this, deep in thought and pain there was no point discussing anything further, so he simply left without another word.

Three hours after he had left his flat to go to the hospital Joe returned, three hours felt like a week to Mandy. She was desperate to hear news of Goose, it was obvious that she had hit the whiskey hard and was in no fit state to go anywhere as Joe had predicted. If Joe was disappointed that she had allowed herself to get half cut he certainly didn't show it. He threw his jacket and keys on the coffee table and sat down wearily beside her. He looked at her, she was now fully made up and was stunningly beautiful. "Were your ears burning love?" he smiled broadly. Mandy looked at him pity in her eyes, "How is he Joe?" Joe got up and made himself a drink, he did not offer one to Mandy. He sat back down "Oh he will survive, it was a mild heart attack, should be allowed out in a couple of days, into the arms of the law, who want to interview him about a hit and run that happened yesterday, it'll just be a formality. We have it covered."

Knowing that a drink was not forthcoming Mandy staggered over to the sideboard and made herself another, she turned her head slightly towards Joe, "And me? What did he say about me, Joe?" not really wanting to know the answer but asking anyway. Joe started to laugh, "Did he mention you? Fucking never shut up about you darling, you now officially have a price on your head, where Mandy Gosling is concerned it is open season." Mandy turned round glass in hand and took a large gulp of her drink, the liquid burnt her throat and then the tears began to flow, she felt her days were numbered.

Joe comforted Mandy, trying to assure her "I won't let anything happen to you love, rest assured. When word spreads every hit man in the land will be after you though, being given permission to take out Goose Gosling's wife anyway they want to will bring them all out the woodwork, all we have to do is get you out the country before they find you."

Mandy cried relentlessly for over an hour, her head on Joe's shoulder, he stroked her hair and offered words of comfort. The tears eventually subsided, she looked up at Joe, "Come with me Joe, come with me to Spain, let us be together, I love you Joe, a part of me always has. All the times we spent together before Goose was released from prison, doing up his flat. The times I wished you would take me in your arms, why didn't you?"

Joe didn't know what to say, it was true he had been attracted to Mandy but he was involved with Janice at the time, Janice had taken his virginity and the sex was incredible, whatever he was or was to become it was in his eyes wrong to have two women on the go at one time, fucking not only them but also with their emotions, their feelings, it was something despite all his faults he would never do, he had seen the pain etched on his mother's face time after time after his father had cheated on her with other woman, and children.

After running words through his head, he decided to focus on the first point of the question and ignore the second. He wanted another drink, this time he offered and made Mandy one. "Mandy darling, I can't come with you, it's bad enough that Goose wants you dead, at least we have a way of getting you away tomorrow before anyone has a chance to fulfil the contract, if I was to come with you Goose would be so hurt that he had been betrayed not only by his wife but also his best friend, we wouldn't last a week before we were caught, Goose would employ a small army to track us down."

Mandy began to sob again. "Think about it love, Goose would spend an absolute fortune to hire men to get us, and who knows his anger is such at the moment that even the kids or your mother could be collateral damage and he wouldn't give a flying fuck as long as he got his revenge and we died." Joe's words sunk in and the realisation hit Mandy, she was to spend the rest of her days or at least until Goose's demise on the run and looking over her shoulder.

Although she wanted Joe in her life all Mandy could do was nod in agreement, Joes words made sense but how could she tell him that she was pregnant and that he was the father, thanks to their little indiscretion in her lounge a few months before. She tried to hide her disappointment but decided not to say anything, it would make no sense to, he had just told her that there was no chance that they could be together, certainly for the foreseeable.

Still trying to justify his decision a short while later Joe asked Mandy about her affair with the banker. Mandy laughed for a full five minutes, tears of laughter were rolling down her cheeks, eventually she composed herself enough to say "There would be more chance of you pulling him than me darling, he is as bent as a nine-bob note. I got the contract to do a makeover on his flat after his wife left him because of his indiscretions with men. He insisted that our meetings were always over dinner at places where he knew his bosses frequented just to keep up appearances." It was Joes turn to laugh, something that they both needed.

Joe and Mandy spent one more night together, they fucked like rabbit's half the night and talked for the other half. Joe had told Mandy about the lie to Goose of her already being in Portugal so she should at least get to Spain without being in any danger or having to look over her shoulder for the time being.

The following morning after checking the coast was clear, Joe walked Mandy to her car, he had wanted to drive her to Peterborough to pick up her passport and then on to Luton where she would get the next available flight to Spain but he knew that with Goose in hospital he would be expected to run the businesses and at least pretend to make an effort organising a search for Mandy and her kids. If he didn't question's may well be asked and his motives could be scrutinised.

Mandy had dressed down, old jeans and a hoodie, she was wearing sunglasses in an effort to disguise herself. They kissed and hugged one last time and then despite the pain both were feeling. Joe sent her on her way. The chances of him ever seeing her again were slim but they would frequently on the phone.

Little did he know that six months to the day she had left his flat she would give birth to a healthy and handsome baby boy in a Madrid hospital, that it was his son and whose name was Joe Junior.

CHAPTER NINE:

August 1992

The Wherry Inn at Rock-Hampstead was in an idyllic location whatever the weather. Today Norfolk was experiencing a mini heat wave so the little pub situated right on the banks of the Norfolk Broads was packed out with tourists, day trippers and locals taking full advantage of the weather. Boats were moored up outside, children playing on the grass verges and play equipment provided, delicious food was being carried out together with beers and local ciders for all to enjoy.

Every one of the fifty or so wooden picnic tables in the beer garden was full of customers.

Marcus Jones enjoyed coming to the Wherry Inn, it was only a few miles from camp and they served the best ploughman's lunch in all of Norfolk the very best local cheeses, ham and pickles adorned the plate together with freshly baked bread.

He sat watching the other customers, he liked to people watch.

At just turned thirty Marcus was handsome and he knew it, his mother was Italian and his father Welsh.

Woman noticed Marcus Jones, his Mediterranean looks, his crystal blue eyes, jet black hair and a five-foot eleven frame that was devoid of any fat, working out at the RAF gym five times a week saw to that, woman couldn't help but notice.

His eyes, hidden behind designer Ray-Ban sunglasses, and without making it look too obvious he was able to observe two woman a few tables over who kept looking in his direction and giggling like school girls, it was obvious that he was the one that they were talking about, the looks they gave were bordering on lustful.

Both of the women were reasonably attractive, one blonde and small breasted, an almost anorexic body in a dark blue cotton dress, the other a brunette, a little on the chubby side but not fat with breasts so large that were trying to escape out of the top of her low-cut yellow flowery summer dress. Marcus hazarded a guess that both women were the top end of thirty in age.

Marcus knew that only three years earlier he would have struck up a conversation with them and would have ended up in bed with either one or both of them this sunny Saturday afternoon pleasuring not only himself but them too. But that was then and this was now and Marcus was a changed man.

His thoughts were interrupted by the handsome waiter who placed a pint of lager and an orange juice and lemonade on the table in front of him.

"Your wife said to bring the drinks over sir, the orange juice and lemonade is for her, she won't be long and said for you not to worry about drink driving as she will be driving home."

Marcus took the cold lager "Thank you."

"You are more than welcome sir, I only wish my own wife was as considerate sir, and as beautiful."

Marcus smiled again "Oh she is that alright, on both counts."

Marcus knew that Claudia was the love of his life, his soul mate. She was so thoughtful, loving and caring. Who else would have said "Don't worry about the drink driving I will

99

drive" knowing that he detested seeing anyone get behind the wheel of a car having had too much to drink? He had campaigned since a teenager for stiffer penalties for all drink drivers.

At the age of thirteen both his parents had been involved in a fatal car crash. His Dad had been driving but the head on crash had been caused by the other driver who escaped with minor cuts and bruises but had left both his parents dead having chosen to drive whilst almost four times over the drink/drive limit.

He remembered at the funeral that everyone was saying what a tragedy it was, a waste of two precious lives with so much still to live for and that the driver should be locked up and throw away the key.

A week later Marcus was told by the Police that the driver received a two hundred and fifty pound fine, a suspended eighteen-month jail sentence and was banned from driving for three years.

What a small price to pay for taking away the lives of his parents.

Marcus had gone to live with his father's sister in London after the death of his parents and his aunt, a spinster had raised him, became his surrogate mum, and he loved her like any son would love a mum. She pandered to his every need, kept him in the best of clothes and always had an ear for his worries and confidences. Sadly, she had died of a massive heart attack a month before he joined the RAF at eighteen. She had smoked like a chimney, drank like a fish and ate like a horse so to Marcus it was no big surprise, but a shock non the less.

Marcus was looking out at the Broads when a day cruiser sailed past.

On the deck were two young girls of about nine who were waving randomly towards people in the beer garden, Marcus put up a hand and waved back.

"Still have an eye for the ladies I see Marcus Jones"

Marcus laughed. He turned round to face his wife.

She handed him his daughter, "there you go one little lady all changed and fed."

Marcus cradled his month-old daughter in his arms and looked lovingly into her beautiful blue eyes, just like her mummy's.

Where Marcus was handsome, Claudia his wife was beautiful in every way. She was a head turner with natural blonde hair, blue eyes, breasts that were neither too big nor small, legs that seemed to go on forever, like Marcus she was five feet eleven and when she spoke, she had a soft voice tinged with a German accent.

Claudia Jones could be mistaken for a model and anyone looking at her would not know or believe that up until just over a month ago she was pregnant, she had trimmed right back to her pre-pregnancy shape.

She sat down, "Got your pint I, see?"

" Marcus smiled, "Thank you Madam."

"I'll get a bottle of wine on the way home; I will express enough milk for missy there so she doesn't get pissed on my tit!" Marcus laughed out loud at his wife's quick witted comment.

He looked down at his daughter, she was beautiful, blonde hair, blue eyes, a little dimple on her chin, she was a mini-Claudia. "Do you feel guilty?" he asked tentatively.

Taking a sip of her drink Claudia leaned forward and put her hand on her husband's.

"No darling I don't, and neither should you. We have been travelling between the camp and Cambridge every day now for the best part of five weeks, we need a break."

"I suppose you're right, besides your parents are there and I do have that meeting Monday early doors about my demob, it will be nice to have a couple of days of normality."

"Yes, your demob, this time in two months you will be out of the RAF and we will be, God willing, starting our new life in Berlin."

"I'll drink to that and how I am looking forward to that with my precious little family." Marcus raised his glass.

Marcus noticed that blondie no tits and brunette big tits had turned their attention away from him, having seen Claudia and no doubt realising that they could not compete against someone of such beauty they were now striking up a conversation with two lads he recognised from the camp. Both were still to hit twenty so fair play to them; they might learn something. After all wasn't that the way he had started, fucking woman more than half his age or old enough to be his mother.

"Right Mrs Jones, I'll down this pint and we'll be on our way, do you want to get the wine from here or the NAAFI?"

"NO, not the NAAFI, they don't sell German wine."

He laughed, "The fact they don't sell the wine or you don't like the manageress?"

Claudia gave him the look that only she could, "Both, I will get it from the stores on the outskirts of the village they sell my favourite and its half what it would cost here."

"Tight arse!"

"Frugal darling, but you can tell me later if I've still got a tight arse!"

They both laughed, loud enough to startle their daughter. He thought that she was going to wake up and begin crying but she soon settled down again. Her small mouth searching hungrily for her fingers.

It was as they were making sure that they had everything, it amazed Marcus how much stuff a new baby needed for an outing, that the white Range Rover pulled in to the pub car-park. Marcus noticed it immediately.

"That's all we need fucking William Cross and his gang of halfwits."

Claudia looked up as the four men were getting out of the car.

"Fucking Cross is an idiot sweetheart, ignore the prick!"

Claudia was always one to say it how it was. Her honesty was pure and second to none.

Having established that they had put everything in the baby bag and nothing was left behind they set off towards the car park, meeting Cross and his company half way.

Cross was accompanied by three of his closest friends and all were dressed in golfing clothes. Cross wore the most eccentric and looked the most idiotic, but this was normal in Marcus's eyes.

He wore the most hideous yellow trousers, a yellow top with a yellow and black patched jumper draped around his shoulders with the sleeves tied loosely around his neck.

Cross was probably the most arrogant, ignorant, big headed person that Marcus had the displeasure of knowing, the two certainly had history.

When Top Gun the movie came out everyone on camp nicknamed Cross "The Iceman."

One thing that could be said about Cross was that he could hold a grudge and payback time for any offence caused to him came when you least expected it.

Whereas Marcus was an aircraft technician in the RAF and a good one at that, Cross was a pilot and didn't he enjoy bragging about how good he was, not just as a fighter pilot but at everything.

As the four got closer Cross and Steve Pearce, another pilot, were arguing obviously about the game of golf they had just played.

Another thing that could be said about Cross was that he was far too competitive and hated losing at anything.

As the foursome got closer the voice of Cross became louder and even more agitated. "You're a fucking cheat Pearce, that club definitely grounded in the bunker on the eighteenth."

Pearce laughed; another thing Cross couldn't bear was to be the butt of any joke.

Pearce looked at the other two companions, Julian Moss and Paul Wright winking "When we get to the bar boys, remind me to ask if they have any more straws old Cross here can clutch at!"

Cross was red in the face now, up until this point they had still not noticed Marcus and Claudia walking towards them. "Fuck off Pearce you cheating piece of shit."

Pearce laughed even louder, knowing that it would wind Cross up even more.

Cross then noticed the pair coming towards them and stopped in his tracks. His anger at losing at golf for the first time this year had enraged him so much this was the last thing he needed. But he soon forgot his spat with Pearce, who even as much as he didn't want to admit it, had beaten him fair and square. But now he had someone else to take his anger and frustration out on.

"Hey up boys look who it is, The Gigolo and the Sour Kraut!"

Marcus, as enraged as he was, knew that this could escalate out of hand and that he had his six-week-old daughter in her carry chair so had to be careful, any other time he would have enjoyed this set to, he wouldn't hesitate in knocking Cross out, after all he had done it before.

Claudia spoke first, "I didn't know it was fancy dress today Marcus" and looking directly at Cross "What did you come as, a Daffodil riddled with black fly?"

Even Crosses three companions stifled a laugh as did Marcus, she was a card to be sure his Claudia.

"Fuck off German bitch" Crosses face was by now a beetroot colour.

Marcus ignored the German bitch comment this time for the sake of his daughter, but chipped in with "No I think they've all come as character's out of Rainbow and we know which one is Zippy don't we?"

Cross was positively fuming by now "Fuck off Jones, fucked anybody else's wife lately?"

Marcus remained calm in his answer "No I think yours was the last, but that was over three years ago, and before that it was his!" Marcus pointed a finger at Wright "And before that it was… oh do you know what there was so many I forget now!"

"Think you are a right clever bastard, don't you?" Cross was spitting his words out so enraged was he, his face getting redder by the second.

Marcus placed a hand on Claudia's shoulder "Let us by and we will be on our way, now Cross."

"Or what?"

Marcus went to hand his precious daughter sleeping in her carrier to Claudia who refused to take her. Even Cross wouldn't be so stupid to cause a ruckus with a small baby in the middle, would he? But she knew that Marcus would kick off if he wasn't holding the baby so to speak.

The raised voice of Cross and the altercation had attracted a small audience who had noticed something was afoot, eyes and ears now focussed on the little gathering.

Claudia stepped towards Cross "Look, Marcus shagged your wife and a few others too, so what, if you couldn't satisfy her someone had to……Pee wee." Claudia moved her small finger up and down mocking the size of his manhood.

Cross raised his hand and went to strike Claudia but as he went to lower it the movement was restricted and he looked around to see Pearce had a tight hold of his arm.

"Don't be a dick William, seriously, you were going to hit a woman, if that wasn't bad enough in front of witnesses, your career will be fucked and that is just for starters, if the old bill gets involved who knows what will happen on top of that, now get rid of the sack of spuds off your shoulder and let's go for a pint or two, come on I'm buying, it's only fair as todays winner!" Knowing that Cross was like a wounded animal Pearce couldn't help sticking the knife in a little bit deeper. He had liked Cross at first but now he questioned himself whether he needed him as a friend that much.

Pearce guided Cross around the Jones and the fracas was over, thankfully.

Marcus couldn't help feeling that it wasn't over completely and that his demob couldn't come a day too soon.

As Claudia drove out of the carpark, the handsome waiter smiled and waved at them and despite the argument they had just had, which had taken the shine off a lovely afternoon, both Claudia and Marcus managed to smile and wave back. Certainly, a friendly gesture as he had witnessed the altercation, guess he could see this loving pair were not to blame.

When they reached the village stores Claudia went in and got her wine whilst Marcus stayed in the car with his new born daughter. The shop keeper a sweet white-haired lady called Mavis who was well past retirement age but who could not give up work as she loved meeting people every day, as a widow with no immediate family it was the only thing that kept her sane. She was a bit of a gossip but harmless enough, she just had to come out and sneak a peek at the couple's new bundle of joy.

Marcus was beginning to wish that he had taken a pee before leaving the pub.

Eventually Claudia made their excuses that the baby was due a feed and that they would have to head back to camp. Mavis reluctantly let them go and waved them on their way.

Camp was about three miles from the village, the country roads were narrow, single tracked with passing places, as always Claudia drove cautiously, on more than one occasion they had both experienced near misses with idiotic drivers driving too fast or a random farm vehicle coming the other way.

They drove along in silence, Marcus cradled his daughter in the back of the car and was watching her as she slept, she was perfection itself, it was pure love and pride that he was feeling right now, it exuded from his very pores.

Claudia was the love of his life but this little lady ran a close second. Marcus was distracted by a shriek from Claudia, it was loud enough to wake baby Erika who started to cry loudly. "That fucking idiot Cross is right up my arse Marcus!" Claudia said hysterically. Marcus snapped his head round in the back seat and saw the white Range Rover with Cross's personal number plate right on the bumper of their Maestro, and then with no warning, he rammed them. Marcus trying to console both his daughter and wife as he looked on in disbelief. "Keep going darling, I don't know what the fucking idiot is thinking of, we are less than a mile from camp, stay calm, keep going love."

Claudia turned a corner and a tractor was right in the centre of the road heading towards them, it was at this point that the Range Rover bashed into the back of the car once more, Claudia had to take evasive action as to not hit the tractor, the forward momentum from the Range Rover hitting the back of the car forced the Maestro to hit the bank at the side of the road and propel through the air, turning one hundred and eighty degrees in the process where it landed upside down in a field.

Claudia was screaming even louder now, Erika was screeching the place down her piercing cries hurting Marcus's ears, then he smelt the smoke just as the car burst in to flames.

Marcus still holding his daughter managed to kick the back window out, but the flames and smoke were too much, the heat was searing and the smoke quickly engulfed his lungs, and then came relief as unconsciousness took over his body instantly stopping his pain and anguish as blackness fell.

CHAPTER TEN:

March 2006

DS McVeigh knocked on the glass door. He could see his Commander sat behind his big oak desk, studying paperwork, without looking up he bellowed "Enter", McVeigh opened the door, walked to the desk and stood to attention.

Commander Henry Cartwright briefly looked up, "Oh never mind all of that man, just sit McVeigh."

Henry Cartwright was nick named the Silver Fox, at fifty-four he still had a full head of hair, all be it completely grey. He was not vain enough to dye it unlike some of his younger colleagues, especially the Commissioner who had gained the nickname Dracula due to his dyed raven black hair, and his two dodgy front teeth.

Cartwright had been in the force all his working life, he had the reputation of being fair, but God help you if you pissed him off, Cartwright was certainly one to hold a grudge, and had a memory like an elephant.

He looked up at DS Patrick McVeigh, he liked him, had admired his work from a far. McVeigh had the potential to go far, so why was he trying to fuck it all up now.

Cartwright placed the paperwork down on his desk, cleared his throat and then became the professional that he was, McVeigh was not going to see the fair side of Cartwright today, that was for sure.

"I had Frank Gosling's solicitor in here just an hour ago."

McVeigh had learnt when to speak and not to speak, it was a skill, saying the wrong word at the wrong time could escalate what could already be a serious situation, so he just gave the briefest of nods of acknowledgement.

"He is claiming that his client Gosling is being harassed by the force, no, I will re-phrase that harassed by you!"

McVeigh cleared his throat but still did not speak.

Cartwright briefly looked down at the notes he had already prepared.

"In the past six weeks Gosling claims whilst driving his car he has had a stop and search conducted fourteen times, and that five of his businesses have been raided by the police."

McVeigh looked at Cartwright, he did have respect for this man, he knew anyone else would not have been so understanding of why his life had been turned upside down in the past three months.

"With respect Sir, the five raids were based on information gathered from tip offs from the general public, and each raid had search warrants issued by those higher up the pecking order than me Sir."

"Don't get smart, one has to wonder about the accuracy of the source, the truth of the information though, do you not think?"

McVeigh remained un-moved.

"Ok DS McVeigh, perhaps you could explain to me why you entered an alert on Goslings' car on the police computer, meaning that it was open season for any patrol that saw the vehicle to pull it over and search?"

McVeigh cleared his throat, "I believed that the car had been used on many occasions for the transportation of drugs, it was also, as we know, involved in a hit and run causing the fatality of one woman, and devastating injuries to her six year old son, the boy had two fractured legs, an arm broken in three places, not to mention the concussion, the bruises, the trauma that will stay with him for the rest of his life, the doctors say his arm will never be completely healed and he will only ever have fifty percent use of it, want me to continue Sir?"

"ENOUGH" Cartwright was out of his chair and leaning with both hands firmly placed on the desk, his face had reddened and McVeigh knew that the one thing he was trying not to do he had failed at, he had over stepped the mark.

Cartwright sat back down, his own actions had been unprofessional, he knew what the man before him had gone through, was going through on a daily basis.

He pulled out a drawer behind the desk, produced two tumblers and a bottle of Jack Daniels. He poured two large measures and pushed one towards McVeigh. Taking a large gulp of his own he continued.

"Men like Gosling are clever, we know that he already pays his workforce a heftier wage than most East End gangs, purely so there are always people ready to step up to take the wrap, to keep him out of the frame, out of jail. Take the hit and run, two days later one of Gosling's employees stepped forward to take responsibility. Said they had been over the limit, panicked and drove off. We're not stupid Pat; we know that it was a set up. Davey Jackson is now doing four years for manslaughter as you know, but he knows that his family is being well taken care of and when he eventually gets out, he will have a pretty healthy bank account. But what can we do there were no creditable witnesses?"

McVeigh gulped his drink, the fact his hand was shaking, did not go unnoticed by Cartwright. This guy before him was a ticking time-bomb, ready to implode any day now.

"The boy witnessed it all, even picked out Gosling as the driver from photographs."

"He was six Pat, that is not an age for a creditable witness, you know that. If he was put on the witness stand even from a video link, Gosling's brief would have ripped him apart. Maybe even have said that his father had coerced him in to saying that the driver was Gosling."

"That six-year-old uncreditable witness was my son, is my son, who had just seen his mother mown down in front of his eyes!"

"Do you not think I know that Pat, that is the only reason you are sitting here now, if you had been anyone else you would be back in uniform and playing Policeman Plod back out on the streets."

Cartwright poured more drinks.

"You are a great copper Pat, you will make DI no problem, and a lot further beside I am sure but you have to let this go. I know how you are feeling, your wife dead, your son recovering, if your son ever does get over this, he will never be the same again. Don't you think I know how unfair this all is? A couple of hours later and only two hundred yards from where the accident happened, we find a travelling salesmen dead, battered to death and calved up like a chicken, found in a seedy bed and breakfast, eye witness reports say that earlier in the day he had openly disrespected Gosling in a packed Stratford boozer, we are not stupid Pat, we know Gosling was responsible, the landlady a right busy body by all accounts, refused to point the finger at Gosling, said she hadn't seen anything yet a week later she is heading off on a round the world cruise!"

Cartwright took another sip of his drink.

"We are members of one of the best Police forces in the world, we need, no rely on evidence. There is an old saying, what goes around comes around. Gosling and his empire will come crashing down one day, you mark my words."

McVeigh finished his drink and placed his hand over the tumbler to prevent Cartwright from pouring another.

"In the meantime, sir"

"In the meantime, Pat, you rebuild your life, take care of your son, help him come to terms with the loss of his mother and get on with your job. Gosling won't pursue the harassment case providing there are no more incidences."

"That is fucking big of him." McVeigh stood "Will there be anything else sir?"

Cartwright offered his hand out to McVeigh to shake. McVeigh hesitantly shook it, where all he really wanted to do was punch him in the face.

He left the office, leaving the door open as a sign of petty defiance.

CHAPTER ELEVEN:

September 2013

Emily McVeigh sat opposite her husband sipping her rich red wine and waiting for the main course to arrive as they made small talk. She waited eagerly for her favourite meal of all time, it consisted of medium rare fillet steak in a mushroom sauce, salad and chips to be placed in front of her.

Her husband sat talking and watching her, she was as beautiful now as when they had married five years ago. Even the birth of their twin sons four years previously had not taken its toll on her hour glass figure and her stunning looks.

Her natural blonde curly hair hung loosely around her shoulders, and her beautiful aquatic blue eyes could melt your heart just by looking at you.

The only thing that she had enhanced and had as he remembered, insisted upon, was having breast implants after the birth of the boys. But even that was not to make them look bigger or false just "To stop them drooping down to me knees in years to come" in her own words.

By being with her she had indeed saved Pat's life, mended his broken heart and stopped him from ruining his career even if she would argue that it was a joint effort.

They had met the day that he had stormed out of Cartwright's office in 2006. She was a WPC working on the front of desk of New Scotland Yard and she had approached him to ask if he was alright when she saw his face as he left the office. When he said that he was as right as he ever would be, she had said "Could have fooled me, you look like you've swallowed a wasp's nest and been fucked by Cartwright bent over his oak desk!"

He couldn't help but laugh at that. The rest as they say is history, although it was too soon after Natasha's death, they had taken things slowly and married two years after that first encounter. A small Civil ceremony, Emily looking even more stunning if that was at all possible, a small gathering of immediate family and their closest friends followed.

Robert, his son with Natasha, took to Emily straight away and now called her Mum. The icing on the cake was the twins who had just turned four, they had their mother's hair and eyes and his handsome looks. They were going to be handsome little buggers and break a few girl's or boy's hearts in the future that was for sure.

Today was their fifth wedding anniversary. The twins were with Emily's mum for the night and Robert was at his grand-mothers, Natasha's mum Margaret in the New Forest for his annual summer holiday. Robert still suffered with limited use of his left arm and he would wake often during the night screaming after nightmares but he was coping well and getting decent reports from school and he was still the apple of Margaret's eye, she loved him dearly.

Natasha's mother had taken to Emily straight away and when the twins were born, she had drooled over them as if they were her own grand-children.

They often all stayed with her and she with them when she visited friends in London and she had babysat all the boys on more than one occasion, sometimes for the weekend to allow Pat and Emily to get away for a few days.

The waiter duly arrived with their main course and he poured the champagne that had been sat chilling for this moment.

Two hours later and both feeling that they were fit to burst, they fell into a black cab to take them home to the house they shared in North London. They kissed, held hands and acted like teenagers all the way home.

Once inside the house they tore off each other clothes and barely made it to the bedroom before they were both completely naked and panting in anticipation of the finale to their perfect evening.

Pat did try not do comparisons between Natasha and Emily. Both had good and bad points. Emily was fantastic in bed as had Natasha been but each in their own different ways.

Emily rode him hard in the super king size bed, droplets of sweat dripped down over her perfect breasts as they both climaxed together.

Afterwards they lay bodies intwined together, sweat dripping down their bodies when Pat's mobile rang. He reached for it and when he saw the name of the caller, he looked at Emily apologetically and simply said "Sorry darling I have to take this."

CHAPTER TWELVE:

Ray Johnson was sat along with the rest of Gosling's elite crew. Including Gosling and himself there were eleven other men.

They were all supposedly the elite of Gosling's operation.

Every first Monday of the month they would all meet for a meal and discuss whatever Gosling had on his mind, mainly business.

The Amid Palace in Forest Gate was an excellent curry house there was no faulting that. Great authentic food and a charming atmosphere, be it still with the flock wallpaper and weird looking statue arms outstretched cheekily sitting by the till!

It was usually closed on a Monday but the owner would always open it for Gosling one day a month as a private function. He was forever grateful to Gosling for protecting his business from the "Pakki haters" in the area who targeted such people purely because they were different in skin colour, the protection came at a cost though, a grand a week in fees.

The table was set out so that Gosling was at the head of the table with the other men six per side.

Small talk about football, girls, Charlie and other drugs were always the main topics.

Ray sat opposite a smack head called Jamie who felt the need to snort Charlie every five minutes.

Joe Whyte who had taken an instant dislike to Ray and reminded Goose at every opportunity that Ray was not to be trusted, his rise in the gang had been too quick, too suspect, sat as always to the left of Gosling.

Ray looked around the table at the misfits and knob heads who made up the elite. He smiled and laughed when he had to. He caught Gosling's eye and made a false toast gesture with his glass.

The starters of poppadom's, pickles, onion bhajis and other tasty morsels were being cleared away when Jamie decided that he would light up a cigarette and requested an ash-tray from the owner Dinesh Khatri.

"Oy Pakki, ash-tray now!"

The owner approached the table; "I am sorry sir, there is no smoking inside the building."

Jamie raised himself off the chair, cigarette alight hanging from his mouth.

"Do fucking what? What did you say Pakki?"

Despite the anxiety he was feeling Dinesh remained calm simply saying in his soft voice with its Indian accent "Smoking has been banned inside public houses and restaurants since 2007" Dinesh was feeling nervous but was sticking to his guns. His voice was visibly shaky.

"Jamie put that fag out and sit down now!"

Jamie looked up the table towards Gosling who had spoken.

Defiantly he smiled "Nah Goose if I want a smoke then I will and this Pakki will get me an ash-tray!"

For someone of his age Gosling could still move fast, he was up and out of his chair and stood by Jamie in split seconds.

He took the cigarette from his mouth before anyone realised what was happening.

"For a start you doped up little cunt, he is from India, not Pakistan and secondly if old bill walked past and saw you smoking that gives them the right to not only enter the building but also poor old Dinesh here could get a fine of up to two thousand quid, let alone the questions the old bill could ask of us. Do you think that would be fair on poor Dinesh getting a fine for your stupidity you prick?"

Ray was enjoying seeing Jamie being put in his place. He had endured a couple of run ins with the jumped-up little runt in the past.

Goose took the still smouldering cigarette and stubbed it out on the younger man's face.

"I will answer me own question, shall I? No, it wouldn't be fair on poor old Dinesh, would it?" Gosling shouting now and right in Jamie's face.

The pain that Jamie experienced was excruciating but he knew that everyone was watching and had to remain the big 'I am' so inwardly winced but still stood with his shoulders stuck back with bravado.

Gosling apologised to Dinesh on Jamie's behalf before returning to his seat and sitting down as if nothing had happened, Jamie had learnt a valuable lesson today but he swore to himself under his breath that one day Gosling would pay for showing him up like that.

The remainder of the meal was carried out without incident and by the time the brandies were bought out everyone, apart from Jamie, had forgotten about the cigarette episode.

Gosling stood and tapped the side of his brandy glass with a spoon.

"If I could have everyone's attention."

No doubt about it when Goose Gosling spoke, everyone paid attention and listened.

"As you all know, the old tiddly winks have been encroaching on to our turf of late, taking liberties in fact, the slit eyed wankers. As you know we went to China Town last week mob handed and tooled up only to find that inexplicably the place was swarming with old bill like, dare I say that they had been tipped off."

Ray smiled inwardly to himself and averted the gaze of Joe Whyte.

"Well lads I am glad to say that tomorrow night we go back and put them yellow skinned bastards in their place!"

Loud cheers erupted around the table, the only people that did not react were Ray and Jamie, whose face was smarting so bad that he felt like screaming but clearly wasn't going to let on about the pain he was feeling.

The evening was coming to an end when Ray saw the kitchen porter come in to the main restaurant area with a tray of clean glasses. It was as the porter was restocking the bar that he and Ray made eye contact, at this point Ray felt the colour physically drain from his face.

CHAPTER THIRTEEN:

Ray Whitehead alias Ray Johnson was a great believer in what goes around comes around and in fate.

After all, hadn't his constant drinking and womanising drove his long-suffering wife Helen to despair and set him on his own path of self-destruction.

It was fate that had seen him arrive home early one day to change clothes for an undercover operation later that day, that had seen him catch his wife in bed with a so-called friend and work colleague Peter Barnes.

And who could blame her after what he had put her through along with their three-year-old son Jake. Never being there to read him a bed time story or when he was, too pissed to make out the words in a book, smelling of cheap perfume from one of his bits on the side.

And it was fate that he had met his best friend from his Hendon days, Pat McVeigh, at a training course, he had jumped at the chance to take on this undercover operation when Pat had suggested it after one too many after dinner drinks that evening.

The day he found Helen in bed he had moved out immediately taking a bed sit on the outskirts of Ipswich and had basically started his own personal journey on the road to

self-destruction.

Although he knew the dangers that an undercover operation could bring, he was of the mind-set that it was better living a life that although it came with risks also had an adrenaline rush, girls, drugs and booze galore and it was to him, a risk worth taking. The alternative, if there was one, was being found dead from excessive alcohol in his bed sit.

And it was true to say that up to this moment he had loved the new life, the classy women he had the pick of every night, the drug fuelled parties and the satisfaction of seeing the looks on the faces of Gosling and Whyte when he had passed on information like the China Town outing.

Yet here he was now, locked in a dingy toilet cubicle in an Indian restaurant wondering how he was going to escape this night alive, yet it was fate that bought him here.

Who would have thought that the lad, whose name he couldn't even remember, would be in a restaurant in a different part of the country from where the incident had happened at the same time as him? Was it God's way of saying "You reap what you sow, mother-fucker!"

McVeigh put the phone to his ear, he stood naked by the bed, he was still semi hard after his seductive and satisfying love making with Emily.

"What's up Ray, it is nearly one in the morning?"

At the other end of the phone Ray was talking fast and nervously. McVeigh had to ask him on more than one occasion to slow down, a mixture of nerves, drink and talking ten to the dozen was making it hard for McVeigh to understand what he was saying.

"I am at the Amid and I have been rumbled, or at least I will be any minute!"

McVeigh while holding the phone under his chin was getting dressed, it was awkward holding the phone and dressing and he nearly over balanced and slipped over on more than one occasion.

"Rumbled, how?"

"A kid I pulled up in the street for possession of dope in Ipswich last year, a student, turns out he is working here at the Amid presumably for the summer break."

Ray was not to know that the young kitchen porter, Gopal was indeed the nephew of Dinesh Khatri.

McVeigh was hurriedly dressing. "So, what makes you think the kid will say anything Ray, maybe he's not one hundred percent sure it was you, did you nick him last year?"

"No, it was just a caution, believe me Pat the way he ran off back into the kitchen he will be telling someone all about it as we speak!"

"So where in the Amid are you right now, the loo?"

"You got it, made out I needed a piss, I was hoping to climb out the window but they have bars on them!"

Whilst McVeigh was talking to Ray, Emily had taken her own mobile phone and was phoning the police station, she got through to the desk sergeant and filled him in on what was happening, she had returned to work after the birth of the boys and was still a WPC so the call was taken seriously, she explained what was happening and that an armed police unit should be sent immediately and that her husband would explain in more detail when he could.

McVeigh winked at Emily and gave her a thumbs up.

"Why the bogs Ray, why not go outside on the pretence of wanting a cigarette?"

"I gave up remember years ago whilst we were at Hendon, that would only have fuelled more suspicion"

McVeigh was now completely dressed.

"Ok Ray, stay calm. An armed unit is on its way. I have been to the Amid on more than one occasion and if I remember rightly the toilets are near the entrance to the kitchen. Make your way through the kitchen and get out the back and run like fuck and hide somewhere. I will be there as soon as I can."

Emily still on the other phone getting regular updates was now demanding a patrol car be sent for her husband immediately.

"Pat, if it all goes tits up explain to Helen won't you, I know we have been separated for almost three years but I never stopped loving her."

"Ray don't talk like that you're going to get out of this, now go!"

Having hung up Ray quickly made his way out of the toilet and headed through the small corridor and into the kitchen serving area of the Amid.

As he entered, he could see an irate Goose holding the young kitchen porter by the throat.

"Fucking lying bastard why would you make an accusation like that?" Goose bellowed.

Goose looked at Dinesh "What sort of cunt you raising here Dinesh, I know he is your sister's boy but he has been in your care for fifteen years or more now, I thought you had more about you than this Dinesh."

Dinesh held his hands in front of him in prayer like motion "Please Mr Goose sir, the boy has made a mistake, please let us forget all about it please."

"What's going on Goose?" Ray had now reached where Gosling and the boy were standing. Unnoticed by anyone, Ray had picked up a small sharp knife from a kitchen unit and hid it in the waist band in the back of his trousers, as he walked towards Gosling and the boy, the steel of the knife was cold against his lower back.

Gosling turned to look at Ray "What's going on is this little dickhead here told his uncle that you are a copper and that he had a run in with you last year in Ipswich!"

Ray despite his nerves, tried to keep calm.

He laughed out loud, "Ipswich, where the fuck is Ipswich?"

Ray noticed a puddle by the boy's feet and the wet patch on his trousers, the lad was scared witless.

Ray could hear sirens getting closer in the distance, nearer and nearer. He was beginning to relax a little, expecting the armed response team to break through the door any moment, but then he noticed no sooner did it appear that the sirens were at their loudest, they began to fade again and the fear that Ray had been feeling began to return.

Ray was trying to think on his toes, "He's obviously confused me for someone else Goose, no harm done, come on let the lad go, I am sure Dinesh here will give us all a brandy on the house to make amends won't you Dinesh?"

Dinesh was nodding furiously "Yes of course Mr Ray, my nephew got confused that is all, please Mr Goose let him go!"

Everything may have been accepted and it all forgotten if despite the fear he was feeling the young lad hadn't shouted "No, it is him, he is a policeman, I swear, as Allah is my witness."

Ray fell to the floor, as the cosh hit him hard on the back of his head, he had failed to notice that Joe Whyte had entered the kitchen behind him. He landed face first in to the urine that the lad had emptied from his bladder moments earlier. And then everything went black.

The owner of the Agra Palace, which was five hundred metres up the road from the Amid Palace was just cashing up. Due to the Amid being closed on a Monday night his takings were always good, it was a good start to the week. It had been a busy night with at least fifty covers.

He almost had a heart attack as he went to put the money in the safe ready to bank the next day, as armed men in police uniforms and riot gear smashed through the front door and stormed the building.

CHAPTER FOURTEEN:

It was now seven am and Pat McVeigh had been at the station since two that morning.

He sat at his desk, his office as messy as ever, files out all over the place, empty glasses, the office looked completely disorganised.

His untidy office had earnt him the nick name Inspector Frost the character played by David Jason whose office was always dis-organised; it was said with jest and he had always taken it as such. Right now, the state of the office was the least of his worries, he was angry, tired, confused and trying to establish what had happened only a few hours earlier.

McVeigh had already played the recording of Emily's call from earlier that morning over and over again so knew that the correct name of the restaurant had been given, so why the fuck was the armed unit storming in on the wrong place.

The head of the Armed Response Unit eventually came to see him, following several phone calls, the officer had told him that the instruction they received from this station was the reason that they had gone to the Agra Palace and not the Amid Palace. The instruction had been given by the on-duty Detective Inspector last night.

As soon as he had said that it all became clear to McVeigh, but had not helped him any or Ray for that matter of course.

McVeigh had at least fifty police officers out already searching property and businesses that Gosling had links with throughout the area. Right now, however he did not know what else to do. His friend of twenty plus years, Ray Whitehead, was on the missing list and it was he, McVeigh that had put him in danger in the first place.

John Walker was a Superintendent and McVeigh's immediate boss. At a couple of years just short of retirement he looked none too pleased as he burst in to McVeigh's office demanding answers as to why an undercover copper was working in his jurisdiction that he did not have a clue about it and why the fuck was his Detective Inspector in police custody.

Whether it was the fact that he was tired, frustrated or the fact that McVeigh knew what Walker really was, but he jumped up from his desk ran towards Walker and pinned his superior to the wall by the throat.

"Shut it you snivelling fucking bastard or I will put your head through this fucking wall!"

Walker was petrified at the actions of McVeigh, what was going on? How much did he know? He tried to stay professional or at least as professional as a bent copper that had been in Gosling's pocket for twenty odd years could be.

"I will have your job for this McVeigh, you see if I don't!"

McVeigh released his hold on Walker.

McVeigh looked at Walker with disgust written all over his face, he smiled "Sure, you will, prick!"

There was a knock at the door and not waiting for a reply to enter, Assistant Commissioner Henry Cartwright entered the room with an air of certain authority.

"Gentlemen, let us be seated shall we and try to conduct ourselves like the professional police officers that we are, perhaps we should all calm down. I talk and you listen, as for you Walker, I suggest you fucking dare not interrupt me and give me your undivided attention or come noon you will be in a cell in your own station, understood?"

Cartwright pulled up a chair "If we are all sitting comfortably, I shall begin."

"First of all, I have requested another three hundred officers from other forces as far afield as Norwich to Newcastle, they will be here in a matter of hours. All to assist with the search for Ray Whitehead. Pat, I know that you want to get out there and search for your friend and colleague so I will be as quick as I can."

"In answer to your question a few moments ago Walker, which I heard approaching the office, in fact half the station heard it closed door or not, it was I that gave the go ahead when Pat approached me for permission to infiltrate Gosling's gang by putting in DS Whitehead undercover. Pat had suspicions of what members of the force, and particularly in this station, could be trusted as they were on Gosling's payroll and he certainly couldn't trust you Walker as you came to light as being a bent copper a short while after Whitehead went under cover, that said Pat did not know who he could trust in any station for that matter."

Walker sat his head bowed and held in his hands, whatever else would happen today he knew that his career was over, it was all about damage limitation now.

"DS Whitehead got to work quickly and was feeding good information back on the shenanigans of Gosling and his band of merry men, that after all was his main purpose, little did we know how many bent coppers he would uncover at the same time, not just at this station but across the Met in its entirety."

Cartwright coughed, "Pat could you ring through for a pot of coffee please, I cannot seem to function properly until at least after my second cup of the day, and it has been an earlier start to the day than normal, there's a good chap."

Cartwright brushed his trouser leg with his hand, removing non-existent fluff.

"Where was I? Oh yes, we soon had the name of three bent coppers working from this station, including you Walker, it also came with photographic evidence, just in case you were wondering how to wriggle out of this!"

There was a knock at the door and on hearing "Enter" from McVeigh, a young WPC brought in the coffee on a tray with cups of course and a few stale biscuits.

Once McVeigh had handed a coffee to Cartwright, he never offered one to Walker, Cartwright continued.

"And now poor DS Whitehead is missing, we can only assume that the outcome will not be good" Cartwright sipped at his tepid coffee.

"And me, what is going to happen to me?" Walker asked, almost begged

Cartwright smiled, almost a grimace.

"One of Her Majesties own is missing and yet here you sit, you snivelling little fuck, excuse my French, and you are only bothered about what is going to happen to you!"

Walker was embarrassed and began to stammer his words when he spoke, something that he suffered from since his childhood whenever he was stressed or nervous and this situation certainly fit that bill.

"Of course, I am worried, please, you have to believe me, I have done nothing for Gosling for many a year, since I made DI, then going on to make Superintendent in fact even when I was giving him information it was not putting lives at risk."

Cartwright looked at Walker, the man disgusted him, any bent copper that had already taken an oath of allegiance but became a bent Bobby disgusted him

"Bull shit Walker, even at three o'clock this morning you were dancing to Gosling's tune. He phoned you as he did, one moment…"

Cartwright produced a note book from his jacket and leafed through the pages.

"Oh yes here we go, as he has phoned you fourteen times in the last four months, we have had your mobile tracked and bugged since we received information that you were taking back handers."

Cartwright finished his coffee and McVeigh topped it up.

"Even last week you met with Gosling along with his driver Ray Whitehead, the day after the unsuccessful trip Gosling and his crew made to China Town. We had Ray wear a bug, we have a full recording of the conversation, so shut the fuck up, hey Pat take that shovel off him, he is digging an even deeper hole for himself!"

Walker suddenly and with no warning burst into tears, he cried so much, bubbles of snot were coming from his nose. Cartwright handed him a tissue, "Shut up, man up and listen!"

Walker tried to compose himself, but he was still occasionally sobbing.

"We know Gosling looked after you. He bought you a villa in Tenerife, albeit in your wife's name, Ray came across the transaction of the funds put in your wife's bank directly from Goslings personal bank account, we checked your wife's account and two days after the funds were received a payment for the exact same amount was sent to a Spanish Estate Agent, strange that don't you think?"

Walker began to cry once more, but one stare from Cartwright was enough for him to control his emotions. "So here is what's going to happen Walker. Detective Inspector Mark Smith was arrested this morning, did you know that he also was on Gosling's books?"

Walker looked up shocked "God no I swear I didn't!" Cartwright raised an eyebrow "We know when you are lying Walker, your lips move."

"Anyway, that is by the by, Pat's wife made a call to the desk sergeant last night whilst Pat was on his mobile to Ray, Pat had already told her what was going on at this and other nicks and he had informed her who she could and could not trust in this nick. However, the desk sergeant passed on the information to Smith after he had called it in to the armed response team.

Smith immediately called the officer in charge of the armed response unit and told them that the wrong location had been originally given, he deliberately gave the wrong information to the armed response unit resulting in a wild goose chase and one which could leave poor Whitehead dead. Now we know that Smith was a bigger fish than you in Gosling's Pond, he is going down for a long time, possibly for conspiracy to murder, we shall see, either way we have enough on him to put him away for ten years or more."

Walker became hysterical, "I swear I was never that involved, just the odd bit of info here and there, I can't go to prison, I will be dead in a week, the number of cons I have sent down over the years will see to that!"

McVeigh was becoming increasingly annoyed with how long this was all taking, all he wanted to do was run operations on finding Ray, get out and search himself if necessary.

He shouted "Shut up and listen for fucks sake Walker!" Cartwright smiled, a cold smile that offered no comfort to the recipient.

"Ok let's wrap this up, sorry Pat, I know how you are feeling. Right Walker, no more sniffles, no more interrupting. I have spoken at length this morning with my superiors and we are happy that you are small fry in Gosling's illicit game. Looking at all the facts we have available, you could say that it will not be in the public interest to take you to court for bribery, possible perjury and tampering with evidence, these are probably the only charges we could get to stick. It could also open up a can of worms. Lawyers for all the crooks you've had sent down over the years would be coming out of the woodwork all over the place, evidence you gave could be bought into question, not a risk we can take, Smith on the other hand has to be brought to justice at whatever cost."

Walker seemed relieved, he puffed out his cheeks.

"Do not look so smug, or I will push your head through that wall like I promised!" McVeigh was once more on his feet staring menacingly at his soon to be former boss.

Cartwright smiled, "that said, Ray infiltrated the gang to get information on Gosling, finding out about bent coppers was just a bonus. There are enough bent coppers who are going to be hauled in over the next few days to warrant the Home Secretary building a special prison just for bent scum inmates!"

Walker's face looked shocked "So what's going to happen to me, am I going down for this or what?"

Cartwright once again played with the imaginary fluff on his knee.

"It is apparent that you don't get bought a one hundred and fifty thousand villa for making a few speeding tickets go away!"

"What do you want from me sir?" Walker just wanted this ordeal over and wanted to be kept out of prison, whatever that took he would do it.

"Outside are two gentlemen who are going to be taking you off somewhere that's nice and quiet for a few days. In those few days you will be writing down every bribe you took from Gosling and the information that he bought for it. In addition to this you will write down every single offence or dealings that you know of that Gosling has done and got away with. He has mugs to take the wrap, yet we know he has got away with murder on more than one occasion. We also know that there are illegitimate businesses out there that he is operating that as of yet, we don't know about as he is too clever by far, we want details and addresses."

Walker looked at Cartwright, "Grass on Gosling, are you mad, I will be dead before the week is out with all due respect sir!" Cartwright just smiled. "And you don't think you will be dead if you end up in prison?" Walker bowed his head, as if in shame.

"Depending on the quality of the information you give us on Gosling, along with the seriousness of the offences you have committed, depends on where you are to spend the rest of your natural days, so do yourself a favour Walker, your career is over either way and you can kiss good bye to your pension my old son, it is up to you now where you want to end your days, a security guard on minimum wage in a budget supermarket or in prison."

"What about my wife, she will be wondering where I am, can I at least contact her?"

McVeigh laughed out loud, "No she won't she is at your villa in Spain where she spends most of her time these days. Probably getting fucked by some young greasy gringo waiter as we speak, we know she has a taste for young Spanish waiters. If we had the time, I would show you the pictures." Then standing up said simply, "Right now we have dealt with this waste of space, can I get back to finding Ray?"

CHAPTER FIFTEEN:

Ray was feeling nauseous. The sack over his head smelt of musty cloth and old potatoes and his head was throbbing.

He had woken not knowing where he was or what had happened, then gradually it all came slowly back.

He heard the moans, groans and crying of someone close to him, he assumed that it was the lad from the restaurant.

Ray had drifted in and out of consciousness throughout the night, when he was fully awake, he realised he still had the knife, he could feel the coldness of the steel on his back. What he didn't know was how to get to it, his hands were tied tightly behind his back.

His emotions were mixed, anger, pity, worry and he just wished the kid next to him would stop his excessive whining. Afterall it was because of him that they were in this predicament, why couldn't the little bastard have kept his mouth shut.

Ray thought of the time he had first met him, he was an arrogant little shit then, thinking the colour of his skin gave him immunity against the police. And when he had spoken to Ray more than twelve months ago every other word was "Like", why did the youth of today have to say the word 'like' thirty times a minute.

"And he like said to me like, what do you want to do like" the lad grated on Ray and he only hoped that his son Jake would not grow up to be a user of the excessive word 'like'.

It was the thoughts of Jake and Helen that helped him get through the night, kept him sane, gave him belief that he may yet get out of his predicament.

His vision was limited through the hessian sack cloth, but he could make out the figure of Joe Whyte and every so often a bucket of cold water would be thrown over him followed by Whyte shouting obscenities at him, telling him that he knew what a cunt he was and that he had sussed him out long ago, even if Gosling had not been able to see it.

Daylight arrived. Ray had begun to work on loosening his hands, jiggling his wrists back and forth, it did seem that he was getting somewhere, albeit slowly.

Sitting there, unsure how to escape Ray heard footsteps go through a door which obviously led to the outside world as the room was filled with a gush of cold air and bright burst of light. Whyte had left the building.

A short while later the door opened once more and he could make out two figures walking past within a few feet. One Whyte, the other one possibly Gosling. He then heard footsteps walking up a metal staircase, heavy footsteps clanking on metal, the sound reverberating round the building which led Ray to believe he was in an empty warehouse.

Through the cloth he could make out another figure to his right, presumably another of Gosling's heavies standing guard.

Thankfully the lad next to him had fallen asleep or was unconscious, Ray was glad of the respite of his moans and groans.

A short time past and Ray was aware of a figure approaching him, it was Whyte he knew because he whispered in his ear that he, Ray "Are a fucking dead man and that you'll be soon be found floating in the Thames or buried alive in a grave" And then Ray felt a pain like he had never felt before, his nose shattered under the blow, he was swept backwards off his feet, still tied to the chair banging the back of his already aching head on the concrete floor, but unlike the blow he received a few hours earlier at least this time he stayed conscious but his head felt it would explode at any moment.

At some point over the next few minutes the heavy that had been standing watch, came over and righted him.

Although Ray knew that his nose was broken and the pain in his skull was excruciating, he afforded himself a smile under the cloth, hidden from view of anyone that could be watching, before the movement of the smile caused him to grimace at the pain this caused to his nose.

Whyte did not know it but he had done Ray a favour. The movement of the chair had loosened the ropes enough for him to release his hands and feel for the blade that he had taken from the restaurant the night before.

Now it was all about biding his time, striking when the time was right, he placed the knife back to its original position and kept his arms behind his back under the pretence of still being tightly secured to the chair.

The noise had stirred the young lad next to him and Ray grimaced as the boy's moaning and crying started once more, he wanted to take the knife, lean over and slit his throat just for the peace and quiet that would bring, but he knew that there were bigger fish to fry, and if he was going to go down, it wouldn't be without a fight.

Ray heard more footsteps on the metal steps, he heard the distant voice of Gosling and another voice he recognised as Pete. Ray had been involved in a few meetings with Pete, had even done a couple of jobs with him, Pete was nothing like his retard of a son Jamie and Ray often wondered why someone as nice as Pete was doing the job he was doing.

The kid was still whining and Ray strained to hear what was being said.

"Billy here's a score, there's a McDonald's near the top of the industrial estate go and get us a double sausage and egg McMuffin and a coffee, I am famished. Get yourself something too. Pete, you take off mate, give him a lift home before you get the food Billy, I will finish up here."

When Gosling spoke, no one dared question whether what he said was right or wrong although Billy and Pete both thought silently, was it such a good idea to leave him on his own with these two?

As if sensing their thoughts Gosling laughed, "Its ok, they're tied up and besides Joe isn't a million miles away."

When Gosling heard the engine start, he moved towards the two figures and one by one he pulled off the sacks that covered their heads.

Gosling laughed his head off when he saw the state of Ray's face. "Joe's handy work I take it mate, looks sore."

Ray ignored the comment and as his eyes adjusted to the light, he knew that he had been in this warehouse on many occasions.

Gosling turned his attention to Gopal, "Fuck you stink boy, best get home and get cleaned up."

Gosling untied the restraints holding Gopal and helped him up, the stench was overpowering, he thought that it was a good job he hadn't already eaten.

Gosling took a handful of notes out of his wallet and gave them to the young lad.

"Walk up to the end of the industrial estate to the main road and flag down a cab, if anyone is mad enough to take you smelling like that. If I find that you go anyone near a copper, and believe me, you are going to be watched, you are brown bread, got it?"

The lad was uneasy on his feet, tired and hungry but he understood only too well what was being asked of him.

"One more thing, tell your uncle that his debt to me is clear, if there are some of us still available to do so he will still receive protection but there is no need for any more payments." Gosling smiled at him, but then caught a whiff of the lad and turned his face up in disgust, the smell was that bad.

The arrogance that Ray had witnessed a year or so earlier was still there as the lad started to rant at Gosling.

"And what do I get like, without me you would not even know you had a policeman amongst your midst like, yet my useless uncle comes out getting all the financial benefit like. I am the one who has spent all night tied up, not my worthless uncle, who is only half the man my father ever was!"

Gosling was taken aback; he did not know if he wanted to put a bullet in this lad's head or pat him on the back for showing some back bone. Common sense soon prevailed though and it certainly was not going to be the latter.

The back handed slap when it came was with such force that the lad was reeling backwards before even realising what had happened.

He lay on the ground having carried a distance of at least five feet. His lip was so split it would need stitches for sure. Gosling was still a powerful force to be recognised with despite his age.

Gosling stood over the boy; a gun pointed down directly at his head. Gosling was angry, angrier than Ray had ever seen him before. Words and spit as he uttered them, flew from his mouth as he went on a tirade against the boy.

"Your so-called useless Uncle flew you over from India when your parents were killed in a car crash. He did it for his sister, your mother even though he could have left you in the hands of your father's relatives. He has fed you, given you a roof over your head and paid for your education and has been through more in his life than you could ever dream of. I have a great respect for him, starting his own business despite the hate mob trying to ruin it before he had even got going, graffiti on windows and walls, petrol bombs through the letter box, shit wrapped in newspaper on his door mat and yet you dare disrespect him after what he has done for you. Your parents died because your useless father was an alcoholic and was pissed out his skull at the time, did you know that?"

Gopal was scared now as this giant of a man stood over him, he knew none of this history.

"Your father used to beat your mother and shag whores down alleyways giving your mother every sexually transmitted disease going, did you know that?"

Gopal could only curl up in a ball, his arms protecting his head and he emptied his bladder yet again, expecting to die any second.

Gosling reached down and hauled the boy up by his hair, not concerned about the pain he was causing or indeed the stench coming from the lad. "Your phone is over there on the table, get it and fuck off, what an ungrateful little cunt you are! When you get home, I suggest you bow down at your uncle's feet for all that he's done for you and give him the respect he deserves – got it?"

Gopal nodded repeatedly and scurried off, grabbing his phone and getting away from Gosling and out of the warehouse as quickly as he could.

Joe Whyte was so tired he had gotten behind the wheel of the old escort van and fallen asleep while waiting for the release of the nephew. He did not see or hear Pete and Billy emerge from the warehouse and drive off.

When he eventually awoke, he decided that he would go to the flat on the Isle of Dogs and get some food and proper rest.

The taking pictures of McVeigh's kids could wait until tomorrow, McVeigh would have his hands full as it was today anyway and as for the nephew, he wouldn't be stupid enough to go to the old bill, even if he did what could he tell them? As he drove off, he didn't look in his rear-view mirror, if he had he would have seen Gopal emerge from the side of the building, go round the back and climb up the exterior fire escape that was in such disrepair it looked like it could collapse at any moment.

Back inside the warehouse Gosling was pacing back and forth, the Charlie he had snorted earlier was beginning to wear off, he felt like he needed a couple more lines.

He cut a couple more on the desk that was a few feet away and snorted both, one after the other. It didn't take long for it to take effect, the buzz it gave was soon racing through his head and he felt that he was in control of the situation once more. He looked down at Ray's mobile that sat on the desk.

"Oh, you are a popular boy, fifty-two missed calls all from someone called Pat, I wonder who that could be?"

Ray was in agony and he felt as if his nose and head were about to explode but he sure as hell was not going to show any weakness to Gosling, especially as he had a surprise up his sleeve, one he would have to act on soon before Billy got back.

"It's me Auntie."

"What am I going to do with you Ray, you have caused me one hell of a lot of aggravation mate, I can't let that go you know that?" Gosling was tapping the end of the gun against Ray's cheek.

"What I want to know though is what have you reported back to your mate McVeigh, not enough to pull me off the streets that's for sure, I mean you've only worked for me for five months, your areas of access were restricted."

Ray had two ways to go, wind up Gosling, but that could back fire as he was doped up to the eyeballs he could just point and fire the gun at any moment, or the second option was to leave him wanting to know more. He carefully thought out his strategy for a second or two then decided to go with the second option.

"Oh, believe me within a week of being in to your inner sanctum I had enough to send you down, with what I've already fed back to my colleagues there was enough evidence to get you put away for a ten stretch but Pat and I decided to play the long game, we wanted more than the bent coppers you had in your pocket, which I found out almost immediately by the way. Then there was the prostitution racket, white slave trading, the loan sharks and drug dealings you had a hand in and much more besides."

Gosling was intrigued by this as Ray had hoped he would be. Ray knew that the time to act was now. "I mean come on Goose you're not as bright as you make out, are you? Me and the lads know that the real brains behind the outfit is Joe, I mean he sussed me out pretty quick didn't he, only you were too thick to listen!"

"What the fuck did you say?" Gosling moved towards Ray gun raised.

"Deaf as well as stupid Goose, come on think about it, you've sent Joe on his merry way probably with access to all your financial assets, I bet he is on his way to Dover to get a ferry to France before moving on to anywhere in Europe as we speak."

Gosling went red with rage and he moved even nearer towards Ray, he pointed the gun at his head, the coldness of the steel prodding into Ray's skin.

Gosling cocked the trigger as Ray swung his arm round plunging the small fillet knife into Gosling's chest, missing his heart by a centimetre. As Ray plunged the knife in, he rolled away to one side just in case Gosling managed to fire the gun.

Gosling, although a big man went down far too easily, a combination of drugs and booze had made him weaker than he normally was. As he fell, dropping the gun and clenching his chest, Ray got up off the floor albeit slowly, his head, nose and full bladder saw to that.

The look on Gosling's face was of shock, not believing that this copper had got the better of him for the second time in a short period of time. Ray kicked the gun across the floor well out of Gosling's reach. He staggered over to where his phone was on the table and dialled Pat.

Pat answered the phone immediately and started to speak, Ray cut him short, "Just listen, Pembrooke Industrial Estate, the derelict warehouse at the end of the estate, I have been here before with Gosling, you should have the address on file, be quick, send an ambulance too, Gosling is going to need it."

Then Ray hung up and threw the phone back on the table before going to retrieve the gun, as he did, he passed by Gosling who was crouched over having trouble breathing, he pulled back one leg and kicked Gosling full in the face with what little strength he could muster.

He then heard the door open and felt that sudden rush of cold like he had earlier, he turned to face the door just as Pete raised his gun and fired.

Ray died instantly the bullet hitting him directly in the centre of the forehead, it was a blessing that he would not have felt anything.

Pete rushed over to Gosling "Come on boss let's get you to hospital, I told Billy we shouldn't have left you on your own, good job I disobeyed orders and came back!"

Gosling smiled at Pete, his breathing was laboured and it was a struggle for him to talk, "Your army training came in handy mate, perfect shooting. He has called the old bill, leave me here Pete, an ambulance is coming anyway. Get rid of his body though or we are all going down for murder!"

Pete heard a car outside "That will be Billy, are you sure Goose?"

Goose coughed and a little blood spurted from his mouth "they were going to catch up with me at some point, may as well not give them the run around, grab Ray's phone off the table and dispose of it, now go!"

As Pete went to get up and move away Goose grabbed his arm "I only wish your Jamie was half the man you are Pete." And then he slipped in to unconsciousness.

CHAPTER SIXTEEN:

McVeigh crawled into bed late that night, he was too tired even to shower let alone eat the meal that Emily had prepared for him. He was mentally and physically exhausted.

He lay down thinking that sleep would overcome him quickly, but his mind was still racing from the day's events and sleep was not forthcoming.

The firearms unit had arrived at the warehouse, it was only eight minutes after Ray had called McVeigh when they stormed in, they found an unconscious Gosling on the floor, the fillet knife still stuck in his chest, it was the knife being left in his chest that at least had given him a fifty percent chance of survival. He was in the process of undergoing lifesaving surgery, an armed unit was stationed outside the operating theatre, guarding him.

Forensics were now going over the warehouse with a fine-tooth comb.

A pool of blood had been found on the floor which could not have come from Gosling and this was what was worrying McVeigh, there was also a heavily urinated patch that was being tested.

Two untouched McDonald's meals along with a receipt had been found on a table in the warehouse along with traces of cocaine, officers were at the McDonalds restaurant which was only two miles from the scene studying CCTV video footage and questioning staff.

Elsewhere over two hundred and fifty police officers from six different police forces were raiding pubs, clubs and other businesses that could be linked with Gosling.

Divers were being drafted in to start a thorough search of the Thames directly outside the warehouse. Ray's phone had been turned off meaning that no one could track it. Modern technology meant that even if a phone was out of charge, it could still be tracked meaning that either the battery or sim from Rays mobile had been removed and presumably destroyed.

Try as he might McVeigh could still not sleep.

***

Gopal Khatri walked all the way home. He was too embarrassed to even attempt to wave down a taxi such was his stench, not that there were any guarantees that any driver would take him. But he clutched his phone in his hand as if it was a life support machine, despite his ordeal, what he had then witnessed after he had been released, he could still not get Gosling's accusation about his father out of his head.

As a young child he worshipped his father, who in his eyes could do no wrong. He never ever saw the side of his father that Gosling had accused him of. Yet if Gosling had been telling the truth, and why would he lie about such a thing, then his uncle had indeed been his saviour and he was feeling guilty about how despicably he had treated him over the years.

His uncle was concerned for the state of Gopal when he walked in, his uncle had not opened the restaurant, not that Gopal thought for one minute that he would.

His uncle could not help but notice that his nephew's clothes were badly soiled and that the lad had a blackening lip, it was swollen and had clotted blood around it.

"You are home, oh thank goodness they let you go."

His uncle gently placed the palm of his hand on Gopal's face, rather than pull away he allowed him to caress his face softly, he would certainly not be bowing at his feet as was suggested by Gosling that he should, but he had at least now a new found respect for the man that had single handily raised him.

"I'll get the first aid kit and clean up your face, you get out of those clothes, throw them away and then you can have a nice hot shower and get some rest." His uncle went scurrying off into the kitchen, shouting "The police have been here for hours, they have gone now but want to speak to you at some point."

Gopal undressed on the restaurant floor. He removed his clothes, his uncle came back and started to clean up his lip. Gopal was not feeling embarrassment standing naked before his uncle.

"Uncle, I need to ask you something."

"The police, oh it's ok, I told them that you had gone out."

"No uncle not about the police, about my father."

Dinesh stopped cleaning the boy's lip, "Your father, what about him?"

"Is it true that it was his fault that he and my mother died, that he was drunk?" Dinesh got a plastic bin liner from under the counter and gathered the soiled clothes off the floor and placed them in it.

"Yes, it is true, he was a good father but sadly not a good husband, we will talk about this later, you need a shower and rest, please Gopal."

"Ok, just answer me one thing, why did you bring me over from India, why not leave me with my father's relatives?"

Dinesh stopped what he was doing and sighed heavily.

"I promised your mother if anything ever happened to her, I would take care of you. I have never married Gopal, never had children of my own, all this, the business, was my child and then you came along, your father's relatives were poor, thieves of the night I could not leave you with them, who knows what would have become of you."

Despite his nakedness Gopal went to his uncle and hugged him close. "Thank you, Uncle, I will take that shower now."

Once inside the bathroom in the flat above the restaurant Gopal locked the door before taking a long hot shower with tears in his eyes, his mobile remained only a few feet away, he would definitely not be letting it out of his sight.

***

Joe Whyte had slept for a few hours, showered and was now tucking in to a recently delivered Chinese takeaway in his new, but temporary accommodation. The flat, although ex-council had been done up inside to a very high standard, and the fridge and cupboards had been well stocked presumably thanks to Techno's hired help.

He got a tin of Stella out the fridge, flopped himself down on the plush corner sofa and flicked on the fifty-inch plasma TV. The local news had just started. Some bird with big tits and whose name he could never remember but who seemed to have been on the telly for years started to talk. Behind her was a picture of Goose, Joe sat bolt upright now, the TV and the bird with the big tits and the forgotten name had his full attention.

"Good evening, reports have been coming in that well-known East End business man Frank Gosling has been taken to hospital with a single stab wound to the chest, our sources at the hospital say that he only has a fifty percent chance of surviving"

Joe listened intently to what was being said, "Fuck, only a fifty-fifty chance of survival" he said out loud.

He picked up his new mobile, found Pete's name in the contacts and dialled, his eyes glued to the TV screen.

A picture of Ray then came up and the news reader said "Police are becoming increasingly worried about one of its officers, who it refuses to name. The police officer has not been seen or heard from since this morning when he phoned his superiors. A spokesperson from the Metropolitan Police has told us that any information they could give us was sensitive, therefore limited, but they were extremely worried for the welfare of the officer. It is believed that the call he made this morning was from the same warehouse that Frank Gosling was found. The Metropolitan Police refused to confirm or deny any link between the two men."

Pete picked up on the fifth ring.

The newscaster was now rattling on about how Goose was a known criminal to the police, but despite several investigations had never faced trial, the most publicised was a hit and run that involved the death of a woman that also resulted in severe injuries to her six-year-old son who survived but with life changing injuries.

Joe flicked on the mute button. "Pete, what the fuck is going on mate? I have the news on, just heard about Goose!"

Pete was at the flat within an hour, he had taken a tube and a taxi in case he was being followed.

Once inside the flat Joe poured Pete a large whiskey, Pete wearily plopped himself down on the sofa, it had after all been a long, exhausting and emotional day.

Pete sipped at the drink and began to explain how the day had unfolded.

"Goose sent Billy to get breakfast, and to take me home. I felt it strange that he insisted on being alone with Ray and the boy, but like he said, you were outside and had his back. When we got outside you were still there so maybe he was right."

Joe took a long swig of his lager "Yeh I was to make sure the Indian lad went straight home, did not go near a cop shop, go on…"

Peter rubbed his tired face.

"Yeh that's what I thought, anyway Billy and I got about a quarter a mile away from the industrial estate, something wasn't sitting right with me, I told Billy as much, a gut feeling so to speak. So, I got Billy to let me out and I walked back. I was busting for a piss and went round the back of an empty unit; I saw you go past in the van so I knew that I had made the right decision to go back to the warehouse."

Joe averted his gaze from Pete, guilt now beginning to eat away at him, the guilt of leaving before the kid had come out and he had followed him to make sure that he went straight home.

"Once I got inside Goose was on the floor, Ray had stabbed him, obviously you had the kid in the van, so there was just the two of them Goose and Ray. Its obvious Ray had concealed the knife, got loose and defended himself."

Joe went to the fridge and got another lager, his mind was racing, why hadn't he stayed? why hadn't he followed or took the kid home? if he had this could have all turned out differently.

"Anyway Joe, I always carry as you know, so basically, I shot Ray, he was dead before he hit the floor. You don't spend a big chunk of your life in the Marines and not be a good marksman."

Joe sat back down, patting Pete on the shoulder. "We sure do owe you one Pete."

Pete downed his whiskey and offered his glass up to Ray for another.

"You sure do mate, I was packing as you called, I'm getting a ferry to France tonight, then on to Spain or Portugal after that, I am going to lay low for a while especially what happened after I shot Ray."

Joe poured Pete another drink, "I'm all ears mate."

Pete took another swig of the whiskey, "Goose said Ray had already called an ambulance and old bill were on the way and that we were to leave him there and take care of getting Ray away from the scene. Billy turned up with the food. We got Ray into the back of the van, drove to Epping Forest and disposed of him. He won't be found for a while. All was good but, on the way back as we approached the outskirts of London, I had Billy pull in to a service station, the only trouble with prostate cancer mate, is when you've got to go you've got to go!"

Joe looked at Pete, "You what? You have prostate cancer. Oh man I am so sorry, none of us knew."

"And why would you mate, not even Jamie or the wife know, it's being treated and I have an eighty per cent chance of recovery, no need to worry anyone about it." He took a large swig of his drink.

"Anyway, as I came out from the services and was walking over the concourse, I could see Billy handcuffed face down and spread eagled over the bonnet of the van and a dozen or more armed coppers surrounding him, I dashed back inside and sat in a bog cubicle for an hour or so until the coast cleared then I got a cab home."

"So, the old bill has the van now, fucking forensics will be all over it like a rash as we speak." Joe asked rubbing his chin with one hand.

"Yeh they must have got the reg from the McDonald's CCTV, it's the only thing I can think of, we shouldn't have left the bag of food and receipt in the warehouse."

"Bloody hell Pete you weren't to know, you were up against it anyway, old bill was bearing down on you."

"Right, I had better get going Joe, me ferry is in four hours, the missus thinks it's a holiday, she doesn't know about Jamie either, talking of which…"

"This is where you call in the IOU mate, we owe you one and now you are going to cash it in." Joe nodded approvingly

Pete smiled "Of course" Pete put the tumbler down on the coffee table in front of him and leant forward so that he was nearer to Joe.

"Jamie has a suspended hanging over him, three years, GBH a couple of years back. It was his first offence, well that he has been caught for. I heard that he is being charged for burglary and assault on the land lady, not sexual assault which is a good thing, life in the nick would be hard enough without being classed as a sex offender. He's going to be on remand and then he'll no doubt do a lump of sorts, with the suspended and the new charge probably five to six years."

"What you saying to me Pete?" Joe looked at Pete, even though he already knew what was going to be asked.

"What I am saying Joe, is let him be, what we talked about this morning, let it go, yes he was a prize idiot, but I took one for the team today mate, let that be classed as paying off Jamie's debt of being a complete and utter prick."

Joe held out his hand, "Done mate, and I'll get Techno to transfer some funds in to your account, lay low in France, an old farmhouse or something in the middle of nowhere for a year or two before you move further afield, you've earned it!"

"That's very kind Joe, Techno doesn't have my account number, I'll write it down."

Joe laughed, "No need, Techno even has the Prime Ministers bank details mate, he is a clever boy that one."

Gopal was playing on Joe's mind, Pete had long gone and he was sat on the sofa, getting slowly pissed and different permutations of what had happened during the day were going over and over through his mind. So, he summoned Techno to the flat. For the second night running Techno had to kick Dyson out of the flat, she was none too pleased.

Techno was at the flat on the Isle of Dogs within the hour, armed as usual with information and a lap-top that never left his side.

After the formalities and ensuring that Techno had a beer in front of him, Joe set out what he wanted.

"Is there any CCTV covering the Industrial Estate where Goose was found?" The request was straight forward enough and opening his laptop Techno got to work.

Within only a few moments he had accessed the CCTV camera at the top of Pembrooke Industrial Estate on Burnaby Road. A few minutes later and he had accessed the recordings from the previous seven days.

"Ok what you looking for Joe?" Techno asked, his handsome blue eyes staring intently at Joe. Joe ashamedly felt a stirring in his groin. Six months earlier the two had spent a night together at Techno's flat.

From the age of ten Joe had known that he was bi-sexual and for fifty odd years he had been in love with only one man, Goose. He dared not share that information with him as he knew that it would not be reciprocated. If he had told Goose, the only thing he would be getting up his arse would be a sorn off shotgun.

"Look from eight o'clock this morning kid." After reminding Joe not to call him kid, Techno scrolled through the recording, stopping when asked to by Joe.

At eight fifteen, Billy's van was seen leaving the industrial estate, a short while later and Pete could be clearly seen walking back into the estate from the main road. Five minutes after that and Joe's van left the industrial estate. Fifteen minutes passed before Billy's van entered the industrial estate once more and then four minutes later it was seen screeching away from the Industrial Estate, smoke bellowed from the tyres as it headed off towards Stratford. Two minutes later police cars and vans, at least a dozen of them roared in to the Industrial Estate at speed, lights flashing and sirens blaring.

For the next two hours Techno scrolled through the footage but try as they might, Joe could find no sign of the young Asian lad leaving the estate.

Techno could sense the tension in Joe, "What's up Joe what are we looking for?"

Joe knew that he himself had fucked up big time, he should've waited for the lad to be released, insisted on taking him home.

"I am looking for a lad that was in the warehouse at the same time as Goose and that bastard Ray, but there's no sign of him leaving, which is making me wonder what he saw."

Techno smiled his perfect white teeth at Joe, and again Joe felt that stirring in his nether regions. "Was he in a car or on foot?" He asked "On foot kid, I mean Techno." "Ok, well there is an alleyway that leads onto the estate from further down Burnaby Road, it's only accessible by foot, he could have cut through from there."

A few minutes later Techno had got into another CCTV that overlooked the area that Techno had described earlier and sure enough Gopal was seen emerging from the alleyway on to Burnaby Road only a few minutes from when Billy and Pete had left heading in the opposite direction for the second time.

Joe was piecing information together in his head, had Gopal witnessed what had gone on? He certainly wasn't still in the warehouse when Pete arrived or Pete would have said surely, so why did he not emerge into Burnaby Road until long after he had presumably been released by Goose?

Joe was even more on edge now, permutations of what could have happened swam round the inside of his head like a shole of crazy fish, causing a severe skull ache "What you like accessing mobiles Techno? I have a feeling that tonight's going to be a long one." Joe placed a hand on Techno's shoulder, Techno patted it gently "Promises, promises."

Techno, now on his third beer, had established that no mobile was registered to Gopal Khatri but had found that two contracts had been taken out in his uncle's name some time ago.

Several minutes later Techno was able to tell Joe that the mobile phone believed to be used by Gopal was switched on and was currently static at the restaurant that his uncle owned, other than that there was no other information that could be given.

"Can you tell what the movements of the phone were today, Techno?"

"I am good Joe but not MI6 mate, that would take some serious software that even I cannot access."

"Do you know if the phone was used to call, text or take pictures or video today then?"

Techno allowed himself a smile before answering. "Again, that is more like software used by the KGB or the FBI mate."

Joe lashed out at a defenceless cushion, taking his anger out on it, "Well there's nothing else for it I'm going to have to go to the Amid and get the phone myself!" Joe looked around for his jacket.

Techno started typing into his lap top, as Joe was about to leave, he stood and stopped him from leaving, placing both hands on his shoulders he leaned in and the two kissed a long passionate kiss.

"If you go Joe, you'll be nicked mate, the old bill will need to talk to this young lad, Ray would have passed on information last night I'm sure that the restaurant will be under surveillance, you get within a hundred yards of it, you will be locked up by mid-night you surely know that as good as me!" Joe broke away from Techno's embrace, "What you suggest that I do, fuck all? If the kid witnessed the murder of Ray, he'll tell the old bill."

Techno once more went towards Ray "And if he does it means that he saw Goose get stabbed by Ray and Pete kill Ray nothing more, it means that Goose will face a lesser charge surely, as for Pete he'll be out of the country by the time they find out with half a million at his disposal." Joe tore off his coat and threw the keys back onto the table, "Ok hot shot, what you reckon I should do?"

Techno was moving towards the flat's bedroom door, which was slightly ajar. "Come to bed of course."

CHAPTER SEVENTEEN:

McVeigh sat at his desk; it had now been twenty-four hours since Ray had disappeared. The investigation was moving at pace, but there was still not a single sign of his friend and colleague being found, dead or alive.

McVeigh flicked through the many pages of the report that had landed on his desk a few minutes previously.

The van that was used by Gosling's henchman was now in the forensics workshop being examined to the finest detail and divers were searching the Thames by the warehouse where Goose was found.

Elsewhere officers had established, by scouring CCTV footage, that the van Billy Roberts had used was spotted on CCTV nearing Epping Forest and officers from the Essex force were searching the area with a fine-tooth comb.

The Uncle and Nephew from the restaurant were now in the back of a police car being escorted in for questioning.

Despite the success of his five-hour operation Gosling was still in an induced coma and far from out of danger.

Elsewhere raids on known Gosling businesses had failed to upturn anything of any significance.

McVeigh was interrupted by his mobile ringing; he glanced down and saw that it was Emily calling so he answered immediately.

McVeigh tried to calm down his wife, she was talking at nineteen to the dozen and was clearly upset. McVeigh managed to calm her down enough for her to explain to him that a few moments before an envelope had been posted through the letterbox at home and that when she opened it there were photographs dated today of her dropping the twins off at school. The pictures, of which there were about half a dozen, showed her with the boys, the boys going through the school gates and individual pictures of the boys as they headed to their respective classrooms. There was also a note stating that McVeigh should visit an undertaker and arrange a triple funeral. She was crying softly and he could almost hear her shaking down the receiver!

McVeigh managed to persuade Emily to come into the station, bringing with her the contents of the envelope, he then got onto dispatch and requested a car be sent to pick his sons up from school immediately and to bring them to the station.

An hour later Emily and the boys were, thankfully safe in the station canteen, the boys unaware of any danger sat drinking milk shakes and Emily was enjoying a nice calming cup of camomile tea, the envelope and its contents were sealed up and on their way to the forensic department.

A WPC was assigned to scrutinise CCTV footage outside the boy's school from that morning.

With his family finally safe McVeigh was able to carry on with his daily duties and proceeded into an interview room to talk to the nephew of the Amid Palace owner whilst a colleague interviewed the uncle in a separate room.

McVeigh looked at Gopal Khatri. He was having mixed emotions, if only the lad had not grassed up Ray perhaps none of this nightmare would be happening right now.

The Asian, was indeed as arrogant as described by Ray, he sat their believing that the State owed him a debt because of the evidence that he had on his person, evidence that would prove that the undercover policeman had been murdered, but that evidence, he felt, came at a price.

"I want protection for me and my uncle, compensation for the business that my uncle will lose, a fresh start somewhere else, a new business for my uncle and a bank account with enough money in to be able to achieve all of that."

McVeigh laughed at the young man before him "Anything else, perhaps a private yacht or helicopter for you sir?"

"Do not ridicule me, I am not the one who placed a policeman into the lair of the gangster am I?" The boy's arrogance was plain to see.

McVeigh was trying not to lose it with this arrogant little prick sat before him

"No, but you are certainly the one who put him in danger, why could you not keep your trap shut, you must have known what danger you were putting him in, did you see him as your money ticket then?"

"I didn't see him as anything and believe me if I had known what would happen to me, the trauma I have faced over the past thirty-six hours I would have kept quiet, I did not ask to see the things that I have had to see believe me or indeed discover the things that I have!"

McVeigh calmed a little, "So what is this evidence?"

163

Gopal thought that he now had the upper hand; "No, not until you promise me what I want, and only then will I hand it over."

McVeigh felt his temper rising once more and a thudding in his temple.

McVeigh looked at Gopal trying to hide his disgust.

"You know Gosling still has people out there right, I am sure he would have someone monitoring your every movement, after all you are a key witness to what went down. I think you need us more than we need you."

McVeigh stood up, "Goodbye Mr Khatri see yourself out." McVeigh went to leave the interview room.

On seeing McVeigh heading for the door, it became pretty obvious to Gopal that perhaps he had overestimated his bargaining chip, he felt his bladder loosen once more but managed to contain it unlike he hadn't on numerous occasions before, he called to McVeigh to come back, panic clearly in his voice.

McVeigh returned to his side of the desk and with both hands on the desk he leaned over, his face red with rage only inches away from the face of the young Indian lad, so close Gopal could feel McVeigh's breath on his own skin. Gopal jumped back with a start when McVeigh bellowed at him.

"Two hours ago, I received a threatening note, and pictures of my wife and kids, my twin boys, the pictures were taken today, you know what that means boy? You think you can sit there and demand things from me you arrogant prick, it means that despite Gosling being near death and fifteen members of his organisation that we already have in custody, there are still people out there who can threaten me and mine, you still want to barter for what could potentially be yours and your uncle's lives?"

The realisation of McVeigh's words slowly began to sink in to Gopal's young mind.

McVeigh was still enraged, "So here is what is going to happen fuck face, you are going to give me whatever evidence you have and then, and only then, will I decide if it warrants for you and your uncle to be given police protection whilst proceedings are underway to get you placed on the witness protection program, and if the information you have does not warrant you getting placed on the program, I will smash your arrogant, smug, ugly fucking face over this desk and turf you out on to the street to face Goslings crew who, and I repeat, are obviously watching you and know you are here, what is to be Mr Big I Fucking am Gopal Khatri?"

McVeigh watched the video footage off Gopal's camera over and over again. Despite the gruesome reality that his friend Ray was dead he felt ashamed thinking that it was not Gosling that had pulled the trigger. The footage was not the best quality so he could not easily make out the face of the gunmen but hopefully the Mets technology department could enhance the image and make it clearer. The footage was enough evidence to prove Gosling's involvement, if indeed he survived and it was enough to send him down for a very long time.

Eventually he handed over the phone and footage to his Detective Sergeant to bag up and send to forensics.

He looked over at Gopal whose arrogance had long since departed. His own rage now gone McVeigh spoke softly this time.

"You and your uncle will be taken to a safe house, arrangements are under way, you will be expected to give evidence at any trial whenever that may be, now fuck off out of my sight."

Not once during the interview with McVeigh had Gopal used the word "like".

***

Sandra Davidson was trying to get her sugar daddy, Lenny the Jew hard, her jaw and knees ached from the amount of time she had been sucking him off, even the Viagra she had slipped into his drink didn't appear to be working.

At twenty-five Sandra had been with Lenny, real name Leonard Kaiser for over three years. In the beginning despite the fifty five-year age difference, it had been fun. Lenny set her up in her own flat which she had furnished to her own personal taste using his gold credit card. All she had to do was be at his beck and call when he fancied a fuck or a dinner companion, which thankfully lately was becoming less and less frequent.

When she wasn't required to be with Lenny, she had her own choice of male companions that could give her everything Lenny couldn't in the bedroom department. Her latest was a doorman from a club in Vauxhall called Lewis. He was muscular, good looking, black and hung like a horse.

The ultimate insult as she was sucking Lenny off was that she heard him starting to gently snore. On the plus side that meant her poor knees and jaw could get some much-needed respite. She left him on the sofa and made herself a vodka tonic in her kitchen which looked like something out of a sci-fi movie with all of its gadgets and units. As she sipped at the drink, she heard the intercom buzzer go and went to pick up the phone.

"Hello?" she asked, wincing at the sudden movement because her jaw was still aching.

The voice on the other end was male "I have an urgent delivery for Lenny."

"Can it wait, he is asleep, come back tomorrow?" she said whilst rubbing her jaw with her other hand. "No, he has requested it tonight, I think it may be some nice jewellery for his girlfriend Sandra."

Not once did it cross Sandra's mind why a courier should know her name such was her excitement at what Lenny may have bought her. "Oh Sandra, that's me, ok I guess you better come up." She squealed a little too excitedly.

Sandra pressed the entry button. She looked across at Lenny who was now snoring louder and was dead to the world. Sandra rushed to the mirror that hung in the hallway, she straightened her hair, undid another button of her blouse to show off her false breasts to their full seductive advantage. If the delivery driver was good looking, she may even get a fuck out of him, Lenny wasn't waking anytime soon, that was a certainty.

There was a knock at the door, she quickly opened it. Her joy at receiving new jewellery and the anticipation of getting a fuck turned to horror as Joe Whyte thrust the gun into her already aching mouth as he forcefully entered the flat.

After Joe had advised Sandra not to scream, he walked her through to the bedroom and ordered her to sit on the bed. He then rummaged through her chest of drawers and finding silk stockings, gagged her and tied her hands behind her back. Sandra, for some strange reason was not afraid, she knew that Lenny was Joes target, not her.

She had met Joe on many occasions although old, he looked after himself, she had often looked at his groin area and knew he was packing more than the average male. Goose was another of her intended targets, but he was too into his girlfriend Isobel, an eighteen-year-old from Scotland who could drink him under the table apparently.

Once Joe knew that Sandra was securely tied up and not going anywhere soon, he went back in to the living room and stood over a snoring Lenny.

Lenny was old, yes, Lenny had made a mistake, yes, but Joe had already made the decision not to torture him as he normally would anyone that had crossed Goose and instead would make death quick and as painless as possible. Besides that, Sandra was right up his street and he may even have time to give her one before he left if he made Lenny's demise quick enough.

Joe knew that he had been spending too much time in the company of Techno the last few days, Techno had practically moved in and although Joe was enjoying laying in the arms of another man, he had decided that he still preferred the attention of a good woman with some fulsome tits, Sandra was going to be that woman whether she liked it or not. Although death was going to be quick, Lenny did have to be made aware of what was going to happen though, so a quick bullet in the head while he slept was not an option.

A glass of water in the face duly did the trick and Lenny woke with a start as the cold water hit his face. It took a few seconds for him to realise what was going on and when he did, he remained cool, calm and collected about the situation he was in.

"It's you Joe, I thought that it would be you who was the one, I wouldn't have expected anything less." If the old man was afraid, he certainly didn't show it.

Lenny pushed his wet hair out of his eyes. "How is Goose? I have been watching the news so know all about it, I do hope that he recovers, I have always liked Goose, so has Sandra, where is Sandra? promise me, you won't hurt her Joe, she has been good for me over the years, bit common but boy what a fuck, when I can get it up that is."

Joe looked at Lenny with interest, he admired the way the old boy was conducting himself, not begging for his life like many much younger than he would be doing. Lenny knew that he had fucked up big time and was prepared to take his punishment like a man.

"You have to understand Joe, McVeigh gave me no option, he had me over a barrel, it was either go along with it or do ten years, at least this way I have had a few months of freedom. That said, it was wrong, please apologise to Goose for me. Can I ask one thing Joe?"

"Sure, Lenny you go for it, I will either say yes or no whatever it is you have to say so you have nothing to lose."

"Thank you, Joe, the keys to my shop and safe are in my coat pocket, please give them to Sandra, the deeds to this place are in the safe, she is to take no more and no less, the remaining wealth I have will go to my nephew, but this place is Sandra's, it is the least she deserves for making an old man very happy, can you tell her that for me?"

While Lenny was talking Joe was screwing a silencer on to the gun he held in his hand. "Course I will Lenny."

And then he quickly raised the gun and fired. The single bullet penetrated Lenny's heart and he died instantly.

Joe calmly walked into the bedroom, untied Sandra and said "Go tidy yourself up in the bathroom then get naked, you've pulled love!" She skipped off to the bathroom, happy saying as she went "As long as you don't expect me to suck you off, my jaw is positively aching!"

Sandra lay with her head on Joe's chest, the birds were singing outside. The penthouse flat overlooked Hyde Park and she often lay here in the mornings listening to natures sounds coming from outside.

Joe had been an attentive, sensitive lover and she couldn't remember the last time she had climaxed so much with a man or a woman.

She was under no illusions, this was probably a one off, she knew that a man like Joe could make her happy but she, like Lenny, had seen the news and knew that every copper in the land would be looking for Joe, his days of freedom were numbered, but the sex had been truly remarkable, she wouldn't forget those orgasms in a hurry.

She stroked Joe's manhood and felt it gradually harden, the pain in her jaw from the night before had long gone so she eagerly took Joes rising manhood in her mouth as he began to stir from his slumber. She then rode him when he was fully hard, within seconds she was coming like a steam locomotive, over and over again.

The pair shared a shower and as she had hoped, two further orgasms followed. She hopped out of the shower and putting on a robe went to make coffee. Within seconds Joe heard a piercing scream, he quickly ran in to the living room expecting to see the old bill. Sandra stood there livid, "Look what the cunts done to me settee, blood all over it, its ruined, three grand that fucker was!"

One of her breasts had fallen out of her robe, Joe instantly thought of Mandy in her living room when they had first made love, he put he thought out of his mind as quickly as it had arrived Joe laughed, "Come back to bed, I'll take your mind off it!" and then Sandra's face lit up and any further thoughts of the settee were quickly forgotten.

Later that afternoon, as Joe had promised Sandra before he left, the Jones brothers turned up at her flat to clean up and dispose of Lenny. She had patiently waited for them after Joe had left despite wanting to rush off to Lenny's shop to claim what was rightfully hers, and a little bit more besides, fuck the nephew, not literally he was a spotty geeky looking boy who she would never go near in a month of Sundays however wealthy he was to become. The apartment in itself was worth the best part of a million plus, but there would still be bills to pay, any cash left in the safe she was having, it was hers for the taking.

The Jones brothers were from Romford, Jason and Jacob, Jacob being the eldest by a year and the most handsome. They were experts at cleaning up situations such as this and would demand high prices for it. Joe had contacted them on the promise of twenty k to make the situation go away. After Lenny had been removed, along with the settee and the carpets had been cleaned together with any other evidence of Lenny's demise, Sandra put on her coat and put the piece of paper with Jacobs recently acquired number and a promise of a date in her purse before setting off to claim her wealth and then to go furniture shopping.

CHAPTER EIGHTEEN:

March 2014

McVeigh saw Helen Whitehead walk into the social club. An hour before they had stood in a cold cemetery in Bury St Edmunds and laid Ray to rest.

His body had been found six weeks before in a small stagnant pond in Epping Forest, it had eventually been released for burial.

McVeigh looked at her son Jake, he was dressed smartly in a two-piece suit and nice overcoat, at only six the boy was the spitting image of his father, you could sense that he was not fully aware of what was going on.

Helen gradually made her way round the room of the hundred or so mourners that were at the wake and who were all sincerely sorry for her loss.

Eventually she made it to McVeigh, Emily was unable to attend due to a heavy bout of flu, he explained as he tried to avert looking directly at her such was the guilt he felt.

Helen was a good-looking woman; he could see that the past six months had taken its toll on her.

Yes, Ray and her may have been separated for three years and she now had a new man in her life, albeit out of respect for Ray, he had not attended the funeral but he could see that the tears, and sleepless nights for the man that she had once loved for so long had caused her to age some considerable years. Jake had been taken off to get pop and crisps by his grandfather so the question when it came was easy to answer for McVeigh.

"Where are we with proceedings Pat?" she asked simply

This time McVeigh forced himself to look at her directly. "Well as you know Gosling's out of danger, and hospital. He is on remand in a secure unit awaiting trial, a date has been set for one month today."

Helen smiled and brushed hair away from her face with her hand, "And the other one, the one who pulled the trigger, what of him?"

"Peter Bennet? Well, he has been found through our friends at Interpol, he is in France under arrest and extradition proceedings are ongoing. We hope to have him back in our hands and the country within a few weeks."

Helen nodded approvingly "And what about Mark Smith? The policeman that virtually signed Ray's death warrant by misleading the fire arms team?"

McVeigh could see the anger etched on her face "He is on remand awaiting trial, along with fourteen other bent coppers that the investigation uncovered, all were on Gosling's payroll. Ex Superintendent John Walker has given us enough information on Gosling to make sure that Gosling never sees the light of day from prison, we are just waiting for the initial trial to be over next month before bringing more charges against Gosling, we don't want to complicate matters by having everything dealt with in one hit."

Helen gave the briefest of smiles, McVeigh knew that whatever happened to Gosling it was never going to bring Ray back and that Jake would still be without a father.

"And what of Walker what will happen to him?" she asked softly.

McVeigh thought long and hard before answering, not knowing how Helen would react and what information he felt he could divulge.

Knowing that Walker had played no part in Ray's downfall he thought it safe to answer. "He cut a deal with the Crown Prosecution Service and my superiors thought it best not to prosecute him. That said, he has been forced to resign from the force, he has lost any rights to his pension and I believe that his wife has filed for divorce, all of his and some of her assets including the villa in Tenerife have been seized."

Helen looked at Pat and smiled, it was a genuine smile. "Don't feel guilty about any of this Pat, Ray was a grown man, it was his decision to go under cover. You know that he loved to role play, the danger, anything so he didn't have to spend time at home with his family" she sipped at her vodka and coke.

"It was his decision to accept but it was me that dangled the carrot I'm afraid" McVeigh said softly.

Helen threw back her head and laughed, maybe a little too loudly, people in the room had turned to look to see what a widow could find so amusing at her husband's funeral.

"I like that Pat, a carrot for a complete and utter ass, very appropriate!"

Jake came running over to his mother and said excitedly that he was going to go and play pool with his grandad and did she want to come too, "Of course, I will darling", she bent down and kissed him on the cheek, "you go and set the balls up and I will be there in a moment."

She turned to Pat and leant in to give him a kiss on the cheek, she smelt of lavender, Pat wondered why Ray had been such a fool where this woman was concerned.

"Keep me updated Pat, but please don't feel guilty anymore, he just isn't worth it" and then she turned and went to find her son, he was the only priority in her life now, she was a good mother, and had been a good wife too, only Ray was foolish enough not to have seen that.

***

Frank Gosling lay sprawled on the bed in his cell.

His trial was to take place in less than forty-eight hours and he knew that whatever happened he was due a long stretch at Her Majesties pleasure, there was nothing he could do to change things now, even with the best briefs that money could buy.

Joe Whyte had fucked up big style, allowing Khatri to film the proceedings and for the filth, the coppers to get to him, Goose had told Joe that in no uncertain terms using the mobile phone that he had at his disposal.

Their friendship was at breaking point which bothered Goose seriously more than the sentence he knew that was coming itself.

The last straw was when Joe had point blank refused to wipe out McVeigh's family, saying that he was many things but not a kid killer, especially innocent kids, who were to be targeted because their father had got one over on Goose.

Joe's comments, and point-blank refusal to carry out what was being asked of him had hurt Goose, his friend of over fifty years who he had the upmost respect for and whom he had never had an argument with was now turning into an enemy in his eyes, some things surely had to be done, whatever the price, it was no time to develop a conscience.

Gosling retrieved the mobile from its hiding place beneath the mattress and dialled a number. The recipient of the call picked up immediately and Goose relayed instructions to the person on the other end of the line as to what to do, he then called Techno.

Techno answered on the third ring, for once he was home alone, Joe had cooled things in their relationship of late and was spending more time in the company of females at the flat on the Isle of Dogs, Sandra Davidson was a regular visitor by all accounts, Joe was besotted with her, the cleaner and cook he had hired, Meryl, also turned out to be a friend with special benefits spending more time at Joes flat then her own of late, only being asked to leave when he had a liaison with Sandra. Joe's morals of stringing more than one woman along at any one time seemed to have gone out of the window. He was now thinking purely with his cock.

Techno listened intently as Goose spoke, "Techno me old son, how are you?" and then not waiting for a response "How much is left in that account I gave you access to Techno?"

Techno did not have to wait to calculate it, he knew down to the last penny, such was his pedantic nature.

"Three million, two hundred and twenty-five thousand and sixty-nine pence." He rattled off the figure immediately without having to think about it.

At the other end of the line, he could here Goose laughing loudly "Fuck me Techno to the nearest mill would have done!" There was a slight pause as Goose digested the information before saying, "Fuck me Techno you've certainly been splashing the cash, I expected there to be twice that amount!"

Techno pondered long and hard whether to tell Goose that Joe had requested three million be transferred into another account so that he could flee the country. Techno felt that he had been well and truly used by Joe, he had scratched an itch and he had now moved on to other things, well Sandra and Meryl to be precise.

He didn't believe that he owed Joe any sense of loyalty so he could go to hell as far as he was concerned.

Techno had spent enough nights in Joe's company to know that he and Goose had stopped seeing eye to eye of late and that Goose personally blamed Joe for the Indian lad being able to stand there and testify against him in a couple of days, probably via video link but testify the boy would.

Techno made the decision to inform Goose everything about Joe that he knew, as far as he was concerned Joe had fucked him over and deserved to get what was coming to him, he took a deep breath and then spoke softly.

"Goose, I feel that there is something that you should know about Joe, he admitted to me that he had slept with your wife and aided her escape after you had put a contract on her head, in addition to that he is heading to Columbia in a few days, with three million of your money, he had me transfer it into another off shore account. He said that since that bent copper Walker blabbed to save his own skin that the businesses were fucked, there's nothing to stay around for, nothing to protect and that it is only a matter of time before the filth catch up with him too." When he had finished Techno exhaled deeply, the damage had been done, there was no turning back now, he had signed his former lover's death warrant, but strangely, he did not feel one little bit guilty about it.

There was a long silence at the other end of the phone, Techno was relieved that he'd told Goose and if Goose was feeling aggrieved by the information he had been fed when he did speak, he certainly showed no signs of it.

"Right Techno down to business, there's something I want you to do for me, do this and the remaining money in that account is all yours."

Techno's mind went into overdrive, what job could be worth over three million? "Ok Goose, what needs doing?"

"That's my boy, knew I could rely on you unlike that cunt Joe!"

Gosling continued with instructions to Techno. "Tomorrow a friend of mine will deliver a package and a letter to you, so make sure that you're in. My friend will give you his bank details, transfer fifty k in to his account. The minute my verdict is announced the following day, you're to take the letter to McVeigh's nick, hand it in to the front desk, then deliver the package to the address that will be already written on it, you got it? And remember make sure that you deliver the package to the address, and the letter to the nick, do not get them the wrong way round, in short, do not fuck up my friend."

Techno, his mind still whirring at what was being asked of him simply asked "Why can't Joe do it? I know that he's betrayed you but I'm just your IT brains after all, this isn't something I would normally do with all due respect Goose."

There followed a full onslaught of verbal abuse from Goose that lasted a minute or more in which Goose called Joe all the names under the sun from spineless to cunt and every expletive in between. Techno wished he had not brought up why he was suddenly a personal post man for Goose, after all he was getting three million plus for it.

Goose eventually calmed down enough to be all apologetic for his outburst. Eventually he was calm enough to give Techno further instructions.

"Whatever you do Techno, make sure while you have the package in your flat you keep it out of the way of heat and do not open it under any circumstances, do I make myself clear?"

The call was ended with Gosling being all nice and thanking Techno for his help over the years.

For a long while after the call Techno sat in silence before he snapped out of his trance and picked up his mobile phone and dialled Dyson's number, he needed a distraction and she certainly could do that. She was naked kneeling on his living room floor with his cock deep in her mouth within thirty minutes from the time she received his call.

Whilst Techno was screaming with delight as he orgasmed, Goose was pacing his cell, an anger boiling up inside him, but he was also fit to burst in to tears of sadness.

He did not ask Techno where he had got the information about Joe sleeping with Mandy, if he had Techno may well have told him it was pillow talk as he and Joe lay in each other's arms after their love making and were exchanging small talk.

Techno had asked Joe outright what his feelings for him were and was he using him to satisfy something that he had kept hidden for so long.

Despite Joe saying that he had feelings for Techno he had told him outright that it was Mandy that was his one true love. He then relayed the information about how he and Mandy had been lovers and that he had helped her flee the country after Goose had taken out the contract on her.

However, Techno had got the information Goose never questioned it but that night after Techno had disclosed it, he cut a sad solemn figure as he sat in his cell and planned the downfall of his onetime best friend.

CHAPTER NINETEEN:

The day of Gosling's trial came round soon enough, the following week it was to be the trial of Peter Bennet who had arrived back in the country and police custody two weeks earlier, he was to plead guilty and by all accounts whatever sentence he received, he would not see out a year in prison. Left untreated for so long, his prostate cancer had taken hold and no treatment could now prevent the cancer from killing him.

Gosling's trial lasted three days and the outcome was inevitable, guilty of conspiracy to murder carried a life sentence. Other charges could have been brought, kidnap for one but the Crown Prosecution decided that the one charge would be easier to get to stick. Sure, enough by a majority, the jury foreman uttered a guilty verdict and Gosling was sentenced to serve a minimum of twelve years.

Young Gopal Khatri had given evidence through video link and his testimony along with the camera footage he had taken on the day, was enough to put the nail in Gosling's coffin. Gopal and his uncle were now in the witness protection program, the Amid Palace had been burnt to the ground two days after Ray's disappearance and as of yet no one had been brought to justice for the arson attack.

McVeigh sat in the courtroom and watched as Gosling went ballistic as first the verdict and then the sentence were read out, he struggled and fought with the guards shouting his innocence and then his eyes met McVeigh's, "You are going to be sorry for this McVeigh, you see if you're not, best get them coffins ready for your wife and boys I am telling you!" he bellowed with rage, spit spurting from his mouth as he was eventually bought under control by the guards and led away down the stairs and to the cells below knowing that his days of freedom and causing fear in to the hearts of the East End public were over.

McVeigh walked into the police station to rapturous applause. The interview he had given on the steps of the Old Bailey was being played on large televisions in the station. Only one reporter had taken the shine off the day's proceedings; when she had asked why so many mistakes had been made that could potentially have saved Ray's life, presumably meaning why was the arms unit sent to the wrong restaurant that night, then on hearing McVeigh's reply, why had there been so many corrupt police officers allowed to work un-noticed in the force and was there was going to be a full police enquiry as to why it was allowed to happen and go unnoticed. He had dealt with the questions as best as he could saying that the Commissioner would be giving a statement later on in the day.

Henry Cartwright put a hand on Pat's shoulder and handed him a glass of champagne, "Well done Pat now that scum is secured behind bars the people of London can sleep easier now. Just that other bastard to find and bring to justice now" he was referring to Joe Whyte who so far had evaded capture, no one knew where he was, there had been no sightings or reporting of his whereabouts at all.

McVeigh still felt uneasy with Gosling's warning still ringing in his ears, whilst Whyte was free his family were still in danger.

The celebrations at the station were coming to a close and people had gradually started to go about their daily duties once more. McVeigh stood talking with Cartwright about McVeigh wanting to reopen the case of Natasha which Cartwright gave his blessing to providing that it didn't take up too many Police hours.

A WPC came up to the pair and apologised for interrupting. She handed McVeigh an envelope. "This was delivered a moment ago at the front desk for you sir."

McVeigh nodded his thanks and opened the envelope; he read the contents and then dropped the glass he was holding along with the contents of the envelope and shouted to no one in particular "Get a squad car and arms unit to my house now!"

He then ran out of the room, giving no explanation as to why.

Cartwright picked up the discarded envelope and the piece of paper from the floor and read it. The letter was made up of newspaper cut out letters and said simply;

"Get the coffins on order, you were warned."

Cartwright took over proceedings with the calm collective manner that was him all over, all available cars and an armed response unit were dispatched immediately to DI McVeigh's home, whilst the envelope and letter were bagged and sent off to the forensics' department.

Meanwhile McVeigh was racing through the streets of London driving like a formula one driver trying to get to home to save his family before it was too late.

CHAPTER TWENTY:

Emily was in the shower she had left the boys playing in the front room and didn't hear the doorbell.

James and Jason were off school due to a teacher training day and she had to fit in things in and around them today.

When their favourite program had come on the television, Horrid Henry, it was a great opportunity for her to at least grab a shower and make herself presentable for when her husband got home, she like others had watched the lunchtime news bulletin and saw her husband's interview, the boys watched it with her and were very excited to see their Daddy on the television.

Unbeknown to her as she stepped from the shower and dried her body, downstairs the boys were arguing who should get the door, eventually Jason went his eyes still glued to the television as he backed out slowly from the room.

He came back into the room and put the package down on the dining table and carried on watching the television just as the titles of the program came on meaning that Horrid Henry had finished for another episode. Jason was annoyed that he'd missed the end and turned his attentions to the package that had just arrived. He had started to open it just as his mother appeared in the doorway, he wondered why she was screaming at him.

***

McVeigh completed the normal thirty-minute journey home in ten minutes.

His BMW sped through the streets and there had been several near misses with other vehicles, cyclists and pedestrians.

As he turned into his road, he could see several police cars coming up the road from the other end of the street, he had screeched to a halt, left the car engine running and the driver door open and had sprinted up the path of his home and was half way up the dozen or so steps that led to the front door of his house before the first police car had come to a stop outside his house.

The force of the explosion from within the house was enough to throw McVeigh backwards and he travelled through the air eventually landing on the bonnet of his own car, every window and pane of glass at the front of the house was blown out injuring police officers as they emerged from their cars and vans. Smoke bellowed from the house as the fire took hold.

A street away Techno, who was making his way to the nearest tube station heard the explosion, felt the rumblings of the pavement beneath his feet and he knew instantly what had been the cause, he leant over a wall and everything he had eaten that day ended up in some poor unsuspecting residents front garden.

***

Gosling had watched the news on his personal television that he had been allowed in his cell, it came at a cost of course having bribed the wings screws fairly substantially. He smiled as the pictures of McVeigh's house and the aftermath of the explosion were shown on the screen. He had the sound on mute.

***

Joe Whyte was in his flat watching the same bulletin, Sandra had her head in his lap and his cock in her mouth, she started to complain as he pushed her roughly off him, so hard she fell on to the floor, she stopped complaining when she saw the enraged look on Joe's face. He leant forward to get closer to the television.

***

Techno arrived home several hours after the explosion via several pubs and could barely stand. He could not believe what he had done, why had Goose set him up for such an horrendous act? He went to the toilet and threw up for the umpteenth time that day, God alone knew how anything was left in his stomach.

***

The phone call Joe made to Goose was short and sweet, Goose had overstepped the mark, they were done, Joe never wanted to talk to him or have anything to do with him again. Joe had his suspicions who Goose had got to do the nasty deed and these were confirmed by Goose himself, Goose had shouted and yelled at his former best friend that he knew that Joe had been fucking his wife and that he helped her get away, he also knew about Joe's plan to take off with his money whilst he was left to rot in jail. Joe went on the defensive and gave Goose a torrent of abuse of his own before hanging up, it was the last time the two ever spoke.

***

As Techno emerged from the toilet for the second time after getting home, he was startled to see Joe standing there, looking directly at him. He could tell that Joe was none too pleased, anger clear to see on his face. When Joe spoke his voice matched that of the look on his face

"How the fuck could you be so stupid Techno, a woman and her two kids, innocents in all of this. And to add insult to injury you blab to Goose about Mandy, then just as matters couldn't get any worse you tell him about me fleeing the country, what the fuck!!" he yelled.

Techno was seeing a side of Joe he had not witnessed before, he felt more bile rising in his throat but managed to keep it down. To say that he was scared was an understatement, he was petrified and in fear of his life.

Joe could see the fear on the face of his former lover, Techno looked deathly white but whether that was because of the realisation of the carnage he had caused that day or because he was scared in the presence of Joe, only Techno knew.

Joe sighed heavily and slumped down on the nearby sofa leaning forward, his head held in both his hands.

"Fucking hell Techno, what the fuck possessed you, two young kids and an innocent woman, for fucks sake man!"

At this moment in time Techno burst in to tears and ran towards Joe taking a seat beside him. He placed a hand on Joe's arm. Through his tears he stammered, "I am so sorry Joe, about everything."

Joe looked at the man beside him, the man that he felt he was once in love with, they had shared a bed on many occasions and Joe was grateful that by doing so it had set him on the right path once and for all where his sexuality was concerned.

Techno was still mumbling apologies through tears and snot.

Joe held his arms open and ushered Techno in to them. The two hugged tight, Techno his head resting on one of Joe's shoulders continued to mumble apologies and start to explain the reasons behind doing what he did.

This only resulted in Joe getting wound up once more. He decided that he was through with the excuses and didn't wait for any further explanations, after all he and Sandra had a plane to catch that night to Spain then eventually working their way country to country with the final destination being Colombia.

Joe pushed Techno gently away from him and in a flash, the knife Joe had concealed under a cushion on the sofa whilst Techno was in the toilet, sliced clean across Techno's throat before he even had time to know what was happening, Joe was at least grateful that the man he had grown so close to over the last six months did not suffer for too long. Techno grabbed at the wound on his throat with two hands but the crimson blood was spurting through his fingers as he gasped for air. Within thirty seconds Techno had slumped on to the floor and was dead.

***

Sandra was at her flat frantically packing. She had chosen to be with Joe, run away with him. She had met up with Jason Jones a few weeks before, yes, he had a magnificent body and big cock but he didn't float her boat, sex was over within five minutes and she never even got aroused let alone have an orgasm. The first night she had spent with Joe was the best sex she had ever had and she didn't want to give that up. They had shared many nights since and each night was not a disappointment.

She would go to Columbia with him and if it didn't work out or like Lenny, he couldn't get it up anymore she would either find herself a Columbian stallion or she could always come back to London and the flat here along with half a million in the bank she had taken from Lenny's safe in cash and jewellery. She had left only about ten grand and a few cheap pieces of jewellery for the geeky nephew.

***

Gosling put the mobile back in its hiding place so that the screws wouldn't find it, not that they would do anything if they did, like bent coppers, they were on his payroll now, he poured himself a large whiskey, another perk from his bent screws. He downed the drink in one, poured another and wept. He had just made a phone call that he never ever would have thought possible.

***

Sandra pulled up outside Joe's flat in a black cab, she told the driver to wait, climbed out and used the intercom to call Joe before returning to the cab.

Five minutes later Joe emerged from the block of flat's entrance door suitcases in hand, the driver helped him place them in the boot of the cab. Joe told the driver to head to Heathrow Airport and leant over and gave Sandra a long lingering kiss, pulling her on top of him.

Before the cab could pull out of the car park a white transit van, its tyres screeching raced in to the car park blocking the cabs exit. Two men got out with sub-machine guns and peppered the cab with bullets, only stopping when their magazines were emptied. Sandra died instantly. The cab driver died later that night on the operating table. When police arrived at the scene there was no sign of Joe.

Two days after the incident the cab drivers widow picked up an envelope posted through her letter box. She wearily bent down to pick it up thinking that it was yet another sympathy card but the envelope was A4 size and quite bulky.

Inside was a letter and one hundred thousand pounds in used notes of all denominations, the note simply said "Sorry, your husband was collateral damage, my sincere apologies, G."

CHAPTER TWENTY-ONE:

JUNE 2014

Less than eight weeks after the explosion and only two weeks since McVeigh had been released from hospital he was fit enough to return to work after making a complete recovery. He had miraculously escaped without broken bones but had lost a lot of blood at the time of the explosion due to lacerations on both legs and a head injury.

The morning he walked back into the station for the first time was to rapturous applause from colleagues who had gathered in the foyer.

Henry Cartwright was there; he had visited him many times in hospital and McVeigh now saw him as a friend rather than a superior. Cartwright shook his hand and the pair went to McVeigh's office.

McVeigh surveyed his office, it was tidy for a start, almost like being in someone else's office, he looked around and scratched his head. Cartwright started to laugh, sensing what was going through McVeigh's mind. "You can thank the new DC for that Pat, gave it a proper going over he did, everything has a place and all that now. You'll meet him soon enough, nice young lad. No doubt he'll explain where everything is."

Cartwright and McVeigh were seated now, "What's it like to be back Pat?"

McVeigh smiled "Like I have never been away!"

There was a knock on the door and McVeigh shouted "Enter" then seeing the uniform of a superior officer before him stood.

Cartwright turned his head. "Hello Barry, nice of you to join us, Pat meet Superintendent Barry Green, he has taken over from Walker. Me and Barry go way back and he is as straight as they come."

The two men shook hands and for the next half hour the three men were deep in conversation about nothing in particular and then Cartwright abruptly stood and said "Right this won't buy the baby a new bonnet, I have a meeting with the Commissioner, welcome back Pat, Barry, been a pleasure adios amigos" and then he turned and left.

Barry Green and McVeigh hit it off instantly, Green was everything that Walker wasn't. "Your new DC is the lad of an old friend of mine who had recommended his son for the job, his father and I spent many years together in the Norfolk Constabulary.

McVeigh raised his eyes he could not stand people on the force being fast tracked because of a senior ranked relative. Barry Green seemed to sense his thoughts.

"I will be honest with you Pat we are very thin on the ground at the moment. The DS and DI I took on to replace those other bastards are both on maternity leave, we still have not appointed a new DCI to replace the one that retired and to make matters worse twenty per cent of the station's workforce are off with food poisoning, sadly an agency chef in the works canteen who we initially thought had allowed red meat to drip over chicken in the fridge, then took it upon himself to do a chicken curry special and gave everyone who had it the shits among other things!" He smiled and rubbed his chin with one hand.

"Turns out he had poisoned the meat deliberately, not enough to kill anyone but as revenge for a detective from this nick being responsible for having his brother sent down for a twelve stretch for armed robbery. No matter how much vetting is done on people there's always one that slips through the net, needless to say that the agency has been kicked out and the chef is on remand awaiting trial."

"Let's hope a major incident doesn't hit the fan then sir." Was all McVeigh could think to say.

Barry Green smiled reassuringly, "My door is always open for you Pat please remember that, I can only imagine what you have been through, the MO and Henry both feel that you are OK to return to work but if it gets too much, please don't hesitate to be open and honest with me and tell me that, no one will think any less of you for it."

He got up shook hands with McVeigh and left, McVeigh began to go through the six hundred emails that had accrued in his absence.

A few minutes after Green had left, a rather young, baby-faced Daniel Phillips came and introduced himself to McVeigh. He was smartly dressed in a two-piece grey suit that looked like it had come from Saville Row and McVeigh's first thought was how a DC could afford such luxury on a policeman's salary. But the lad seemed pleasant enough.

The next couple of hours were spent with Phillips showing McVeigh how the filing system he had created worked. The morning flew by and McVeigh asked his new DC out for lunch. He liked him, despite the fact that he knew Phillips was only a DC because of who is father was, but the young detective reminded him of himself at that age, he was keen, lived alone and loved fashion, hence the suit and was the son of a former Deputy Chief Constable, hence the fast track up the ranks.

Over lunch at a boozer round the corner from the nick, due to the incident, the canteen at the nick was still closed waiting for Environmental Health to give it the green light to re-open, hence the excursion to the pub instead.

McVeigh asked what else other than tidying his office the DC had been doing and was not expecting his response.

"I have been looking into the killing of your first wife sir."

McVeigh was just about to put a fork of steak and kidney pie in his mouth and then stopped, taken aback by what had just been disclosed. "Really, was this authorised and if so by who?"

"Oh yes sir, I wouldn't have done it otherwise, Assistant Commissioner Cartwright gave me the assignment personally and it had Superintendent Green's backing by all accounts."

McVeigh continued with his meal, he noticed that Phillips had hardly touched his Caesar salad, it also turned out he was a health and fitness freak.

"Did you find anything?" McVeigh asked cautiously, hoping that the DC had, but apprehensive of hearing what it might be.

"Yes sir, plenty" he looked cautiously around him "But I am not sure this is the place to disclose my findings."

McVeigh stood instantly; his meal half finished. "Ok as I've suddenly lost my appetite and you are obviously not going to eat your rabbit food, lets head back to the office and you can tell me all about it."

Once the pair arrived back at McVeigh's office, DC Phillips produced a photo from a manilla envelope, it showed Gosling seated behind the wheel of a car that was taken from a speed camera. "This shows Gosling caught speeding within two miles and five minutes from the accident that killed your wife sir."

Phillips then produced a court document from the envelope "As you are aware twenty-four hours after the accident a man came forward and claimed that he was the driver not Gosling. My investigation found however that at the time of the accident the man, Davey Jackson, was in court facing a charge of GBH, the Magistrate adjourned the case to a later date. The time that he was attending court was eleven fifteen am sir, ten minutes before the fatal accident, the court as you can see from the heading at the top of the document is Romford Magistrates. There is simply no way he could have been the driver, unless he had a time machine or a DeLorean."

McVeigh was feeling mixed emotions, he was angry that this information had not come to light sooner, but pleased that they had Gosling bang to rights, that said he was impressed with Phillip's ability as a DC and in the way that he investigated and gathered evidence.

"Why was this not picked up at the time by the investigating officer?" At the time of Natasha's death McVeigh's head was all over the place he couldn't even recollect who was on the investigation team as he was keeping a vigil at his son's hospital bedside for days.

DC Phillips cleared his throat and almost embarrassed said. "The leading member of the team investigating the hit and run was a PC John Atkinson, based at Stratford nick sir."

McVeigh looked at Phillips with a puzzled look on his face, "Never heard of him, is this relevant as to why it was covered up?"

195

Phillips looked at McVeigh, his new mentor who he already knew that he was going to learn a lot from. He cleared his throat.

"Six weeks ago, PC Atkinson was found guilty at the Old Bailey of fraud and corruption. He was one of the coppers found to be on Goslings books, in short, a bent copper sir, I have discovered at the time of the investigation in to the hit and run of your wife and son that evidence against Gosling to being the driver was buried, presumably by Atkinson. PC Atkinson was also the officer that found Gosling on the floor of his living room after Gosling had suffered a heart attack"

McVeigh needed a drink, at last he could get closure for the murder of Natasha and the maiming of Phillip, but it wouldn't change anything, it wouldn't bring Natasha back or give Phillip one hundred percent use of his arm again, or make the nightmares he had stop but the knowledge that Gosling would end up with a full life term and never see the light of day from a prison gave him some satisfaction.

Phillips looked at his new boss, pulling a bank statement from the envelope and handing it to McVeigh. "One other thing sir, this shows a payment of one hundred thousand pounds paid in to the joint bank account of Davey Jackson and his wife Jane on the day of Jacksons sentencing for being the driver that caused the accident, it was deposited from Frank Gosling's bank account."

McVeigh looked at the DC, now seeing him in a different light, in his mind he was harsh to judge the young DC who was proving to be a good detective and had a very promising career ahead of him, with or without his father's leg up on the career ladder.

"Who have you told about this, your finding's?"

"No one sir, I was under strict instruction that whatever I discovered was to be shown and discussed with you and only you first, at the end of the day it was decided that Gosling would not be going anywhere any time soon so my findings could wait until your return sir"

McVeigh stood, "Right it's my first day back, I am tired, and hungry let's try going for that meal again, this time a place of your choice, as long as it's not raw fish and they do more than rabbit food."

Phillip's laughed, he liked McVeigh, it was going to be a good partnership, he could sense it.

CHAPTER TWENTY-TWO:

Julian Moss whistled to himself as he drove to work. He was happy, very happy.

Later that day he was meeting up with his long-time lover Sally Jeffries. They had been having an affair for over six months and both knew that it was just sex, pure and simple. Sally had told him that she would never, ever leave her husband of over twenty-five years, her husband was a wealthy banker and part time lay preacher. Moss didn't know whether it was the fact that she loved her husband so much, or it was the two million pound plus mansion with its own indoor pool on the outskirts of Watford and the penthouse flat he owned in Hammersmith which was the reason she would not leave him.

It didn't bother him either way, when they were together it was the best sex that he had ever experienced and he was not in the slightest bit guilty of cheating on his wife, he owed her no loyalty whatsoever, after all hadn't, she cheated on him all those years ago with that gigolo whilst Moss was away on secondment in Kuwait? Despite her indiscretion they had decided to make a go of it for the sake of the children, but with the children both at university now and despite he and his wife staying together, he felt that it wasn't working anymore, this is why he had jumped at the chance to set up another branch of the business in Manchester. Once it was all up and ready to go, he would tell his wife that he was moving and she wasn't welcome to join him.

Sally was a church goer and charity worker and that's how they had met; he had employed her as a charity co-ordinator and the two had hit it off straight away. To anyone else she was the prim and proper wife of a lay preacher and a charity worker, a Miss Jean Brodie type, but to Moss when he got her in the hotel bedroom for the first time, she became

Linda Lovelace, never before had he known a woman to talk so dirty during sex, there were more F's and C's than a classroom full of Tourette sufferers. The first time she was screaming so loud that the occupants of the next room were banging on the wall and he had to use one of her stockings to gag her. This had excited her even more, she insisted that he tied her up all the time after that.

Every time they met, she would dress up, she loved role play, today she was meeting him at the hotel dressed as a nurse, in full uniform that she had acquired from a fancy-dress shop. If anyone had filmed one of their sex sessions it would make Nine and a Half Weeks look like a Disney movie.

Happy by Pharrell Jones came on the radio and Moss turned it up loud and whistled even louder, he did not see the motorcyclist this morning or any of the last three mornings that it had been following him.

Moss pulled up as the lights turned red, it was a hot morning and he had the window down, he didn't use the cars air conditioning as it tended to dry his contact lenses out.

The motorcycle rider with its pillion passenger pulled up alongside his BMW X5, he was too engrossed in the music to notice but then looked sideways just as the pillion passenger pulled out a handgun and fired several shots through the driver's open window.

***

McVeigh walked into the station to be met by Superintendent Green and DC Phillips.

"Good morning, sir, you're in bright and early, you too Phillips." McVeigh couldn't help notice that Phillips had a different suit on from yesterday, it was a dark blue suit, again from Saville Row he suspected.

Green came straight to the point "Morning Pat, there has been a shooting in Stratford, a motorcyclist fired into a car before speeding off. I know that it's only your second day back but we need the Met's most successful detective on the job so I was hoping that you could be the investigating officer accompanied by Phillips here."

McVeigh looked at Green, he had decided the day before that he liked him but why was he doubting him, asking him if he would take the case, did his boss think that he should not have returned to work so soon? It hurt a little, maybe his superiors including Cartwright doubted his ability now.

"Of course, I'll take it sir, the MO would not have thought it safe for me to return to work if I wasn't capable of carrying out my duties."

Green knew that he had put his foot in it, this was not what he had intended, he wanted to explain but thought that could wait for another day. Forensics were at the crime scene, traffic had backed up for miles and he wanted the best detective the MET had to offer on the scene, so all he said was, "Good, Phillips here has all the details he will fill you in on the way."

When McVeigh and Phillips arrived at the scene, uniform had managed to divert the traffic and the X5 had been placed under a blue tent that forensics always tended to use. Onlookers had gathered but were being well kept back by police tape and a dozen or more uniformed coppers.

McVeigh approached the tent just as a man in the tell-tale forensics white boiler suit and attire came out. "Pat good to see you, well I say that but it's a shame it wasn't under different circumstances." The forensic officer cheerily yelled.

McVeigh looked at James Matthews, he had known him for years and he was in McVeigh's opinion the best forensic scientist in the country. "James, how are you?"

Phillips was watching the meeting and wondered if one day he would be able to have the same attitude as this pair, here they were at a murder scene and it was as if they had bumped into each other whilst out shopping in the local supermarket aisle.

"I'm good thank you Pat, oh I haven't seen you, well since so long."

McVeigh smiled, "It's ok James, you can say it, since you attended the scene when Natasha and Phillip got run over."

James had been the forensic officer that fateful day and McVeigh had not seen him since, he quickly drew a line under where the conversation was going. "Ok, what we got then James?"

James seemed relieved that the conversation had moved on and McVeigh had got straight down to business.

"We have a white male, aged fifty according to his driving licence, name of Julian Moss, the car is registered to X-Service Recruitment, a company based in Chelsea so presumably his Company car. Three bullets, one to the head, that's the one that killed him, another two one to the shoulder, another to the chest. We believe that six bullets were fired in total as there were three bullet's we retrieved from the holes on the wall by that chip shop over there. I can tell you this Pat, this was not a professional hit, whoever fired the gun from such a close range is not an expert marksman."

McVeigh nodded and turning to DC Phillips, "DC Phillips take a look at what CCTV is available, either shop keepers, business premises or local authority."

"James, do we know the calibre of bullets yet?"

"Yes 9mm, my first thought is a Glock, or could be a Sig."

"Police use both those types of guns, don't they? "McVeigh asked as a matter of fact not insinuating anything, he was not expecting a response and neither did he get one "what possessions do you have from the car or the driver other than his driving licence?"

James returned to the tent and handed McVeigh an evidence bag inside were a wallet, car keys, a mobile phone and a packet of cigarettes, lighter and some loose change.

The uniformed officers present had already started to take witness statements and within three hours McVeigh was back at the station along with DC Phillips going over what information had been gathered so far.

McVeigh looked inside the wallet retrieved from Moss's person, as well as the usual credit card and business cards there was two photos, one of Moss standing with a woman, a young boy and a young girl in front of the Eiffel Tower, the other a photo of a naked woman who was not the same woman in the family photo taken in Paris.

"Maybe he was having an affair and the woman's husband found out."

DC Phillips suggested, McVeigh looked at him, he was showing initiative, he liked that, "Or the wife" he smiled. "Ok young Daniel, get in touch with Moss's credit card company and his phone company I want all records from the last six months, then get in touch with the liaison officer who has been assigned to look after Moss's wife, do we know who it is?" Phillips looked at his note pad. "Yes sir, WPC Arnold I believe."

McVeigh nodded approvingly.

"Good, she's a good officer, if anyone can extract information from the wife it will be her, not as good as my Emily, but good nonetheless, and while you do that I'm going to go and visit X-Service Recruitment."

CHAPTER TWENTY-THREE:

McVeigh sat in front of William Cross, the MD of X-Service Recruitment, his office overlooked the Thames and was in the heart of Chelsea, an impressive view greeted him from the window.

The man was in his early fifties, dyed black hair and had the physique of a twenty-year-old, so obviously worked out and looked after himself, unlike McVeigh, only that morning Emily reminded him that he could do with losing a few pounds.

DI McVeigh felt that he was a pretty good judge of character on first meeting someone. Despite being given the news of Julian Moss's death, Cross struck McVeigh as being arrogant and a man that was very much up his own arse.

"I wonder if you could tell me Mr Cross, what role Mr Moss had within your Company?"

It was not difficult to see that William Cross was upset, but not at the fact his colleague had been killed, more of the fact that his death was a massive inconvenience, the day's events had certainly got to him.

"Julian was a partner, joint partner, there are four of us all equal shares, twenty five percent each. I am the Managing Director, Julian the Charity Co-Ordinator Director, Steve the Financial Director and finally Paul is the Recruitment Director, we were due to launch another branch, now I suppose I will have to go and do that myself until I can find a manager to take it over and run it."

Despite the disclosure that there were four equal partners McVeigh couldn't help feel that Cross was very much the ruler of the company, he was the head of the organisation, whatever the titles.

"Charity Director? I thought that this was a recruitment agency."

Cross sipped from his water glass

"Oh yes, it is, we recruit only Ex-servicemen and woman, but a few years ago we were alarmed by the amount of ex-service personnel living rough on the streets through no fault of their own, it is hard for people to adjust to civilian life, especially after some of the atrocities many have witnessed, so with the help of government grants, donations and sponsorship we now offer them accommodation and get them back to work, or work with them to get access to benefits and housing, that and the fact it comes with very lucrative tax cuts, grants and contacts."

McVeigh noted this down, Cross was already getting under his skin.

"Commendable, I suppose, now when you say X Service recruitment, I take it that this does not mean mercenaries sent abroad to fight in wars and coups and the like?"

Cross afforded himself a laugh despite the fact that one of his so-called closest acquaintances had just been murdered.

"Hold your horses there DI McVeigh, I wish, there is far more money in supplying soldiers to small countries to start a coup, I am obviously joking. No, DI McVeigh, we primarily service the hospitality industry, waiters, waitresses, chefs, bar persons that sort of thing, also drivers, body guards, stewards at concerts etc, believe me it is all above board."

The fact that Cross could joke was beyond McVeigh and it only went to show the calibre of the man before him.

"I am sure it is Mr Cross, what can you tell me about Mr Moss's private life?"

Once more Cross gulped at his water, he was sweating and McVeigh noted this but did not know why.

"He was going to leave his wife, she cheated on him many years back, if you ask me, he should have kicked the whore out years ago, I know I did mine when she did the dirty on me. His marriage was dead in the water but they stayed together for the sake of the children, they're grown up now, like I said earlier we are in the process of expanding, first Manchester then Edinburgh. Julian was going to leave Sophie, his wife, go to Manchester after finding suitable premises then set up the Manchester branch and run it, typical Julian, in all the years I have known him he always let you down."

McVeigh couldn't believe the attitude of this prick sat before him. "Do you know if Mr Moss was having an affair?"

"That I don't know, we were always too busy running the business to mix as friends like we used to, although we did get together on the last Sunday of every month for a round of golf, which I always won by the way."

"Used too?" McVeigh asked inquisitively.

"Yes, we all used to be in the same squadron in the RAF, all pilots, we left at the same time, our base was due for closure so we got out a year before it did, about nine years ago, we all went on a golfing holiday to Dubai for a month and while we were there we came up with this brain child, when we returned, we set this place up, three of us are originally from London so it made sense to have the business here, that and the fact I got this place for a pittance, right place right time so to speak."

McVeigh duly noted this, "Do you know who may have wanted Mr Moss dead?" McVeigh studied Cross closely for any reaction; his facial expression however remained the same.

"Me, for leaving me in the shit!" Cross bellowed a laugh; he was obviously the type of person to laugh at his own jokes, however bad or inappropriate they were. Cross could see the seriousness on McVeigh's face, so stopped laughing.

"If he told Sophie he was leaving her maybe she did, but to be honest she is a weak woman, thick as shit and couldn't function without a drink, but that's only an opinion DI McVeigh."

Every moment spent in the company of Cross only made McVeigh realise how much he really did dislike the man.

McVeigh pulled out a photocopy of the picture that he'd found in Julian Moss's wallet, he had had it edited to show just the woman's head, face and shoulders, he placed the picture on the desk in front of Cross.

"One last thing Mr Cross, do you recognise this woman?"

Cross picked up the photo and looked closely before placing it back on the desk.

"Yes, that is Sally Jeffries, she worked as an assistant to Julian." Then he leant back in the chair his hands on his head, "Fuck me, you are not telling me that she and Julian were having an affair, what a lucky bastard, I wouldn't mind giving her one!"

McVeigh took the photo and placed it back in his jacket, "I am not telling you anything Mr Cross, I merely asked if you knew the lady, and now you have confirmed you do, perhaps you could save me some time and give me some contact details for her."

Cross jumped up from the desk and began to panic wondering back and forth in his office "No you cannot contact her, well not at home anyway, if she and Julian were having it off her husband cannot find out, he is a CEO of a bank at Canary Wharf, that bank sponsors the charity, generously I might add, that was the only reason she got the job, bored housewife with an influential husband. Her husband is also some kind of preacher at the weekend, his church donates every month, if you have to see her it must be discreetly and away from the marital home, this cannot come out, he will pull the plug on financing us!"

McVeigh liked seeing Cross squirm, his panic was enjoyable to see.

"Mr Cross, I will contact her where and whenever I want, as for her husband, he like many others, including you, are a suspect in my book so do not tell me what to do, how to do it, where to do it, get my drift you arrogant little fuck, now get me the contact details, please."

Cross was shocked to be spoken in that manner by anyone, let alone a DI from the Met but in truth McVeigh had spoken to him like so many other people he had crossed paths with had wanted to but were too afraid of the repercussions, but to be spoken to like that, especially by a high-ranking police officer grated on him, he had been well and truly put in his place.

Back at the station McVeigh and DC Phillips were in McVeigh's office. Phillips was showing McVeigh the CCTV footage that he had obtained. The motorcyclist and pillion passenger could be seen pulling up alongside Moss at the traffic lights and the pillion passenger, the gunman, could be seen rapidly and rather frantically shooting into the car before the bike sped off. The footage only confirmed what witness statements had already said, motor bike, two people, shots fired, one dead Julian Moss.

After watching the footage several times McVeigh then requested what Phillips had found out from the phone and credit card records.

DC Phillips produced several A4 pages, he had highlighted points of interest using a yellow highlighter pen. He handed the phone records to his superior,

"You will see sir that one number has been called or texted almost a thousand times in the past six months, we have ascertained that it is not his wife's number."

McVeigh studied the pages, he then produced his note book and finding the information that Cross had given him on Sally Jeffries and compared the numbers,

"Bingo, that number belongs to Sally Jeffries, what about the credit card records?"

DC Phillips produced yet more pages, "We know that once, or sometimes twice a week Mr Moss has paid for a hotel in Kensington, The Grove."

McVeigh was piecing together information in his mind, Moss and Jeffries were having an affair, that much was obvious but would that be enough for her husband or his wife to warrant a hit on him. Looking at the footage and going by what James had already told him it was not professionals who carried out the shooting. By all accounts Mr Jeffries was a high-ranking CEO and God-fearing person, the idea of him organising the killing was remote, which left the wife, Mrs Moss.

"What has WPC Arnold been able to report back Daniel?"

DC Phillips consulted his note book, "Mrs Moss admitted that she had an affair years ago and although her husband had forgiven her, things had never been the same between them again. She suspected that her husband was the one having the affair of late, but after her own actions years ago didn't feel that she had any right to confront him on the matter. She has also admitted to being an alcoholic, her heavy drinking only started when the children went off to university, her husband was always out and she rattled around in a big house all on her own, WPC Arnold doesn't think that the wife would be capable of organising a hit on her husband, we know she was not one of the two on the motorcycle she was at a hair salon at the time, this has been confirmed so she has a solid alibi."

McVeigh looked at his own notebook,

"Her affair confirms what Cross had to say, he is one arrogant fuck by the way Daniel, if we need to interview him again, you can have the pleasure, I was this close to throwing him out his office window into the Thames below!" McVeigh squeezed his thumb and index finger together to illustrate.

"What next sir, where do we go from here?" Phillips asked. He knew what he would do but didn't want to appear too eager and step on his superior's toes.

McVeigh stood up, "I go home, albeit a temporary one while they repair the bomb damage on the other one, to my loving wife and children, I have been told to take it easy remember, it has been a long day, tomorrow we'll get Sally Jeffries in for questioning but something tells me that the reason Moss was killed goes back to something that we are yet to discover, I believe that something from his past has caught up with him, but what could he have done that was so bad to warrant being killed?"

Phillips scratched his head, "And me sir, what would you like me to do in the meantime?"

It was apparent to McVeigh that Phillips had nothing to rush home for and wanted to continue with the investigation.

"You Danny boy, you get to go to The Grove and find out who Moss was with on his frequent stays, I think we already know the answer to that question but let's get it confirmed, see you in the morning son."

Phillips nodded and then asked apprehensively "Can I ask that you do not call me Danny Boy sir, my father calls me that and I hate it"

Phillips had shown balls, made his point and he went up even further in McVeigh's estimation's.

***

Sally Jeffries was a good-looking woman, immaculately dressed and not a hair out of place. She was more beautiful than she looked but for some reason she played down her appearance, whether this was because she was a lay-preachers wife or because she was in mourning for her lover, McVeigh could not tell.

She had come to the station immediately when requested to do so by a WPC that McVeigh had asked to call her, discretion was assured for now.

McVeigh and DC Phillips sat opposite her and the WPC that had called her sat next to Sally to offer reassurance and comfort if needed. She had declined having legal representation present. She was not under arrest or a suspect and could leave whenever she wanted, she had been assured of this.

During the interview she openly admitted that she and Moss were lovers, she tried to justify that by explaining that although her husband was a good man, a good husband and father he could not offer her what she wanted in the bedroom department, she confirmed that she and Moss would meet at the Grove, which DC Phillips had already found proof of the previous evening. In front of him were several photos retrieved from the hotel's CCTV of Moss and Jeffries together in the hotel's reception area, all timed and dated. But there was no need to use them, as she was open and honest with them both from the outset.

The only time Sally showed any sign of distress was when McVeigh asked if her husband had found out about the affair and could he be capable of murder. She had broken down at this point, but McVeigh believed that it was because her husband may be dragged in for questioning and the affair would be discovered, rather than the fact that she believed he could be guilty of killing her lover. The young WPC had calmed her down and then fetched her a cup of tea.

The interview continued when she was calm enough to do so, McVeigh gave reassurances that her husband being questioned would only happen if there were sufficient grounds to point the finger at him as being a suspect, which seemed unlikely given the circumstances.

There was a knock on the interview room door and Superintendent Green entered without waiting for an answer, he approached DI McVeigh and handed him a piece of paper then apologising for the interruption, left the room without uttering another word.

McVeigh looked at the paper, then handed it to DC Phillips, both men looked shocked at what was written on it. They both stood immediately. McVeigh looking directly at Sally Jeffries "Mrs Jeffries, thank you for coming in, we have no further questions for you, and we believe that we will not have to talk to you again, or indeed your husband for that matter, so rest assured your secret is safe with us."

Sally stood up "But I don't understand, only a few minutes ago you said that you may have to bring my husband in for questioning, what is going on?" She turned to the WPC for support, for answers but they weren't forthcoming.

McVeigh was collecting all the paperwork he had in front of him, the note that Green had brought in was on the table in clear view of Sally, she looked at it then understood why the interview had been called to a close. The WPC also read the note, it simply said "Another shooting, another murder in the private car park of X-Service Recruitment"

As McVeigh left, he turned to Sally Jeffries and simply said "I'm sorry for your loss." Afterall who was he to judge or condemn two grown adults having an affair, just because it was not something he would do?

CHAPTER TWENTY-FOUR:

McVeigh and Phillips stood outside the erected blue tent in the X-Service Recruitment car park donning protective overalls, mask and gloves. Once the proper attire had been donned, they walked in to the tent.

It was apparent that the victim, Paul Wright was dead, shot twice at close range as he went to get in his Jaguar.

James Matthews was once again the attending forensic officer and he confirmed that the bullets were of the same calibre as the ones found at the Stratford shooting site.

McVeigh and Phillips emerged from the tent. McVeigh spotted the CCTV cameras overlooking the car park and sent DC Phillips into the main office to look at the footage.

McVeigh phoned his boss Barry Green and filled him in on the findings so far, McVeigh wanted to know when he was getting more manpower, after a second killing the case was growing fast and more hands were needed. Although Phillips had the makings of a good detective, he was still inexperienced and now that there had been a second murder, they needed to act fast.

Green had promised to draft in a couple of Detective Constables from nearby police stations along with a handful of uniforms who were bordering on becoming detective material. They'd be at his disposal and present at the daily briefing tomorrow morning.

Satisfied, McVeigh hung up and went to join his colleague inside the office of X-Service Recruitment just as William Cross was coming out. He was laughing and joking, he was with a young female companion, he stopped instantly when he saw McVeigh approaching.

McVeigh for the second time in twenty-four hours was disgusted by the attitude of the man in front of him. "Can I ask where you are going Mr Cross?"

Cross looked at the young girl beside him, unbeknown to McVeigh she was Cross's PA Monica Watson, a twenty-five-year-old beauty with legs up to her armpits and perfectly sized breasts and an hour glass figure who Cross had been trying to get into bed from the day she had started working there. A feat that he managed to achieve the previous weekend, smugly turned back to McVeigh,

"Lunch, not that I have to explain anything to you DI McVeigh."

McVeigh could not believe what he was hearing, a second Director of the company had been killed a day after the first and Cross was going out to eat, what the fuck was wrong with the man, had he no scruples?

"Lunch will have to wait, Mr Cross, I want you to accompany me to the station for questioning."

Cross, whether it was to act big in front of his new girlfriend or because he was genuinely appalled by the request flew into a rage. "What, am I a suspect, are you arresting me, this and the way you spoke to me the last time we met is totally out of order!"

Monica on more than one occasion had asked Cross to calm down, she placed a hand on his arm but he shrugged it off angrily and his rage continued.

When he had finally finished waving his arms around and shouting McVeigh simply said, "Finished throwing your teddies out the pram now have we?" And then when no reply was forthcoming,

"I am not arresting you Mr Cross, but I would like to question you, surely you must find it strange that two people that you set this Company up with have been murdered in the past two days, who is to say that you are not in danger of receiving the same fate along with Mr Pearce? But by your actions and attitude on the two occasions we have met, who is to say that you are not the one who organised the killings, and before you fly in to another hissy fit, think long and hard whether you accompany me to the station under your own free will or whether I cuff you and treat you as a common criminal, choice is yours Cross, I don't give a fuck either way."

Cross walked back to the office, Monica looked at the rather handsome DI in front of her and wished that it was his bed she was in every night and not that of Cross.

Inside the building Cross had been to get his coat and car keys, he demanded that Monica phone his brief to meet him at the station and then stormed out of the building.

Phillips joined McVeigh, "I see what you meant about him sir" McVeigh laughed out loud, "He is a character for sure, how did you get on with the CCTV?"

"I have the recording here sir, it's the same bike that was used in Stratford, a Honda CBR 600F, one thing though sir, the driver and pillion passenger have switched positions from the last murder, I'll have to check that with the stills from yesterday but I am pretty certain of it, when Moss was killed the motor cycle passenger was shorter than the rider, but not this time."

McVeigh couldn't help but be impressed with DC Phillips, and felt guilty that he had told his boss that he was inexperienced, he placed a hand on Phillips's shoulder,

"Good work Daniel, you finish up here, take witness statements from everyone that works here, start with her." McVeigh nodded towards Monica Watson who was sat at her desk, "I will head back to the station and interview Mr Charisma, laughing boy fucking Cross, we have established that the other surviving partner is out of the country, apparently, Mr Pearce is on honeymoon and doesn't fly back until tomorrow evening."

***

McVeigh sat in his office with a tumbler of whiskey, he should go home but there was nothing to go home for. Emma had taken the twins to visit Margaret and Robert for a few days. DC Phillips knocked on the door and entered. McVeigh produced another tumbler and poured a whiskey ushering Phillips to sit.

The DC took the glass and sipped the drink offering his thanks, he hated alcohol but did not to want appear rude to his boss. "How did you get on with Mr Cross sir?"

McVeigh leant back in the chair as far as it would go and took a gulp of his drink,

"Oh yes Mr Cross. He was even more arrogant and smug in the company of his brief, gave me fuck all other than a headache."

"Do you think he is a suspect sir?"

Phillips was direct and to the point, McVeigh had already noticed in a short space of time that his new DC was not one for small talk.

"To be honest no, as much as I would like him to be, I would love to send that bastard down, no, I think that someone has it in for Cross and his partners, we'll interview Pearce when he lands tomorrow."

DC Phillips took another sip of his drink, the taste of the liquid was burning his throat and making him feel nauseous. "So other than Pearce, what next sir?"

McVeigh lent forward and poured another drink, Phillips instantly put his hand over the top of his own glass.

"Lightweight, I've spoken to the Super he is going to give us a couple of DC's and some uniforms to help with the investigation, we will have a briefing in the morning, I want one of the newly assigned DCs to look at the employment files of X-Service to look for any disgruntled employees."

Phillips was learning a lot from McVeigh, after what the man had been through, he still remained very professional and focussed to the task at hand.

"I want a couple of the uniforms to do a wider search of CCTV from both murder scenes, that bike doesn't just turn up at a crime scene out of fresh air, it must have come from somewhere, hopefully the officer's might be able to tell us exactly where from."

Phillips nodded, "And us sir, what are we going to be doing?"

"Steve Pearce's plane touches down late afternoon, get his address and be waiting on the door step for him, his address is in the file, get there for five o'clock, that should be about right, by the time he lands, gets through customs and makes his way home, I don't want Cross contacting him and revealing too much in advance. Superintendent Green has requested the military files of our four ex RAF men from the MOD, they're due to be couriered over tomorrow morning. The last base they were stationed at has now closed down, several hours of Green pulling his very little hair out, being transferred from the

RAF headquarters, back to the MOD back to the RAF etc by all accounts he had been passed from one department to another to track down their service records and get the required permission for six hours straight, well he did offer to help."

Phillips stood up and despite knowing that he would leave the office, go to the gents and throw up he downed the whiskey in one go. "Ok sir, I'll say goodnight, I am off to the gym, just one more thing, if I may ask sir, what have you done about the information on Frank Gosling sir?"

McVeigh smiled, "Nothing yet, like you pointed out he is not going anywhere in a hurry so it can wait, this case we're on takes precedence, good night, Daniel, enjoy your exercise, oh and if you don't like whiskey just say, your face is greener than The Hulk, now go before you spill your guts on me Axminster!"

Phillips felt the bile rise in his throat, turned and ran. McVeigh laughed out loud, a right belly laugh, and poured himself another Irish whiskey.

CHAPTER TWENTY-FIVE:

The following morning and as Barry Green had promised, four uniformed police officers now dressed in civilian clothes and a couple of DC's drafted in from North London were sat in the briefing room along with DC Phillips and Superintendent Green. DI McVeigh entered and was pleased to see that unlike Walker, Barry Green was a man of his word.

McVeigh explained in detail about the two murders, that they were linked and what he expected from the new recruits, he then handed over to DC Phillips who nervously stood before the audience in the room, talking to more than one person at a time was new to him.

He flicked on the TV that was rigged up to a projector, the image of a motorcycle appeared on the screen. "We know that the motorbike our suspects were on at the time of both murders, is similar to the one shown here a Honda CBR 600F, sadly it is not an uncommon bike, about eleven thousand are registered in the UK today."

Phillips clicked on to the next slide, two CCTV images side by side.

"The image on the left is from the Stratford shooting the one on the right from the Chelsea shooting. You can see from the first image on the left that the rider is taller than the pillion passenger, however the second image shows that the two have changed positions. The second killing was more accurate, by someone who knows how to use a handgun whereas the first was a little erratic, even from close range three shots missed the victim completely."

McVeigh and Green nodded in unison, they were impressed with their new DC, Phillips clicked on to the next image a photo of a gun.

"From the images we managed to get of the gun being fired and the bullets retrieved we now know the gun is a Glock 17 and not a Sig Sauer as was originally thought. Both guns are commonly used by the UK police force, not that it means anything, it could just be coincidental, the Glock 17 is a common handgun and weapon of choice used by most of the UK's firearm clubs."

One of the Detective Constable's who had been drafted in, Johnny Miller, a policeman with many years on the force and who was born and raised in the East End spoke,

"No offence, but Glocks are a criminal's weapon of choice these days too, they are so easy to come by, you can get your hands on one for less than a bag of sand these days."

DC Phillips looked confused momentarily, DI McVeigh laughed, "Excuse DC Phillips, he is originally from Norfolk, a bag of sand is a grand, i.e., £1000"

DC Phillips blushed, but did not let his embarrassment from the sniggers that went round the room affect him in any way.

DC Phillips looked to McVeigh to take over and to tell the uniforms and DC's what he wanted from them but he simply smiled, "No DC Phillips, you carry on, you are doing a splendid job." Phillips nodded his thanks, cleared his throat and continued.

"We need a couple of you guys to look into whether there have been any thefts from Firearms clubs and ranges recently, especially stolen Glock's. Another officer is to go to X-Service Recruitment and liaise with their HR department to see if any employees have been sacked recently and may have a vendetta against them, although as a company that employs ex service personnel and takes homeless people off the street and finds them work and accommodation, this is a long shot. Mr William Cross, Managing Director, has been offered police protection and declined, so at least with one of you there it will offer him at least some protection, by all accounts he is a difficult man and has not been the most sympathetic to the murders, he and his three co-owners go back twenty or more years, so for him to see two of their deaths as a hindrance rather than that of losing a close friend and business partner should tell you all you need to know about him."

Phillips was growing in confidence and wished that his father could see him now, the man that had interfered and got him this promotion when in fact all he had wanted to do was to prove himself on merit.

"We also want one of you to look at the social media accounts of all four owners of X-Service Recruitment, we know Julian Moss was having an affair and that his marriage had been dead in the water for quite some time after his wife had an affair years before by all accounts, we also know Cross divorced his wife after she too had an affair, Pearce and Paul Wright we don't know anything about their private lives, we do know that Pearce is gay and is on the way back from his honeymoon with his new husband, maybe one DC could interview Wrights wife, but take a WPC with you for the wife's moral support, not yours. The remaining two of you, we would like to look at CCTV footage leading up to and away from the murder scenes, I apologise in advance what a laborious, tedious task this will be, but any information is better than what we already have, sir?"

McVeigh stood up and took over.

"Thank you, DC Phillips, the DC here will be interviewing the other director this evening when he returns from his holiday and both myself and Superintendent Green will be checking into the four owners of X-Service Recruitment previous careers in the RAF, let's get to it shall we?"

McVeigh assigned each officer with their tasks and the brief was over.

***

DC Phillips was in Notting Hill, about a hundred yards away from the home of Steve Pearce, he sat in his battered Mini.

The car certainly looked out of place in such a wealthy neighbourhood.

The house was a Victorian three-story which from the outside appeared to have been modernised. The neighbourhood stank of wealth, nice cars on the drive, children attending private schools, the people that lived here were wealthy bankers, TV stars, architects and footballers to name but a few professions.

Phillips had looked into the life of Pearce and his new husband, Benedict Collins, Collins was older than Pearce by ten years and was an art critic and author.

Through an app on his phone, Phillips knew that the plane had landed on time so he just had to sit and wait it out for the newlyweds to arrive. This was one part of the job he disliked, sitting, waiting, in his mind it was an unproductive waste of his resources, the sort of job a couple of uniforms could have been assigned, but his boss DI McVeigh was in charge and he was not going to contest a request from him.

Shortly after six o'clock a SAAB 93 pulled onto the drive of the house, Phillips had been taking bets with himself as to who would carry who over the threshold, he smiled to himself at his own humour.

Collins and Pearce were getting luggage from the boot of the car when Phillips noticed a motorbike enter the top of the street at speed, he quickly turned the keys in the ignition. His car due to its age was not the most reliable of vehicles and it refused to start, he cursed himself, he had had the radio on low for the past two hours and it must have drained the battery.

Phillips got out of the car as quickly as he could and started to run towards Collins and Pearce's house just as the motorbike stopped directly by the newly married couple and was completely helpless to do anything as he witnessed the pillion passenger raise a gun and fire off two shots. The motorbike then quickly turned round in the street and headed back in the direction that it had come from. By the time Phillips made it to the house, out of breath despite the personal fitness levels he kept too, Pearce lay dying on the drive, his distraught husband kneeling beside him.

***

The following morning back in the briefing room, McVeigh and Phillips looked forlorn as McVeigh filled the rest of the team in on the previous night's events, a slide came up of Pearce laying on the ground on the drive of his home in Notting Hill.

"Steve Pearce died at the scene moments after being shot twice in the chest at close range by a motorcycle pillion passenger. The bullets match those used in the killings of Julian Moss and Paul Wright, DC Phillips witnessed the event but was sadly unable to prevent it, and despite giving first aid at the scene could not prevent the death of Mr Pearce."

A young uniform who had spent the previous day trawling through video footage leading to and from the Stratford shooting site, and had been bored rigid, eagerly asked, "Does this mean William Cross is a suspect now?"

McVeigh gave him a discerning look "No why would it, if anything we now have to keep round the clock surveillance on Cross and give the prick protection whether he likes it or not, one of the unmarked police car units from a South London nick has offered to help out with a car and manpower and will discreetly watch Cross from a distance as of nine o'clock this morning."

McVeigh was interrupted by a gasping out of breath Superintendent Green running into the room, in between gasps of breath he managed to say "It's too late for that; Cross has just been discovered dead in his office by his PA when she opened up this morning."

***

William Cross sat at his desk drinking whiskey, everyone else had gone home including Monica who had refused to go to dinner with him and had been giving him the cold shoulder since the death of Paul, well fuck her, he would get a new PA and a new bed partner, no one fucked him over, he called the shots.

His ex-wife had tried to wear the trousers all those years ago, and look how that turned out, she was now living on a council estate in Derby with her painter and decorator husband and she was working in a launderette to make ends meet.

William Cross needed no one other than himself. He heard the front doorbell go and got up to go to the main reception door, he had ordered a curry from the local takeaway and he expected it to be that or a delivery from a courier who had been running late and had tried to deliver when seeing the lights on.

He opened the door to the helmeted rider in black leathers,

"Well, where is it? where is my fucking curry, I am starving?"

It was only then that he saw the gun pointed at him.

Cross was frog marched back to his office where he was tied up to his chair, a second helmeted motorcyclist who Cross noticed walked with a severe limp, walked into the office to accompany the first. When he was sure that Cross was secure, he took off his helmet his back to Cross, the first rider handed him the gun and then he turned to look directly at Cross. It gave him great pleasure in seeing the colour drain from the face of Cross,

"You, this has to be a fucking wind up?" was all that Cross managed to say as the gun was raised and one shot was fired. It hit Cross directly in the centre of the forehead. The gun man handed the gun back to his fellow assailant.

"All that shooting practice paid off!" he said laughing out loud. His assailant laughed back.

"Sure did, four down, one to go!"

The shooter replaced his helmet before leaving Cross's office, both men now laughing out loud as they left.

CHAPTER TWENTY-SIX:

The CCTV footage from the exterior of X-Service Recruitment had picked up the first assailant entering the building quickly followed by the second, the second assailant walked with a noticeable limp. The interior CCTV showed Cross being forced to go in to his office, but what it did not show was anything directly from what happened inside the office.

Cross was killed at approximately nineteen thirty hours, an hour or so after Pearce if the timing on the CCTV of the motorcyclists arriving and leaving the office was anything to go by.

McVeigh sat at his desk, confused, frustrated and generally pissed off. Nothing of any value had been found by the uniformed officers so far, no disgruntled employees had been found, no decent video footage of the bike, no extraordinary material retrieved from Facebook, Instagram, Twitter and the like, they had come up against a brick wall and although the investigation was ongoing, they had up to this point, literally nothing to go on.

McVeigh was struggling with the service personnel files of the four owners too, Green had lost interest in helping long ago.

All four victims had spent several years in the RAF, all were pilots and had all flown in the first Gulf war, and partly the second.

They had been deployed to Kuwait for a short period of time training Kuwait pilots, but nothing in their files showed anything of significance as to what would cause a gunman to end their lives.

He pushed the files to one side; it was hard going and right now he would even contemplate swapping tasks with the uniforms trudging through video footage.

The knock at the door and DC Phillips entering was a needed respite, although when Phillips spoke, McVeigh soon changed his mind.

"For fucks sake Danny we are in the middle of a quadruple murder investigation, you know we are short on manpower as it is yet you are insistent that you need to take your fucking holiday!"

DC Phillips could see how pissed off his superior was but he thought to himself that it was better to piss off his superior rather than his father so no, fuck him.

"I know that it's not good timing sir, but first sir, at the risk of repeating myself it is Daniel, not Danny. With all due respect sir this holiday was booked six months ago, and again with all due respect sir, it is too late to make other arrangements."

McVeigh poured himself a drink, for the first time since they met, he was clearly disappointed in his new DC.

"Ok, point taken about the name, and ok you lose a few quid on a holiday, are you not insured for flights and stuff, fuck me I will give you the money myself if you're not!"

DC Phillips didn't want to ruin the relationship that had developed between himself and McVeigh but on this occasion, he would have to stick to his guns. The pain of disappointing his father would be far greater than that of disappointing his DI.

"Every year my father and mother fly to their second home in the Caribbean sir, every year I go to Norfolk, house sit and take care of the animals, look after the horses and dogs, it's too late to arrange anyone else to do it."

"Daddy, I might have known, for fucks sake, you are only here because of Daddy's influence and if I refuse, he will be on the phone to Green no doubt, ok just fuck off, go on your jollies and get out of my sight!"

McVeigh knew that he was being unfair, Daniel Phillips had shown his true worth to him, he was going to turn out to be a good copper on merit, not because of who is father was, he knew the young detective didn't want to live in his father's shadow, his father had pulled unwanted strings as far as Daniel was concerned.

DC Phillips left, he wanted to stay and argue the point with McVeigh but having seen the rage etched on his DI's face thought wiser of it, hopefully when he returned in a fortnight everything may have blown over, as it was, he didn't have to wait long. He had pulled in to services on the A11 to use the toilet and get a coffee, he checked his phone, there was a message from DI McVeigh it simply read "Sorry for overacting, enjoy your time off, regards Pat."

***

It had been a week since the last murder, that of Cross and still he had nothing. A tired and stressed looking McVeigh sat at his desk burning the midnight oil looking through the military records of the four murdered victims once more.

The uniforms appeared to be getting nowhere with the video footage from the hundred plus hours of various CCTV footage at their disposal, the HR files from X-Service. social media interaction or anything to suggest that the four had seriously pissed someone off, enough to kill them. McVeigh was concerned that three of the victims had been shot either getting out of or into a car. Cross was the only one to be shot away from his car, although his car was the only car in the car park at the time, was he clutching at straws, was this significant? But then again what else did he have to go on?

Despite the late hour two of the uniformed officers knocked on the door, interrupting his train of thought, he beckoned them in. They were the two poor souls who had spent hours trawling through CCTV from the first two murders and then the third and fourth.

"What you got for me gents? something to get us out of this black hole we have sunk in to hopefully."

The older of the two PC Sean Osbourne stepped forward and spoke for the two of them, "We got lucky sir, we have found footage from outside a multi-story in New Barnet, it is just behind the Sainsburys store sir, it is of the bike leaving and entering on the days of all four murders, unfortunately the cameras inside the multi-story are out of order and have been for some time by all accounts."

McVeigh leaned forward with interest to look at the photos that were all laid out in front of him, they were all timed and dated, he studied them with interest before turning to look at the two officers.

Osbourne looked at McVeigh who waited in anticipation for what the two had to reveal.

"After the murder in Stratford we managed to track the bike back to New Barnet, I am not going to lie, it was hard going and if I am honest sir, brain draining but despite some blank spots in the CCTV coverage we did it, probably more my luck than judgement but the result is still the same. Once we got it located to the multi-story it was easier to discover that the bike left and entered the multi-story on the days of the other murders and within a certain time frame either side of those murders"

There were eighteen photos in total. Each showed the bike used in the killings leaving then entering the car-park, a time and date was displayed on each of the photographs, all related to the days of the murders. Other photos showed the bike on days leading up to the murders so had killers done reconnaissance beforehand?

McVeigh was impressed "This is good work gents; And don't put yourself down, luck does not come into it. You poor buggers have spent hours finding this information out".

The second officer, a baby-faced PC who looked about twelve, laid eighteen more photos on the desk in front of McVeigh, they showed images of a white Ford transit van.

"This van is seen entering and leaving the building at least an hour before and after the murder's sir, apart from the day Cross and Pearce were killed and its nearer to three and a half hours before it returned to the car-park, it is also seen twelve times either side of the motorbike leaving and arriving on days leading up to the murders."

DI McVeigh leaned forward, excited with the information presented to him, did they finally have a breakthrough in the case.

The young officer could see the elation on his superior's face so continued.

"Within ten minutes on each occasion after the van has entered the multi-story the motorbike has left, as is the same when the motorbike has returned, the van leaves within that ten-minute time frame or as near as. The plates on the van are fake and belong to a Mini Cooper but it could be that this van is used to transport the motorbike, seems too coincidental not to be."

McVeigh leant back in his chair.

"Have you found the owner of the car that the false plates belong too, they might be just stupid enough to use the plates off a car they already own."

The elder of the two officers smiled, "Already looked into that sir, the mini was scrapped five years ago sadly, belonged to an old couple in Milton Keynes"

McVeigh shrugged his shoulders, "Oh well, worth a punt but seriously this is good lads." McVeigh picked up the photos from his desk and thumbed through them, "A lead at last, now gents you know what's coming next?"

Seeing the disappointment on the officers' faces was enough to know they had pre-empted the next request that was coming.

"You got it, track the van using CCTV from the multi-story and see how far you get. I wonder why they use the same car park, two killings in Chelsea, one in Notting Hill and the other in Stratford maybe they're from outside of town and it's easier to use the bike from there to get through the traffic, you don't need me to tell you how to suck eggs boys, get to it, and great work thus far."

McVeigh returned to the records in front of him, pleased now that some form of breakthrough had been made, but that didn't tell him why the four men were targeted and killed in the first place.

The records in front of him were full of nothing but praise for the four former RAF men, all had been awarded the Gulf War Medal and the Kuwaiti Liberation for Services Medal during the Gulf War conflict.

Then McVeigh found something that could be nothing, but worth investigating as there was a slim chance that it could be a reason for the murders.

He discovered it purely accidentally whilst looking through the file of Julian Moss for the umpteenth time, after further investigation he then found the same information in the files of the other three.

He took his bottle of Irish and a tumbler from the desk drawer, poured himself a large measure, fired up his computer, which he rarely used other than for checking emails. He clicked on the internet icon and began typing in the search engine bar. He had a feeling that tonight was going to be a long one.

At four o'clock the next morning McVeigh turned off the computer and went to lay on the sofa that he had in his office, he could see no point in going home now, Emily would understand, she'd gotten used to it over the years.

Mary Barker, a WPC, woke McVeigh with steaming hot coffee, it had not been the first time that she had found the DI asleep on the sofa over the last couple of weeks.

She spied the empty Jameson bottle on the desk and put it in the plastic wastepaper bin. His drinking was getting worse but who was she to judge after what he'd been through. McVeigh wearily raised himself into a sitting position and thanked the WPC for the coffee. He would go and have a shower in the gent's rest room and then head off to the canteen to have a hearty breakfast now that Environmental Health had deemed it fit to reopen, but first he looked at the file of information he had collated the previous night.

Once showered and fed McVeigh conducted the morning briefing before heading back to his office, at the briefing he had not given anything up other than the white van.

Miller, the detective working through the employment files at X-Service, said that it was a slow process as there appeared to be a high turnover of staff and that there were still two to three thousand more files to go through, Monica was helping apparently. He made the comment that she appeared to be a lot happier and more forthcoming now that Cross was off the scene. McVeigh had decided before the meeting not to disclose the information he had stumbled across last night, he wanted to be sure, he was already paranoid that Barry Green thought that he may have lost his edge as a top detective since the explosion.

Once in his office, McVeigh picked up the phone and dialled the number of an old colleague who was based in Norwich with the Norfolk Constabulary, once the formalities were out the way, "How are you?" "Sorry to hear that you were caught up in an explosion" "How are the wife and kids etc?" McVeigh then got down to the real reason he had called.

Ten minutes later McVeigh placed down the receiver with the promise of his request being with him within twenty-four hours by courier. He then turned his attention back to the file he had collated from the early hours of the morning.

He spread out the news clippings he had retrieved from the internet and had printed them off in the early hours of the morning, Marcus Jones was convicted of causing death by dangerous driving in May 1993. The accident took place in August of the previous year but Jones had spent several months in hospital so was therefore classed as unfit for trial until the following year.

Jones had been sentenced to five years in prison for killing his wife and six-week-old baby girl following an accident on a country road half a mile from the base he was stationed at, RAF Collinshall.

Jones was found to be twice over the legal drink drive limit. The judge said that if it was not for the fact that he would have to bear the pain of his actions for the rest of his life and that the accident left Jones in a wheelchair, the sentence would have been for a lot longer.

Four men based at RAF Collinshall who witnessed the crash and tried to get the victims out of the burning wreck were key witnesses to the trial.

Two of the four, Stephen Pearce and Paul Wright had both been nominated for a bravery award after having both received severe burns to their hands and body as they tried in vain to free the woman and child from the burning wreckage.

It is believed that Jones managed to crawl unaided from the upturned burning vehicle.

Mr Jones was given a dishonourable discharge from the RAF following the accident which happened just three weeks before he was due to leave the service, he therefore lost any entitlement to his pension.

McVeigh put the various printed articles back in the manilla folder, was there something in this, did it warrant his time but what else did he have to go on? He would read the case files when they arrived from Norfolk and make a decision then.

CHAPTER TWENTY-SEVEN:

As promised the case files from Norfolk arrived at eleven o'clock the following morning. McVeigh lay out the contents of the box file on his desk but only after locking his office door to ensure that he would not be disturbed or prying eyes saw what they shouldn't. When he saw who the investigating officer was on the first page of the file, he knew that not only was his hunch correct, but he was also right to have locked his office door.

The box file contained statements taken after the crash and photographs of the crash scene itself. McVeigh was glad that he had not eaten when he saw the photographs of Claudia Jones and her young daughter, both unrecognisable as human beings, the daughter looked nothing more than a doll that had been tossed on to a fire and left to burn, and her mother looked like a discarded mannequin.

Eventually when he felt that he was able to continue, McVeigh turned over the photographs and put them to one side and began to go through the statements.

On reading Marcus Jones statement, Jones had pleaded innocence from the outset, he denied being the driver, it was his wife. He stated that it was not an accident and that it was William Cross that had caused the crash deliberately as he had chased them from the village after following them from The Wherry Inn and the village stores.

Jones was insistent that their car was run off the road by the pursuing Cross after Claudia had to take evasive action to avoid an oncoming tractor on the narrow country road.

McVeigh could find no statement from the tractor driver.

Jones had also stated that the barman at the Wherry Inn could vouch that it was Claudia driving because as they left the pub car park he had waved, and when they had stopped off at Collingshall Village Stores for a bottle of wine for Claudia, the lady who owned the stores had come out to take a look at their new born daughter, she could vouch that Claudia was behind the wheel of the car.

McVeigh could find no statements from the store owner or the bar man.

McVeigh had read enough witness statements to know that the four now deceased RAF servicemen's witness statements about the events of the crash were fabricated.

They were too precise, too alike, normally you would have a few "Maybe, I think so, I cannot remember etc," the statements were virtually word for word identical details of their version of events to what had happened.

Another thing that was disturbing McVeigh was the fact that all of the statements had been written in the same handwriting, only being signed individually by the four witnesses. McVeigh had matched the writing up to that of the investigating officer.

Then there had been a statement from the investigating officer himself. He had claimed to having seen the crash after driving back from dropping his wife off at work, where she was the Catering Facilities Manager at the RAF camp.

The only question McVeigh had on his mind now was, why would a member of Her Majesty's constabulary want to nail this accident on an innocent party, if indeed what Jones had stated was true, why were there three vital witnesses' statements missing?

McVeigh lent back in his chair, tempted to pour a whiskey, for once he refrained and got to the task at hand.

The RAF had wanted to do an internal trial and court martial rather than go through the criminal courts but due to the seriousness of the incident, Norfolk Constabulary had insisted that the trial should take place at Norwich Crown Court, the death of a six-week-old baby at the hands of a drink driver was in their belief, "In the public interest".

Several hours later McVeigh was still piecing together his own interpretation of what had actually happened in Norfolk on the day of the fatal crash that took the lives of Claudia Jones and her young daughter and ruined the life of her husband, an innocent man it would seem. A man that had his life ruined that day, but was that a reason after all these years to turn him into a killer on a self-destructive course for revenge? And if he was confined to a wheelchair, would he be able to, unless he was the man that had arranged for others to do it for him.

***

Henry Cartwright was none too pleased at being woken up at three thirty in the morning by his phone ringing. He listened to what McVeigh had to say and at six o'clock was on the road to Norfolk having been unable to get back to sleep.

***

WPC Mary Barker was not ugly but she had a certain look that wouldn't turn heads either, a bit of a plain Jane, she brought McVeigh his coffee at seven o'clock thinking that she would find him slumped on the sofa again, along with an empty bottle of Jameson. She was quite surprised therefore to find him bright eyed and bushy tailed sat at his desk and not a glass or bottle in sight. "Morning Mary" he said cheerfully "Thanks for the coffee, I have to go out, can you ask the Super to do the morning briefing?" Mary looked at McVeigh, he was incredibly handsome and she always had butterflies in her stomach when she was in his presence. "Where shall I say you've gone sir?" she asked as she placed the coffee in front of him, the smell of his aftershave was making her tingle all over and she hoped that she would not embarrass herself by tipping the contents of the cup all over him. "Just tell him it's a follow up hospital appointment I'd forgotten about, a little white lie won't hurt, will it?" and when he winked at her, she thought she would faint.

***

McVeigh pulled up outside the current known address of Marcus Jones. After his release from prison and whilst on probation he had lodged in a hostel in the city before moving to his current residence.

The house was in a small village just outside of St Albans and from the outside looked like a small cottage. As he locked his BMW, he took in the surroundings and immediately noticed that there was a wheelchair ramp that led up the steep pathway to the cottage, could this be a wild goose chase after all.

McVeigh rang the doorbell and waited, still unsure as to whether this was a complete and utter waste of his time and police resources.

Eventually the door was opened and McVeigh had to lower his gaze to make eye contact with the man before him sat in a wheelchair. Having seen photographs the previous day, McVeigh knew that the man in the wheelchair was Marcus Jones.

McVeigh introduced himself, showed Jones his warrant card and was invited in.

As he walked in McVeigh observed the stair lift that led up the stairs from the hallway. Once fully inside the cottage McVeigh could see how deceptive it was from the outside, it was a lot bigger than he had first thought.

The cottage had minimal furniture and the open plan kitchen, diner and living room had obviously been renovated to a very high standard to allow wheelchair access. The kitchen units and cooker were a lot lower than normal kitchens would be so had obviously been adapted for Jones to use whilst in his wheelchair.

Marcus Jones was more than polite to the policeman that had turned up uninvited and unannounced at his home, although he was wondering why the need for the visit.

The niceties out the way, McVeigh sat and drank the coffee that Jones had made him. McVeigh had to do a double take of a photograph framed on the mantlepiece, it showed Jones in his wheelchair, and beside him a young man in motor cross gear standing by a trial bike with a trophy in his hands, at first sight he thought that it was a photograph of DC Daniel Phillips, but on second glance he saw there were similarities, but nothing more.

Marcus Jones was still a handsome man despite the tragedy's that life had thrown at him.

He returned from the kitchen with his own coffee and facing McVeigh said simply "Ok, DI McVeigh how can I help you?"

McVeigh had with him a folder with information that he had extracted from the police files sent from Norfolk, he had highlighted the specific points of interest, he only wanted to ask what was relevant. Nothing more.

"I am investigating the murders of four men in London that took place over a seventy two hour period two weeks ago, all were separate incidents but are all related, we know that the four men owned and ran a company together and were also ex serving members of the RAF and were indeed colleagues. They have known each other for at least twenty years."

If Jones was wondering why the DI was telling him this it didn't show on his face. "So why are you interested in talking to me DI McVeigh?"

McVeigh sipped at the scolding hot coffee, burning his lip in the process "Because Mr Jones, you knew the four men."

Jones raised an eyebrow "I did?"

McVeigh was trying to read Jones; he generally knew if someone was feigning surprise or trying to hide their guilt but he was struggling with this man sat before him.

"They are the four men that you were stationed at Collingshall with at the same time, it's also the four men that you accused of causing the death of your wife and daughter all those years ago, well Cross anyway. The other three were passengers in the car but still hold a form of responsibility for giving false statements, if it is true."

"Of course, it is fucking true!" Jones flew into a rage at the mere mention of Cross's name, "Cross caused the crash and then I was set up by that fucking DCI who investigated the case, the others just went along with it but were all responsible, two of the fuckers even got a bravery award, did you know that DI McVeigh, and I can hand on heart, tell you without any remorse that I am glad the bastards are dead!"

McVeigh was astonished by the outburst, never before had he seen so much hatred in anyone's eyes, if Jones was not in a wheelchair, he would think without a doubt that he was the shooter, and even if he wasn't, the hatred shown was enough to put him in the frame as he could still have arranged it all.

McVeigh ignored the outburst and looked down at his notes, "Your statement said that the barman, the shop owner and the tractor driver witnessed your wife driving, is this true?"

Marcus Jones tried to calm himself, he should never have flown into a rage like that, if the DI did not have him as a suspect before, he did now.

"Yes, DI McVeigh" the words were spoken more softly, all signs of anger now gone, on the outside anyway, but he was still raging within.

McVeigh looked at the man before him, "Why did your solicitor not bring up in court about the three vital witnesses, information that could have proved your innocence?"

Jones was feeling the urge to rant and shout again, but he took deep breaths trying to keep a lid on his anger. "The trial was months after the accident, the RAF had taken some bad press, how it had allowed one of its own to become a child killer, a small baby killer, they appointed some junior solicitor from the RAF, I was guilty before the trial even started, in the public's eye at least, the RAF wanted it to all to go away as quickly as possible."

McVeigh nodded his head as if in agreement, but wondering why someone who insisted they were innocent allowed the RAF to sell them down the river without some sort of fight.

"One last question, or two actually, why did the DCI investigating have it in for you, enough to commit in what is in essence a serious crime, falsifying statements and hiding evidence, and why did Cross try to run you off the road that fateful day?"

Jones moved the motorised wheelchair over to a drink's cabinet that was in the shape of a globe, "I am having a drink, you want one?"

McVeigh shook his head, "Not on duty, thank you all the same, you carry on though."

Jones looked at McVeigh, the hatred still there in his eyes albeit subsided, "I wasn't fucking asking your permission I intend to."

The drink made; he came back to his original position facing McVeigh, he took a large glug of the spirit, "Cross didn't try to run us off the road, he succeeded! As for the copper, I had an affair with his wife, she was manager on the base for all the catering facilities, he found out about it. As for Cross, well I fucked his wife too, and Moss's and Wright's, Pearce was as bent as a nine bob note so not his, satisfied? Until I met Claudia, I would fuck anything with a pulse, she changed me, made me from the boy I was into a man and those bastards took her away from me, the love of my life. One other thing Detective Chief Inspector, I lost both my parents in a car crash, due to a drink driver, I would never drive a car even after half a shandy, something else that went unheard in the court that day."

***

McVeigh started up his car just as a phone call from the DC who was looking into files at X-Service came through. "Sir, I need to see you, I've discovered quite a bit this afternoon, may be best if we discuss it in person, face to face." McVeigh was intrigued, "Sure I'll be

244

back at the office within a couple of hours." There was a slight pause, "No sir, with all due respects not the station, maybe the White Hart round the corner from X-Service Recruitment." McVeigh looked at his watch it was just after three "Ok, let us say five." Then after another slight pause, "Ok sir, oh Monica Watson will be with me sir" McVeigh hung up.

Whilst McVeigh was talking on the phone to the DC, he looked back over to the cottage and saw that the cottage had a garage attached, he could see that the garage door was slightly ajar. After the call had finished McVeigh pulled away and drove about two hundred yards down the road, parked up and walked back towards the garage. He peered inside through a window at the side of the garage, which meant he would be unobserved from the cottage if anyone came out.

Inside the garage he could see that it had been fitted out as a gym; treadmill, rowing machine, exercise bike and weights to name a few items and then on one of the shelves McVeigh spotted a motorcyclist's helmet and protective gear the sort that riders would wear hanging on a hook below it. McVeigh had never been one for technology but he was glad that his phone was able to take pictures. He was tempted to go through the open door but decided against it in case he was observed by anyone.

CHAPTER TWENTY-EIGHT:

Monica Watson could turn heads, her beauty and stunning figure, aided by the appropriate tight clothes saw to that. She felt men's eyes on her wherever she went and even if the attention was not wanted sometimes, it gave her a thrill.

The twenty-five-year-old walked through the bar of The White Hart to the ladies' rest room and sensed the men who frequented the trendy Chelsea wine bar had eyes only for her at that moment in time.

She had gone ahead of DC Johnny Miller so as not to attract attention from those at the office.

Monica looked at herself in the mirror in the ladies' toilet and touched up her makeup, not that it was needed, but Monica was always striving for perfection.

She would use any man to get what she wanted in life, she wanted the career, the money, nice holidays, a beautiful home, designer label clothes and a life of luxury. She had thought that the man to offer her all that was William Cross, but he had got himself killed.

Always the entrepreneur, she decided that even that would not stop her. He had given her a key to his penthouse apartment in Holland Park sensing that the police would be in no rush to search his flat, she had gone there a few hours after his body had been discovered by her and after answering the police questions. After finding Cross dead she called the police but only after emptying the office safe of ten thousand in cash along with a few stocks and shares that were stored there.

When she entered the flat, she quickly got to work and rifled through draws, filing cabinets and cupboards. She found another safe and hoped that Cross would be predictable and use the same combination number as the one in the office, low and behold it opened with ease. She was now sitting on over a hundred grand in cash, another fifty thousand of stocks and shares and the best part of eighty grand of jewellery and watches.

With her make up finished and to her satisfaction she took a pee, she wondered if DC Johnny Miller was there yet, she liked him, not that it would amount to anything, he was after all only a policeman, could offer her nothing anything like the life she strived for. But he was handsome and knew how to please a lady. They had got close; he was single and the previous night she allowed him to share her bed. She was only after a good fuck and he did not displease, a succession of orgasms left her completely satisfied. The last man to please her like Miller had last night was Erik Strasser, an accountant that was in the office a few months ago and who could possibly be the killer of Cross and the others. The thought of how he had pleasured her and that he may be a killer made her wet and excited. She placed her hand below and brought herself off quickly to a massive orgasm. With one more check of her makeup she headed out to the bar to meet up with Miller and his boss, another handsome man who she thought would be fun to get into bed.

DC Johnny was already seated and had already got the drinks; he raised a hand when he saw Monica come from the toilet area. He watched as she walked towards him, she had on a yellow silk dress and it was obvious by her erect nipples sticking out she was not wearing a bra, little did he know why her nipples were so erect, they came towards him like protruding bullets. She sat down beside him, she smelt gorgeous and he felt the first stirrings in his groin.

They passed small talk and she touched his arm or leg at every possible opportunity, throwing her head back at his silly jokes and leaning forward as much as possible offering him a peak at one or both of her nipples at every opportunity. They were so wrapped up in each other's company they were startled when a voice behind them said "Not interrupting anything am I? "

DC Johnny Miller went into professional mode immediately standing up, "DI McVeigh, let me get you a drink sir."

McVeigh asked for a Jameson and water and as the DC went off to the bar, his face red with embarrassment, McVeigh sat opposite Monica Watson. "Miss Watson, how are you? well I hope after all that you have had to endure?"

Monica smiled; she had endured worse. The man before her intrigued her, he was handsome, fit and the sort of man she would go for in an ideal world. Johnny had told her a few things about him, he had suffered a lot but still looked good on it. As McVeigh looked at her, she wondered did he even notice her beauty, have any feelings about the way she looked, or was Pat McVeigh a one-woman man?

DC Miller quickly returned and handed his superior his drink and sat back down beside Monica.

McVeigh took one sip of the drink and added more water from the jug that was supplied with it. "Ok what you got for me and what is it with all this cloak and dagger stuff?"

Miller looked at Monica and she in turn back at him, he produced a notebook, found the relevant page and started to read. "About six months ago X-Service recruited an accountant, after the previous one had just upped and left."

Monica lent forward, McVeigh didn't appear to notice that this was a seductive movement on her part towards him, "She didn't just leave DI McVeigh, she was sacked by Cross, Sally Jeffries brought to light that money was missing from the accounts, two hundred k to be precise, Carol the accountant was the fall guy, that and the fact she had also slept with Cross, she said she knew nothing about the missing money, and she was being blamed as she had stopped sleeping with Cross in case the affair was discovered by her husband. Cross sacked her, but didn't report the missing money."

McVeigh wondered where this was leading, the fact that Cross slept with his accountant was not evidence enough to get himself and the others killed, two hundred k missing however and not to report it to the police was suspicious in anyone's eyes.

Miller noticed the look on McVeigh's face. "So, the new accountant was put in place quickly. Recommended by Sally Jeffries, she had worked with him in the past apparently, Cross was always meticulous before employing new staff, he would vet them, get references etc before they were even allowed on the premises, the new accountant was a guy called Erik Strasser, he was allowed to start immediately due to the urgency of requiring an accountant, Carol the previous accountant having been sacked. He soon settled into the company and was a good accountant by all accounts, excuse the pun."

McVeigh noticed how Monica threw her head back and laughed, these two were banging each other that was for sure, but his disappointment in DC Miller for being unprofessional could wait.

Monica uncrossed and crossed her legs again seductively, a move that did not go unnoticed by McVeigh this time, it was obvious it was not just a bra that was missing under that dress. She rang her tongue over her lips, another movement no doubt for the benefit of McVeigh. She talked softly, seductively even.

Miller looked at his notes again, he too had noticed the flirtation on Monica's part and was in truth jealous. But it was Monica that spoke.

"Strasser was sacked on the spot after just six weeks, his references when they arrived were less than adequate, his CV had been fabricated and he lied about who he was apparently, that's all Cross would tell me. After Erik had left, Cross discovered that his safe had been opened and certain items removed, it happened when Strasser was the only one in the office, CCTV proved that, although that footage has now been wiped clean. A search of his computer history after he had been shown the door showed that he had downloaded information on the Directors, names, address, car registrations etc and a further hundred k had gone missing from the company's accounts."

McVeigh cleared his throat. "There is no CCTV in Cross's office so the footage will have only shown him entering and leaving the office, not opening the safe directly, I cannot get my head around how at least three hundred k had gone missing from the company books and that it was not followed up or reported on."

Monica leant forward once more, "I had a fling with Strasser, DI McVeigh, it only lasted a couple of weeks, a bit of fun, he never stopped asking questions about Cross and the others, where did they live, have they ever told you about their past lives, that sort of thing, he was obsessed with them. What DC Miller has not told you yet is that in his safe Cross had an illegal firearm, a Glock."

McVeigh now leant forward, downed his drink and gave the DC money to get another round in.

When Miller was at the bar McVeigh looked at Monica, and not for the first time noticed how beautiful she actually was, her skin was flawless, her eyes a piercing blue, he also noticed that she was the sort of woman that could wrap a man round her little finger. "You and Cross had a thing, Miss Watson; did he tell you where the gun came from?"

Monica sipped at her wine and tossed her hair back with one hand, McVeigh could see why Miller had succumbed to her charm. "I opened the safe one day to get out some papers and saw it, he didn't seem that bothered that I had seen it but did offer an explanation. He said that an airman in Kuwait had given it to him, Cross smuggled it back into the country and it was a keepsake, a souvenir nothing more he had said."

Miller returned once more with the drinks. McVeigh offered up his thanks, "Have you an address for this Strasser by any chance DC Miller?"

Miller once more returned to his notes, "The address he gave was either an old address or a false one sir, people back at the nick are trying to trace him now."

McVeigh looked confused, "Ok if people back at the nick know about Strasser, why the secret meeting?"

Miller went to speak but Monica placed a hand on his arm to silence him. "Please Johnny let me." What she thought that she would achieve by divulging the next piece of information instead of DC Miller was anyone's guess, maybe she thought that McVeigh would be so grateful he would take her to the nearest hotel and fuck her rigid, or would see her in a different light enough for her to get close to him such was her mentality, the way she thought or fantasised.

Monica leaned forward once more so that McVeigh had a clear view of her nipples, licking her lip with her tongue once more, "DC Miller told me that as far as you are concerned X-Service was owned equally among the four diseased Directors, this is not true, DI McVeigh if you had asked one of your officers to check with Companies House you would have seen that there are indeed five owners."

Monica enjoyed seeing the look on McVeigh's face, deep down he was enjoying the view of her nipples so was quietly disappointed when she sat back upright after dropping her bombshell, but he quickly erased that thought from his mind.

Monica went in to her bag and produced an A4 print out and handed it to the DI. It was a fact sheet of the company produced from Companies House web-site, the fifth owner was highlighted,

McVeigh did not let his face disclose his true feelings right now but simply said "Fucking hell, good work you two, I am famished do you two love birds want to join me for dinner?"

Miller and Monica knew that they had been rumbled, and although both her and Miller had agreed immediately, Monica could not help thinking that she wished it was just her and McVeigh going for dinner but if she ended up with Johnny in her bed again tonight, any cock was better than no cock.

CHAPTER TWENTY-NINE:

McVeigh was in the incident room at six o'clock the following morning, as he was updating the incident board the team began to arrive. Henry Cartwright was keeping Superintendent Barry Green out of the way on the pretence of discussing staff shortages. Despite the heavy night they had each endured, Johnny Miller was the first to join McVeigh. The two of them along with Monica had shared a pleasant evening at an Indian Restaurant of McVeigh's choosing and despite the fact that Monica had flirted with McVeigh all night, it was Miller that ended up in her bed, but little did Miller know that it was McVeigh she was fantasising about the whole time he was satisfying her. Miller was certainly feeling the effects of the alcohol and the lack of sleep today, Monica was a man eater in every sense of the word.

McVeigh had printed off pictures of the gym equipment, motorcycle helmet and bike gear he had found at Jones house the previous day and these were on the board along with a picture of Jones out of the police file from Norfolk. There was also a silhouette of a man's face with a question mark and Erik Strasser written underneath.

The rest of the investigation team slowly drifted in one by one all wondering why an early meeting was required.

McVeigh started the meeting and only stated what he wanted the others to know, the fifth owner of X-Service and the investigating officer of the crash in Norfolk was not disclosed. Henry Cartwright had been to Norfolk and retrieved the court files to the Marcus Jones case after cutting through several yards of red tape and these were now in McVeigh's office for him to read after the briefing.

DI McVeigh started the morning briefing when the last of the team arrived and took their seats. "Ok now we have a suspect, Marcus Jones, but as yet we do not have enough grounds to arrest him, there is also a second man, an Erik Strasser, we have a name nothing else."

Murmurs went round the incident room.

McVeigh turned back to the board, "Marcus Jones was involved in a car crash in nineteen ninety-two, he was charged, tried and convicted of causing death by dangerous driving whilst under the influence of alcohol, the accident left Jones in a wheelchair, his wife and baby were not so lucky, they died. Jones always said leading up to, and throughout the trial, that he was not the driver, it was his wife and that he had been set up by the investigating officer after the crash, the four main witnesses at the trial were our four dead Directors. Jones is adamant that Cross was the driver of a vehicle that was pursuing his, Cross was the cause of the accident, deliberately running them off the road"

The baby-faced PC who had been looking at all the CCTV footage asked "Do we know who the investigating officer was and why Jones would think he was being stitched up sir?"

McVeigh looked a bit apprehensive, wondering in his head what to disclose, "We do, Jones had an affair a few years before the accident with the investigating officer's wife, he also admitted to me that he had affairs with three of our victims' wives, Jones was a bit of a Gigolo back in the day by all accounts."

When the PC realised that no name for the officer was forth coming, he asked "If Jones is confined to a wheelchair, how would he manage to get on and off a motorcycle sir?"

255

McVeigh sighed heavily, "Well that should be pretty obvious, you yourself discovered that a van was being used to transport the bike to and from New Barnet, obviously something in the van enables him to get on and off, but let us not forget the gym equipment in his garage, maybe the gym is for someone who lives with Jones, or maybe the wheelchair is a front, we know one of the gunmen walked with a severe limp from the footage shown, shortly before Cross met his demise, we have asked a judge to get us an order to request medical records, maybe Marcus Jones is not as badly crippled as he makes out. I will be in a better position to know more when I get those records."

McVeigh wanted the meeting brought to a close quickly, the sooner people were on the case instead of sitting in a room the better, and he wanted to see what the trial records showed.

"DC Miller has finished his investigation at X-Service so along with the two officers who have been on CCTV monitoring will look in to finding this Erik Strasser and what, if any connection there is between him and Jones, I have already put Jones under surveillance, using man-power from St Albans nick, luckily there is a river in front of his cottage, popular with anglers, so the undercover is pretty straight forward without raising suspicion. In addition to this we are also trying to establish if the motorcycle helmet and gear I found in Jones garage matches that of one of our motorcyclists."

There was a knock at the door and WPC Mary Barker walked in dressed in civilian clothes, she looked a lot more attractive out of uniform. McVeigh smiled broadly at her, "Hello Mary, gentlemen for those of you who don't know this is WPC Mary Barker she will be joining us to look in to Sally Jeffries, Mary has arranged to meet up with Mrs Jeffries today and will look into Sally's background a bit further. We know that Mrs Jeffries was having an affair with Julian Moss, we also know she is the one that highlighted money had gone missing from the accounts of X-Service, throw in to the mix she was the one that recommended Erik Strasser to replace the sacked accountant, so there may be more to this woman than meets the eye!"

McVeigh pointed to a picture of the white van, "The rest of you, we need to find this van, it could well belong to Strasser or Jones, the motorbike too, notice on the side of the van two distinctive dents and faded signwriting, forensics are working on that now. Now I know that could be any white van in the country but the sooner we know who owns it, the quicker we find Strasser, find him and the quicker we solve the case, let's get to it."

McVeigh left the room and immediately returned to his office, he set about studying the court records, the door locked once more.

After several hours McVeigh realised that the records did not really disclose anything of use and he felt a little deflated, unlocking his office door he was putting on his jacket getting ready to go to the canteen to grab a bite to eat when a WPC whose name he could not remember knocked and entered, "Excuse me sir, there is a phone call for you on line three, a Miss Monica Watson."

McVeigh nodded his thanks, when the nameless WPC had left, he picked up the phone, "Miss Watson?"

There was a giggle at the other end of the line, McVeigh was wondering what Monica was wearing today, he just couldn't help himself.

"Call me Monica please," McVeigh tried to block out the day before, how he had felt himself getting aroused by the woman flashing her tits at every opportunity. "Monica, how can I help you?" At the other end of the line, he could hear her laugh once more.

"I have been thinking DI McVeigh, I don't know if it is important or not but I went to Erik's apartment one night, and he rode a motorcycle to and from work."

McVeigh jumped up "Really, why didn't you say this last night, Miss, I mean Monica where is this apartment?"

Monica was slightly offended that McVeigh had taken this attitude with her, she felt like all those years ago when her father used to chastise her and more besides. She could feel herself blushing, that she had been nothing short of reprimanded by DI McVeigh. She composed herself before answering.

"I know how to get there from the office, we went on his bike after work, but I don't know the street name or anything, its somewhere in Camden."

McVeigh was locking the court files in his draw and looking for his car keys "Are you at work now Monica?" she responded with a nod and then realising he couldn't see her giggled, "Yes, DI McVeigh."

McVeigh laughed softly "Call me Pat, I will be with you as soon as I can, try and think long and hard about the route he took you Monica."

With that McVeigh hung up and dashed out of the office. Monica leant back in her office chair and smiled to herself, the excitement of seeing DC… Pat again set her juices flowing once more, the way that he had reprimanded her was long forgotten as she headed off to the ladies' restroom.

***

Monica Watson walked out to McVeigh's car. It had taken him longer than he thought to get across town to her the traffic was hectic.

She wore a white silk dress, as she got nearer to the car he could see once again she wore no bra and as he could see no panty line meaning she probably wasn't wearing panties either, he felt the first stirrings in his trousers, Emily would kill him if he ever disclosed such thoughts. As Monica slid into the passenger seat, the dress rode up showing her wonderful slim thighs, she was truly beautiful and smelt delicious. McVeigh tried to think of Emily, anything to stop his rising manhood and from taking this beautiful woman in his arms and kissing her.

They made small talk, as he drove, now on first name terms, McVeigh thought of what a lucky bastard Miller was.

They headed off towards Camden. Monica would try to direct him to the flat as they got nearer.

Before they had set off Monica showed McVeigh the pictures, she had printed off from the CCTV of the company's car park, which was never wiped for at least six months after recording unlike the interior cameras.

McVeigh instantly knew the bike in the pictures was identical to that used in the shootings, he called in the number plate to be checked at base, his feeling was it was the genuine number, not fake like the ones used in the shootings.

When they got to Camden Town itself, Monica was directing McVeigh left, right, carry on, a few times she made a mistake and giggled like a little girl, it only made her look more beautiful.

After about thirty minutes of driving round she suddenly shouted "Stop, that's it, that flat up there." She pointed to a warehouse that had been converted into luxury flats.

McVeigh drove a few hundred yards past the flats and parked up.

He turned the engine off and turned to face Monica, the sunlight caught her hair and he felt the stirrings down below again, "You stay here, if he's in and spots you, it could be game over, so the top flat you say, are you sure?" She smiled and touched his arm, leaving her hand there longer than was necessary, "Of course I'm sure Pat." McVeigh took hold of her hand and placed it gently back in to her lap, patting it slightly, her hand was soft, not like his big manly hands, for a moment he let his mind wonder and envisaged it wrapped around his cock, "Ok, wait here."

McVeigh walked back to where the building was and made his way up the staircase to the top flat not using the lift that was available. When he was standing outside the front door, he noticed the name plate Erik Jones on the wall, he called DC Miller and told him to change the name on the search, Erik Strasser was an alias, or that was what he assumed. Three times McVeigh pressed the bell, it was obvious that the occupant was either out or did not want to answer, he crouched down and peered through the letter box, he looked at his phone ringing, saw it was Monica and chose to ignore it, he heard a motorbike and then

he saw Erik Jones standing behind him demanding "What the fuck are you doing?"

McVeigh recognised the man in front of him as the one in the picture at Marcus Jones

home.

CHAPTER THIRTY:

DI McVeigh and DC Miller interviewed Erik Jones after his solicitor had arrived and had spent time with him alone presumably to establish the facts and advise him accordingly.

McVeigh showed Jones a picture of the motor cycle that Monica had given him from CCTV footage at the car park of X-Service.

"Do you recognise this bike Mr Jones? It is a Honda CBR 600F, for the benefit of the tape I am showing Mr Jones a photograph taken in the car park of X-Service Recruitment when Mr Jones worked there."

Jones lent forward looking at the picture, he arrogantly shrugged his shoulders "Yes, it is my bike."

McVeigh produced another picture of what appeared to be the same bike, this time the picture was from CCTV footage obtained from a business close to the Stratford killing site, "And this one, for the benefit of the tape I am showing Mr Jones a picture of a motorcycle taken from CCTV footage near a murder scene in Stratford."

Jones solicitor whispered into the ear of his client, after a pause Jones only muttered "Not sure."

McVeigh lent back in his chair arms folded, if that was the way he wanted to play it, today was going to be a long one.

"I can tell you now Mr Jones we can confirm the bike in both pictures is one and the same, forensics highlighted that there is a small stone dent on the fuel tank, it is identical in both pictures along with some scuffs on the exhaust."

Jones solicitor whispered in his client's ear once more, whatever he had said caused Jones to just murmur "No comment."

McVeigh placed a photo of a white van in front of Jones, "Do you recognise this van Mr Jones?"

Erik Jones had now leant back in his chair he also folded his arms, showing no interest in the questions being asked of him any longer, "No comment."

Miller leaned forward, "You should recognise it, evidence has just come to light within the last thirty minutes that it is registered in your name, it used to belong to a window cleaning company, before you bought it six months ago."

Jones feigned looking bored, "No comment."

McVeigh looked at Miller, "DC Miller please play the footage."

Miller set up a video on a lap top and turned it round to show Jones, "This footage shows a man walking dressed in motorcycle gear into the office of X-Service Recruitment, shortly afterwards a Mr William Cross was shot dead, notice the man walks with a slight limp, you walk with a limp don't you Erik?"

"No comment."

McVeigh sighed, "This is getting a bit boring now Erik, what is your relationship to Sally Jeffries?" Jones lent forward now, he looked as if he was about to talk, but after his solicitor urged caution, he simply replied "No comment."

"And your relationship to Marcus Jones?" "No comment."

McVeigh had taken about as much as he could, just as he was about to explode with rage there was a knock at the door and Mary Barker poked her head round the door, "Can I have a quick word sir?"

After the usual small talk for the benefit of the tape McVeigh left the room and talked to Mary outside briefly before returning to the room.

"Maybe the man in the footage with the limp is Marcus Jones, what you reckon DC Miller?" Miller smiled, "Or at least one of the ones on the motorbike boss."

Erik Jones stood up and leant over the table ignoring the pleas of his solicitor, "No fucking way, my dad had nothing to do with it, he has been through enough, it was me ok, I killed the bastards, not my dad!"

McVeigh and Miller between them managed to calm Erik Jones down enough for him to retake his seat. After a glass of water, he poured his heart out from what he had been keeping pent up for so long, and when he finally finished his confession, he was glad that it was all out, that he did not have to carry the burden around any longer, revenge had been extracted that was all that mattered, his story when it came was heart rendering and even McVeigh felt sorry for what Erik and his father had to endure and carry with them over the years.

Erik Jones was still in hospital in Cambridge when his mother and twin sister had been killed in a crash caused by Cross.

When his father was in hospital and then prison, after he was well enough to leave hospital, Erik had been taken off to Germany by his mother's grandparents. He had been renamed Erik Strasser.

His grandparents were convinced that Marcus was responsible for the deaths of their daughter and granddaughter, despite his father's insistence that he was innocent and had been framed.

When his father was released from prison, legal proceedings began to gain access to his son and when the boy was seven, he had started regular visits to the UK to spend time with his father and his aunt, his aunt was Sally Jeffries, nee Strasser, she was Claudia's sister. At the age of twelve, his grandfather died and a year later his grandmother, Erik inherited a small fortune. Erik and Sally were the only beneficiaries as the only two surviving relatives.

He moved to the UK to be with his father at the age of thirteen.

His father spent years telling him what had happened to his mother and sibling and a hate grew inside him for the injustice that had taken place.

Not once did he ever doubt what his father had told him as being the truth, his aunt had always believed that his father was innocent.

His father, despite being told that he would never ever walk again, had battled all the odds and through regular exercise had managed to walk unaided all be it with a severe limp, he kept up the pretence of having to use a wheelchair as he did not want his benefits to be cut.

Erik's father had very little money, no service pension and his grandparents on his father's side had a house in Tuscany which his father reluctantly sold to buy the small cottage outside of St Albans.

Erik went to college and studied accountancy, bought the apartment in Camden with his inheritance, gave some money to his father and plotted revenge against Cross and the others.

The breakthrough came when he had found the four had set up X-Service Recruitment. With the help of his aunt and her rich husband, the pair were able to get into the company as employees, his aunt first and then him.

He had falsified his CV, but sadly Cross discovered the lies and more importantly who his father was, but not before he had stolen the gun and ammunition from the safe in Cross's office and all the personal details of the four directors, along with discovering information about the fifth owner.

Erik found it quite amusing that he had transferred one hundred thousand pounds from the companies' funds into an offshore account he had set up in his father's name just minutes before his sacking, telling Cross that he wouldn't do anything about it because the truth would out.

His aunt had already stolen the two hundred thousand that the previous accountant was deemed to have stolen. Although she felt bad that Carol had to take the wrap, the funds were in the same off shore account that only his father had access to. They had lied to his father as to where the money came from, so he was totally blameless in the theft.

Despite the four directors being involved in the death of her sister and niece, his aunt had an affair with Julian Moss.

On a long train ride to Manchester that the two had shared, Moss had poured his heart out to her, how Cross was a bully, how they had all covered up the accident under duress from the investigating officer and Cross. She saw Moss in a different light after that and they started an affair shortly afterwards.

Erik had challenged his aunt about it, but all she would say is that she had sexual needs, her husband and she had an open marriage, Erik's dear old uncle prefers boys by all accounts, all Sally had said was if it got her nearer to the truth, who was anyone to complain?

Sally would meet Moss mainly in hotels but when his wife was away, she would go to his house too, she also visited the homes of Cross, Pearce and Wright when they invited her and her husband for dinner parties and was able to snoop around and get information on them.

X-Service Recruitment and the charity were a front for the company's main business, Cross and the others employed specific ex service personnel to traffic drugs in to the UK from all over the world, it certainly brought in big bucks, his aunt had said that once at Cross's apartment she accessed his safe and found there to be more than a quarter of a million in cash inside.

Erik Jones had told McVeigh and Miller that he had a memory stick at his apartment showing every drug shipment that had been brought in to the country, and a list of names in the UK that the drugs were supplied to up to the point of his dismissal.

The total received for smuggling in and supplying drugs so far over the years was over one hundred million pounds.

After the confession McVeigh, although feeling sorry for Erik, his father and his aunt simply asked "So who was the other person on the bike Erik?"

Jones had smiled, "No comment. Although you are the detective work it out!"

McVeigh looked closely at Erik, deep down he still felt Marcus Jones was involved more than was being let on. Erik almost sensed what McVeigh was thinking.

"All you… all you need to know is that I was the gunman, my aunt taught me how to shoot, she used to be an expert marksman back in the days of growing up in Germany, taught by my grandfather. My Dad had called to say you had paid him a visit. I knew it was only a matter of time before you caught up with me, so I warned my aunt. I was heading back to my apartment to get clothes to do a runner when you caught up with me. My aunt and her husband are now laying on a beach somewhere, her husband will just be thinking it is an impulse holiday, she will break the news gently to him but either way she is free from prosecution or extradition. I am the man in the video, my limp was courtesy of a bad trial bike accident, I am guilty of all of the murders, but you caught me before I could get to the fifth man, oh well his time will come."

McVeigh smiled, it was his turn now to have the upper hand "That is where you're wrong Erik, your aunt is in a cell downstairs awaiting interview." The look of horror on Jones face was priceless, one of shock.

McVeigh looked through the paperwork in front of him, "Before I charge you with the murders of Cross, Moss, Wright and Pearce, what if any involvement did Monica Watson have in all of this?"

Jones smiled broadly, and lent back in his chair, positioning a hand in his groin. "That Monica, one hell of a bird right, you've seen her, right cock teasing whore she is." Jones looked to Miller who had gone bright red, he leant forward putting his arms on the desk, "No fucking way man, you've fallen and succumbed to her charms haven't you mate?"

Miller excused himself from the room, the embarrassment was too much to take. When Miller had left the room, Jones looked at McVeigh, "That woman taught me positions in bed I didn't even know existed, be careful though she is a viper, a dangerous maneater, she would fuck a tramp if he had wine and the boozers were shut and she wanted a drink. Bet you haven't been to Cross's flat since his death have you DI McVeigh?"

McVeigh neither confirmed or denied the question.

"Monica would have done, as soon as your backs were turned, bear in mind my aunt has been in that place of his, stocks, shares, cash and jewellery in that safe, thousands of pounds worth, bet you a quid the safe is empty now thanks to Monica!"

A short while later Erik was charged with the four murders of the owners of X-Service Recruitment and was to go to court in the morning where he would be placed on remand. The headache for McVeigh and his team now was finding out whether it was Sally or Marcus on the bike along with Erik, they knew that Sally was being interviewed at the time of Paul Wright's killing so was it both of them taking it in turns or was there the possibility that the second person was someone completely different, someone that they were yet to discover and that Erik was telling the truth, that his father was not involved at all.

After interviewing Sally Jeffries, the only thing that she confessed to was stealing the money and falsely blaming Carol the previous accountant, despite a barrage of questions the only thing she repeated was 'no comment'.

CHAPTER THIRTY-ONE:

At the following morning briefing DI McVeigh looked tired. He told the assembled officers about Erik Jones; Marcus Jones and Sally Jeffries were the two suspects as to who the second motorcyclist was and that they would have to pull out all the stops to find out which one. McVeigh advised them that Marcus and Sally may have alternated for the different killings so it could be both, or it could be that there was another suspect waiting to be discovered?

Using the photograph from McVeigh's phone, forensics had matched the motorcycle gear and helmet hanging up in Marcus Jones garage as being the same worn by one of the motorcyclists in the shootings. This in itself did not prove Marcus was involved, Sally could have left it in his garage.

The fact that a van was used to transfer the motorbike prior to the killings was bugging McVeigh. All the killings had taken place on a weekday and McVeigh knew that during the week Sally lived in the heart of the city, Erik lived in Camden, so why would they travel to New Barnet in the van first unless it was easier for Marcus Jones to mount and dismount the bike, that and the fact New Barnet was nearer to St Albans than the city.

Officers were requested to look at all video images that had been compiled of the suspects and see if the images could be identified as either Marcus, Sally or someone else entirely.

When McVeigh finished the briefing, he was not expecting progress to happen as quickly as it did. His mobile rang, it was one of the undercover officers based outside Marcus Jones house. "He has walked from his home to an industrial estate on the outskirts of the village, he went to a lock up and drove out in a white van, I have pictures I'll send them to you now." The officer, who was experienced with over twenty years on the force said excitedly.

McVeigh asked "Where is he now?" There was a pause, McVeigh repeated the question, his voice louder than he had wanted it to be. "That is the problem sir, we followed him on foot from a safe distance, when he came out in the van, we had to run back to get our vehicle, by the time we did that the van had disappeared, we have…" The officer was not able to continue as McVeigh had hung up. The officer slightly embarrassed, forwarded the images of the van to McVeigh's phone immediately hoping that damage limitation was the best way to save face on this occasion.

McVeigh got the images and despite his frustration and anger at the officers babysitting Marcus, was able to put out a bulletin on the vehicle not having a clue where Marcus Jones was heading.

Throughout a frustrating day for McVeigh who had charged Sally Jeffries with theft but then having to release her on police bail, McVeigh had wanted her charged with conspiracy to murder, her husband had employed one of the best briefs in London to represent her, he ripped McVeigh's theory apart and McVeigh knew without more evidence the CPS would throw it out in a heartbeat. Chances are she would get off with the theft such was the brief's reputation, he would get the charges dropped on a technicality of some sort.

The one piece of good news came from Mary Barker who had studied the footage of the gunmen, gunpersons entering X-Service offices prior to the shooting of Cross, going by the height of all three suspects she noticed that both suspects in the footage walked with a limp, the second more prominently than the first, and along with the photographs taken from Marcus's garage of the motor bike gear, she was able to identify the man that they thought was Erik was indeed Marcus, with Erik being the leading man going into the office.

Alerts had been flooding into the station all day of the white van's location, the order was to track the vehicle and driver, but not to apprehend it, the Glock pistol was after all still unaccounted for despite an extensive search of Erik Jones apartment and Sally Jeffries home.

The van had been seen on the A414, the A1(M), the A505 and it was only when it was spotted on the A11 heading East that McVeigh knew where the final destination was going to be and called in an armed unit to pull the van over and apprehend the suspect.

McVeigh got the news a short while after that Marcus Jones had been apprehended near Thetford, he had given up without a struggle, a pistol and ammunition believed to be the Glock used in the murders was found on his possession.

Marcus Jones under armed guard, was being escorted back to London; the van was being transported to forensics at nearby Wymondham police headquarters.

Marcus Jones stated to the arresting officers that "He had been heading to a house outside of Norwich, to finish the job that he and his son had started and kill the fifth owner of X-Service recruitment who was the investigating officer in the crash all those years ago," after Marcus had made that comment he remained silent all the way back to London.

CHAPTER THIRTY-TWO:

McVeigh and Cartwright sat drinking Jameson's in McVeigh's office. The two were close friends and had a certain respect for each other that went beyond their positions in the police.

"Good work Pat, you've still got it son" Cartwright winked.

McVeigh was feeling tired, signs showed in his face that he had become a little haggard of late, the bags under his eyes could be sponsored by Tesco they were that big. He promised himself a holiday when all loose ends were tied up. He smiled at his friend, "Not quite finished yet though is it, Henry?"

Cartwright shifted uncomfortably in his chair, "No I suppose not, what time does his plane land tomorrow?"

McVeigh leant over to look in his diary, "Twenty-three fifteen tomorrow night, Gatwick North terminal."

Cartwright nodded, "I'll take a few armed officers with me, just in case he's been reading or seeing the news, should be ok though."

McVeigh leant downwards and produced documents from his desk drawer, it was the folder that Daniel Phillips had given him, but it now seemed thicker for some reason, he handed the folder to Cartwright in silence. After several moments of murmurs from Cartwright he looked up at McVeigh, "Fucking hell Pat, who authorised this?"

McVeigh poured them both another large scotch knowing that they would both need it.

Sipping his drink McVeigh looked at his boss and friend, he didn't want to go behind his back, but in his eyes Gosling, at the time had already been cleared of murdering Natasha he was not prepared to take the risk that he would get away with anything else.

"The Governor of the prison Gosling was sent to is an old friend. Before Goslings' trial and while he was on remand between us, we arranged for a screw on Gosling's wing to befriend Gosling, get him whatever he wanted, cigarettes, booze and more importantly a phone. The screw, a man with many years' service is as straight as a die, a chap called Harry Boothroyd and he was happy to do it. We drew up a document which we all signed in case it went tits up stating that Harry was working undercover, with the governor and my specific permission and blessing."

McVeigh could sense that Cartwright was not sitting comfortably with the information he had seen and the explanation he was being given. Ignoring Cartwrights anxiety McVeigh carried on.

"The mobile phone given to Gosling was being tracked and monitored from the Governor's office, all incoming and outgoing texts along with calls were monitored and more importantly recorded. We know that Gosling ordered a hit on Joe Whyte, we only ever found the bodies of Whyte's girlfriend Sandra and the taxi driver, Whether Whyte survived the initial shooting and was taken away to be tortured and finished off elsewhere is anyone's guess, but it's fair to say that whatever his demise, Whyte is probably pushing up daisies on the Mud Chute or somewhere similar now."

Cartwright silently held up his glass for a refill, which McVeigh happily obliged.

"We know Gosling ordered an explosive package to be delivered to a guy called Techno, we also know that Techno was found dead, his throat slit, in his luxury apartment overlooking Tower Bridge twenty-four hours later by his girlfriend, Whyte was more than likely the knifeman. Although we do not have specific names mentioned of the target for the explosive device, we do have an address, mine, it is fair to say that was the package that was delivered to my house."

Cartwright shifted uncomfortably in the chair "So why were you unable to prevent the package being delivered if you knew that it would be imminently?"

The look on his face told Cartwright everything he needed to know.

It was some time before McVeigh could answer, at one point the anguish on his face was so bad that Cartwright thought that the man in front of him would burst in to tears, eventually McVeigh had calmed down enough to answer.

"The Governor, Samuel Forbes had taken a couple of days leave to attend his daughter's graduation in Edinburgh. Like I said, the recording equipment was in his office and it was locked away in his desk draw. Sadly, and this is the part that will eat away at me for years to come by the time he listened to the recording it was too late"

And then McVeigh could hold in his emotions no more and tears strolled down his face as he sobbed uncontrollably.

Cartwright was up out of his seat in an instant and went immediately to McVeigh and put an arm round his shoulder and pulled McVeigh towards him, "There, there son, let it go, get it all out" he said like a father would to a small child.

It took a while for McVeigh to recompose himself and when he had it was like the incident had never happened, but an even stronger bond had just been formed between the two men.

Cartwright had returned to his own seat after a toilet break and as usual went to stroke away the imaginary fluff on his knee, "And the evidence related to the death of Natasha and the injuring of Phillip?" he continued looking through the contents of the envelope.

McVeigh took a large gulp of his drink, just the mention of Natasha's name filled his head with bad memories that he wished could be erased.

"As you well know Henry, you gave him permission to look in to that. DC Daniel Phillips reinvestigated the case and found the evidence whilst he was waiting for me to return to duty, well that and when he wasn't destroying my office, you know I still don't know where everything is!" Cartwright gave a loud laugh that came from the belly at that remark and the disappointment Cartwright had felt by McVeigh crossing the line with his governor friend was instantly forgotten.

"Ok let me get tomorrow night out the way Pat and I'll arrange a visit with Gosling and his brief at the prison and we can charge him accordingly. I could send a detective but I want to see the bastard squirm for myself."

McVeigh produced another envelope, "DC Phillips has true potential you know" McVeigh pulled out an A4 piece of paper that was filled both sides with business names and addresses and handed it to Cartwright. The older man studied it, the paper was filled with the names of all the businesses that Gosling was using for his criminal activities, from money laundering to prostitution.

Cartwright scratched at his head, "He sure does, makes you wonder why his father felt that he needed a leg up in the force though, the boy has the potential to go far."

McVeigh pointed a finger at the paper that Cartwright was holding, "The last business name on that list is interesting don't you think?"

Cartwright had to do a double take, "Fucking hell, it sure does Pat"

"WPC Mary Barker is working on it as we speak, trying to find the connection, there must be one." McVeigh refilled their glasses and for the remaining few minutes it took for the two men to finish their drinks was done in silence; it was a time to reflect not to chew the fat for the sake of it.

***

The following morning McVeigh, accompanied by WPC Mary Barker knocked on the door of a flat in an apartment block of the smart residency area of Fulham. They could hear footsteps approaching from within. Monica Watson answered the door, she wore only a silk robe, when she saw who was at the door she smiled widely, "Oh it's you Pat" and then seeing Mary "And who is this?"

McVeigh flashed his warrant card, "its DI McVeigh, Miss Watson and we were hoping that you could let us in for a word or two." Sensing the seriousness in McVeigh's voice and the concerned look on his face, Monica Watson's attitude changed. "Oh well do you have a search warrant DI McVeigh? or if it is a word you want, I'll accompany you to the station, not in the privacy of my home." Mary Barker took great pleasure in showing the woman in front of her the search warrant, and then Mary smiled even more broadly when she saw that Monica Watson's expression quickly changed to that of someone who looked like they had swallowed a razor blade.

Once inside the apartment Monica asked to be able to go and put something sensible on, even this was done in such a way to keep McVeigh's attention, she left the bedroom door open far enough and knew that he would be looking as she let her robe drop to the floor and see her in all her nakedness. McVeigh once more felt the stirrings below.

After what seemed like an hour and having given herself a complete makeover, Monica returned to the open plan living room. As usual she looked stunning and as she walked in front of the living room window, he could see that once again she wore nothing underneath the light blue silk dress, her material of choice it would seem. Having been kept waiting for so long McVeigh was agitated and not in the mood for any more games, dismissing out of hand offers of tea or coffee and fucking bourbon biscuits.

A search of the flat gave them the evidence they were looking for, receipts for jewellery given to a pawn shop, stocks and shares all in William Crosses name and almost one hundred and twenty k in cash. The likelihood of theft standing up in court was going to be a hard case to win, knowing Monica Watson she would say that they were gifts and that the money was hers and she would be able to prove it, falsely or otherwise, but this was more about McVeigh clearing his conscience for having inappropriate thoughts about this woman over Emily, Monica was a woman that he had let get under his skin, a viper who could not hold a candle to Emily or indeed Natasha but he had allowed her to turn him on just by looking at her.

Even if she disclosed in court about her relationship with DC Johnny Miller, McVeigh couldn't care less, although he understood how the DC had been weak, hadn't he nearly succumbed to her charm himself, almost grabbing her in the car and pulling her into him for a kiss moments before setting off to find Erik's flat in Camden, only coming to his senses as an image of Emily flashed before his eyes.

Three hours later under arrest, Monica was presented to the desk sergeant and her whole charm offensive began once more, like McVeigh and Miller before him the desk sergeant was reeled in like a helpless fish.

CHAPTER THIRTY-THREE:

Fourteen months after the explosion that killed Emily and the twins and nearly took his life, DI Pat McVeigh returned to work.

He had spent ten months in hospital, most of it in an induced coma, and had been resuscitated at least fifteen times being told by the medical team looking after him that he was a walking miracle.

After another three months in a recuperation hospital arranged by the Police Federation and undergoing physio on a daily basis, there followed a month-long holiday in Spain, McVeigh could not bear to go back to Cyprus his destination of choice where he had shared many happy times with Emily and the boys.

Having been given the all clear by the federations medical officer he now felt the time was right to get back to work and put all that had happened behind him.

The nightmares wouldn't stop he knew that, the pain wouldn't completely go away, normal would never be a normal that he once knew but he had to at least try.

DI McVeigh walked into the station on his first morning back, he immediately felt a sense of de je vu but unlike before on this occasion, there was no crowd to meet him to cheer and clap him, Henry Cartwright was there of course placing a firm hand on his shoulder "Welcome back son."

The two headed off to McVeigh's office, the few people they passed offered a murmured "Welcome back sir" or "Good to see you" in truth, many couldn't look him in the eye because they were at a loss for what to say.

On the way to McVeigh's office, they passed by the glass fronted office of the new Superintendent, sat in front of him was another man in a Saville Row suit. Seeing him look in the direction of the Superintendent's office, Cartwright turned to McVeigh and simply said "That is your new Super Barry Green, I will introduce you to him later."

McVeigh was still looking in the direction of the two men, "and the suit that is with him?" McVeigh asked innocently.

Cartwright coughed as if the words had got stuck in his throat, "All in good time dear boy, all in good time" was the only comment McVeigh got.

Once in his own office Cartwright looked confused and perplexed when McVeigh passed no comment or showed no reaction to how tidy his office was compared to its normal organised chaos.

Once seated McVeigh looked around, there was that feeling of de je vu again.

WPC Mary Barker knocked on the door and entered with coffee for her two superiors, she smiled warmly at McVeigh and he in turn smiled back, "Good to see you Mary, how are you?"

Mary blushed slightly, McVeigh had that effect on her, she had a secret crush on him and seeing him again for the first time in over a year that crush had never gone away. She left without further ado as she could feel herself reddening even further when McVeigh touched her hand to stop her pouring the coffee, "It's OK love, I'll be mother" and then he smiled broadly and winked at her.

Alone once more the two men got down to business, McVeigh had been out of the game for far too long and there was so much to talk about.

McVeigh looked at the man who he had classed as a friend rather than a boss, he cleared his throat, "Before we start, I would like to thank you Henry, Margaret, Natasha's mother told me how every Sunday you would go to the New Forest and pick up Phillip and bring him to see me at the hospital before taking him back again a few hours later via a McDonalds."

Cartwright blushed slightly "It was the least I could do dear boy, it was a pleasure, Phillip is a lovely boy, a credit to you, I hoped that the sound of his voice would be of help to you and your recovery."

"You went the extra mile Henry, literally, I also know that you visited me privately at least every other day, Winston, the auxiliary nurse told me, and thank you for employing a professional photographer to video Emily and the boy's funeral, I haven't brought myself to watch it yet, but thank you anyway."

Cartwright was a darker shade of red now, the man who sat before him he felt he owed a debt to from their very first meeting, where in his own words discussing it with his wife of thirty years afterwards, he had told her with a heavy heart "I have let him down."

McVeigh having said what he felt needed to be said "Right Henry let's get down to business."

McVeigh opened a desk drawer and placed a manilla envelope in front of Cartwright, "In that file you will find transcripts from phone conversations and texts that Gosling made from prison, he can clearly be heard saying my address to one of the recipients on one of those phone conversations." McVeigh explained about his governor friend, the friendly helpful screw and how the calls and texts had been monitored but sadly, not discovered in time to prevent the explosion.

When Cartwright had finished studying the information that had been presented to him McVeigh waited a moment for the information to sink in. If Cartwright was disappointed that McVeigh had gone behind his back, he didn't let it show.

McVeigh then opened the draw in his desk once more and handed Cartwright a sealed manilla envelope, "You'll need this also" as McVeigh handed the envelope over, he could see that Cartwright had a worried look on his face, thoughts raced through Cartwright's head, had McVeigh been in the office already perhaps yesterday evening and written out his resignation.

Cartwright looked at McVeigh "Dare I ask what is in it?" McVeigh smiled, something that he had not done much of recently "Only one way to find out, open it."

As Cartwright studied the contents, the photograph of Gosling behind the wheel caught by a speed camera within three minutes of the fateful hit and run causing the death of Natasha and the injury to Phillip along with the other evidence collated by DC Daniel Phillips, McVeigh watched Cartwright for his reaction, non-appeared to be coming so McVeigh continued. "DC Daniel Phillips has been working here, he is the one that you and Superintendent Barry Green gave authorisation to look into evidence surrounding Natasha's death and Phillip's injury, that's what he came up with. He was under strict orders to show me first, but the funny thing Henry, today is my first day back, how would I

284

know what was in that envelope, it has not been opened yet, and how would I know that DC Daniel Phillips was my new DC and responsible for tidying the office, I also knew that Barry Green is my new superior, long before you said."

Cartwright looked at McVeigh wide eyed, thoughts raced through his mind, all he could say was, "Fuck the coffee, get that Jameson out your draw and pour two large ones!"

Cartwright didn't know what was going on, how McVeigh who had spent months in and out of a coma would know what he knew, there was one thing that he felt sure he didn't know though, the only thing was how to tell him.

Cartwright crossed his leg and swiped the usual imaginary fluff off of his knee. "It is true, DC Phillips was your new DC, he was placed by Superintendent Green as a favour, Phillips father was a Deputy Chief Constable of the Norfolk Constabulary before taking early retirement, he is the man currently sitting opposite Green right now, he and Green go way back. Green needed a new DC so it was an easy decision to make, Green was happy that he was helping out an old friend, along with filling a vacant position, DC Phillips father was happy that his son was being given an opportunity to fast track up the career ladder."

Cartwright paused, took a sip of his drink, swiped the imaginary fluff away again and looked McVeigh squarely in the eyes, "Thing is Pat, DC Phillips was shot and killed five months ago whilst off duty" Cartwright saw McVeigh's mouth open in shock.

McVeigh calmed himself before requesting details on the demise of Daniel Phillips whom he had never met, in person at least.

Cartwright explained in detail that Daniel Phillips was on leave and that the shooting took place on the drive of his father's house just outside Norwich, he had been house sitting and looking after the family pets whilst his mother and father were away.

When he had finished, McVeigh poured more drinks and shifted uncomfortably in his chair, he still had aches and times of excruciating pain caused by the injures he received from the explosion. "Who is investigating?"

Cartwright looked at his friend, the pain was easy to see on his face, he didn't know however if it was physical or because of the news that he had just dealt him.

"Norfolk police are on it, he was shot twice at close range getting into his father's Jaguar, parked on the drive. Sadly, the investigation appears to be getting nowhere fast, five months since it happened and no one is any the wiser as to who did it or why for that matter, no leads, no suspects, fuck all in fact."

McVeigh sighed heavily, what he was about to say could have him locked up in a psychiatric ward for the rest of his days and if it had been anyone other than Henry Cartwright sitting in front of him, he may well not have said it at all.

"Let me help them out, save them some time" McVeigh cleared his throat knowing that what he was about to say could cause no end of problems for all concerned but mainly him, he could end up being sent to a psychiatric unit for tests or his career could be ended in an instant. Eventually his heart and mind, who had been battling each other for a few minutes decided to say what he knew, but at what cost. Needing courage, he took a large mouthful of his whiskey.

"Daniel wasn't the target; the target was his father. He was shot by two men who turned up on a motorbike, the pillion passenger was the shooter, the weapon was a Glock and the ammunition was nine-millimetre bullets."

Cartwright's head which was fuzzy before, was now reeling, how would McVeigh know this? CCTV and forensics had already proven what he said was true, Cartwright had an update report delivered to him every day by courier from the Norfolk Constabulary.

McVeigh could see that Cartwright was confused and in truth so was he. There appeared to be a long moment of silence and McVeigh could see that Cartwright was thinking about what he had said, he was probably thinking what is the hotline to the looney tunes bin, I have another inmate for you. After a few minutes of silence that seemed like an hour, McVeigh broke the silence, "Who is investigating the shootings of the X-Service Recruitment directors?"

If Cartwright was confused before he was mentally delirious now; "What shootings Pat, other than a few youth gang stabbings and shootings, the norm these days unfortunately, there have not been any other murders in the city for weeks, months even."

It was McVeigh's turn to be confused, what the fuck was going on, was he going mad? He fired up his computer and did a google search in silence, within two minutes of searching, the printer on the other side of the room whirred into action. He rose quickly and almost ran across the room to collect the paper that was coming through its rollers. He handed the document to Cartwright, "This is proof that Edward Phillips, Daniel's father is the fifth owner of X-Service Recruitment, give me more time and I will have other things to show you."

Cartwright looked at McVeigh, he honestly didn't know what to think, the medical officer had assessed Pat and ensured him that he was fit to return to work, but how would he know the things that he did, he had let him down in the past, he wanted to give him the benefit of the doubt. He could either call for the men in white coats to come along with a straight jacket or give him the time he had requested. He got up and locked the door, "Ok Pat, but I'm not leaving you alone, and we don't want to be disturbed, so crack on son"

CHAPTER THIRTY-FOUR:

Despite Barry Green trying to enter McVeigh's office and introduce himself four times, Cartwright had raised a hand to usher him away and three hours later Henry Cartwright sat and ran his fingers through his good head of hair. He looked at all the facts that McVeigh had printed off and whilst he did that, McVeigh talked him through it. He explained about the car crash in Norfolk back in ninety-two when Jones had been framed by Edward Phillips.

"Normally a DCI would not investigate a road crash like that but a kid had gone missing from a holiday park in Great Yarmouth and all available units, including traffic police, were out and about looking for her. Phillips was in the area, even though he was off duty he was first on the scene even stating that he witnessed the accident. Four years before the crash, Marcus Jones had an affair with Phillip's wife and believe me having seen both Jones son Erik, whom he had with Claudia and seeing Daniel Phillips I would say that it is a fair bet that Daniels father is not the man he thinks, thought he was, he and Erik are the spitting image of each other. Phillips superiors allowed him to see the investigation through"

Cartwright had a splitting headache, he couldn't think straight, "So that's the reason that he falsified evidence, withheld evidence, didn't fully investigate the crash and falsified statements." He leant back in the chair "What about X-Service?"

McVeigh handed Cartwright another piece of paper off the printer tray it showed a photograph of five dead men in army uniform lying in a make shift grave, "That picture was taken six years ago in Columbia, it made international news headlines, five British nationals were found in a shallow grave, each with a single bullet wound to the head. They were discovered after the Columbian authorities carried out a raid on a known drugs cartel property." McVeigh could see that Cartwright was confused as to why he was being presented with this information.

"All will become clear Henry believe me" McVeigh said hoping that the confusion on Henry's face would ease.

"The authorities killed forty of the Cartel's gang and seized heroin with a street value of over one hundred million dollars. These men in the picture were employed by X-Service Recruitment. One of the cartels surviving gang members disclosed to the Columbian police, after the discovery of the bodies, that the five men had tried to rip off the Cartel and were caught stealing more heroin than they had actually purchased"

Henry looked at the picture again, "Edward Phillips was he in on this, knowing that the company he was part owner of was being used for these illegal activities?"

McVeigh eased his friends mind, "I would say no, annual dividends paid out to him as a silent partner would suggest not, in fact I would be surprised if any of the directors knew what Cross was up to. When we visit Erik Jones flat, I can get hold of a memory stick that has every transaction of every shipment that was brought in to the country and who it was passed on to, times, dates, places and how much for."

Cartwright sighed a deep sigh, "I have to ask Pat, how do you know all this, you have been out the game for fourteen months?"

McVeigh smiled, "You mean am I a looney tune or is this all for real?" Cartwright laughed "Well you said it son."

McVeigh rose from his chair, "I'll try and explain, but can we go get lunch? I am famished, I have eaten like a horse since getting out of hospital."

Cartwright stood up "Good idea, but we'll go out somewhere, I don't trust the canteen after twenty percent of the station staff are off sick with food poisoning due to a dodgy curry!" McVeigh smiled and simply said "Yes I know."

Before they went for lunch Cartwright felt that it was only polite that McVeigh and Green should be introduced to each other, it was a small introduction and the meeting was over in less than five minutes. After they had left, Barry Green wondered to himself why he had not been invited out to lunch and why had Cartwright looked so pale and worried.

The two men ate in silence in a pub just round the corner from the station, it had been a heavy morning for both men, there was a lot to get their heads around. The meal finished; McVeigh broke the silence that had been throughout the meal. "Do you believe in the afterlife Henry or apparitions, ghosts, de je vu, precognition or whatever the fuck this might be?"

It was a simple enough question but one that Cartwright found difficult to answer immediately and with no thought, eventually after summing up everything in his head he spoke, "I haven't given it much thought dear boy, too much going on with the living, let alone the dead." As soon as he had uttered the words he regretted them, here sat a man before him who had not even been able to attend the funeral of his wife and twin boys, murdered by the same man that had killed his first wife and maimed his first child.

McVeigh sensed Cartwright's embarrassment "It's fine Henry, no need to walk on egg shells around me, I'm not about to be carted off to the local nuthouse, though I cannot explain how I knew about the things we discussed this morning but I'll try and make sense of it all."

Cartwright called over the waiter and ordered a bottle of Jameson and two glasses, he had a feeling this was going to be a long afternoon. Cartwright listened without interruption as McVeigh spoke and the more, he talked the more he believed him.

"Whilst in hospital in the coma on more occasions than I can remember, I was in a brightly lit corridor with several doors, none of which had handles. At the far end of the corridor was a bright light but however hard I tried to make my way up the corridor towards the light, the distance was not getting any less, then I would be back laying in my hospital bed. After I came out of the coma and started to recover, I was told by the medical team looking after me that I had been resuscitated at least fifteen times, so it's safe to assume that I was in this corridor at least fifteen times and each time they pulled me back, back from the brink of death."

Cartwright nodded and poured more drink "Go on…"

McVeigh sipped at his drink, other than a few glasses of wine in Spain with his evening meal he had gone months without alcohol and he was already feeling light headed.

"In the beginning I used to wake and see Emily and the boys at the end of the bed, all immaculately dressed, Emily always made sure the boys were smartly dressed, we would have normal conversations, the boys would even jump up on the bed and give me hugs. Emily would kiss me before she left. But then towards the end of my induced coma, Emily and the boys would still be at the end of the bed but on these occasions, they would be covered in blood, bruises and ripped clothing, black ash and burns all over their bodies, on these occasions there would be no hugs, no kisses and no words." Cartwright reached out and put his hand onto that of McVeigh's and patted it slightly, "Go on dear boy, you are doing well."

"One day I was visited by DC Daniel Phillips, he was with Emily and the boys, he was dressed in shorts, trainers, and a running vest, not one of his normal Saville Row suits. I knew he was a keep fit fanatic, his white vest was blood stained, with a black hole in the middle of his chest, a bullet hole and half of his head and face on the left side had been blown away."

Cartwright gulped down his drink and poured another, he'd told McVeigh that Daniel Phillip's had been shot twice but not that it was once in the chest and once in the side of the head, he also had not mentioned that Daniel Phillips had been wearing running gear, he broke out in a cold sweat, he suddenly felt nauseas and took out a handkerchief to dab his brow.

McVeigh looked at how the colour had physically drained from Cartwright's already pale face in front of his eyes, it was pure white, a deathly white. He topped his friends' glass up, both were now a little tipsy, perhaps that was the best way to handle this.

When Cartwright had got some of his colour back, McVeigh felt it safe to continue without putting his friend at risk of a heart attack or causing him to collapse in front of him.

Henry Cartwright just looked blankly at McVeigh, had he gone bonkers or was what he was saying clearly feasible, either way he knew that he was getting slowly bladdered.

McVeigh interrupted his train of thought as Cartwright poured yet more drink.

"Here is how I see it Henry, I feel that Emily, the twins and Daniel cannot move on, dare I say in the spirit world, unless justice is served. What if Daniel was showing me what happened after his death? Will Marcus and his son eventually be going after the remaining four X-Service owners, or because they fucked up by killing Daniel, after all it was dark and they were only going on the car registration number and address alone, they thought it was Daniel's father getting into the car, Daniel died because of mistaken identity. If they had seen the news after the shooting, they would know that they had got the wrong person, maybe it's thrown them, the guilt might be too much and they won't pursue taking revenge on the others".

McVeigh paused and took another drink of a quickly depleting bottle.

"I am no expert on how a killers mind works and what triggers it Henry, but that is what I honestly feel. We know that the Directors at X-Service Recruitment are safe from harm for now, the murders that I was investigating, albeit in my head, my mind, all took place within three days of each other, and Marcus Jones was apprehended on his way to Norfolk to kill Edward Phillips within a few weeks of the four killings. Although it has been five months since Daniel's death that does not mean the directors at X Service Recruitment are out of danger and that they may well be a target soon for Marcus Jones and his son.

It is fair to say, and please do not ask me to explain because I don't know how any of this is possible, but Daniel wanted me to witness the murders in reverse order."

Cartwright and McVeigh sat in silence, neither one of them daring to talk, both of their minds working overtime. It was Cartwright that broke the silence and that was only to call the waiter over for another bottle of whiskey.

CHAPTER THIRTY-FIVE:

The following morning and with both men nursing hangovers from hell, McVeigh and Cartwright met with Superintendent Green. They kept the explanation for the arrests that were to be made that day as simple as they could, after all Cartwright had nearly popped his clogs the night before through shock and disbelief, even questioning whether McVeigh had over indulged on box sets of Randall and Hopkirk (Diseased) whilst he was recovering.

As far as Barry Green was concerned Cartwright simply told him that they were acting on information from a reliable source.

Officers from St Albans police station were to go to Marcus Jones home and arrest him on suspicion of murder, another group of officers from their own nick were to go to Camden Town and arrest Erik Jones as well as doing a thorough search of his flat for the memory stick and any other incriminating evidence.

When Marcus and Erik Jones were safely in police custody, they were to be transferred to Norfolk Police Headquarters in Wymondham to be interviewed by the police investigating the murder of Daniel Phillips.

McVeigh along with DC Johnny Miller, who had been drafted in from another station along with several other police officers, were to go to X-Service Recruitment. Cartwright had applied and got a search warrant without having to give too much away, the fact he and the magistrate had been golf buddies for a quarter of a century meant the warrant was issued without too many questions being asked.

McVeigh and Miller, backed up by a dozen or more police officers, stormed in to the X-Service Recruitment office.

The receptionist almost wet herself with fright as they burst in.

McVeigh and Miller headed immediately to Cross's office, Cross had the phone in one hand and was trying to do up his trouser zip with the other when they entered and from the little conversation McVeigh heard he knew it was Cross's brief on the end of the line. McVeigh, rather none to gently, snatched the phone off him and slammed it down on its cradle.

Monica Watson came crawling out from under Cross's desk and was as beautiful as McVeigh had remembered, albeit she was a slut and want to be thief, she went to walk out of the office, not embarrassed at all by being caught under the boss's table.

She smiled at the handsome DI before her, she didn't know why but she had a feeling that they had met before, the young DC with him bore a resemblance to someone she had met before also, but she could not quite place where.

The DI called her back as she approached the door, "Before you go Miss Watson, I believe that you have a key to Mr Cross's apartment, perhaps you could give it to me, I would hate to have to arrest you for going to his apartment and tampering with potential evidence before my officers can get to search it."

Monica Watson did not question how the DI already knew her name, or the fact that he knew she had a key but it concerned her. She had pre-empted that if she and Cross were ever to split up, that she would be out of a job and out on her ear in a heartbeat, that is why she had an additional copy of the key made to his apartment. So, she quickly obliged with the request knowing that she would still have access, she went to her office retrieved the key from her bag and came back to give it to McVeigh smiling broadly as she did so. McVeigh felt the stirrings down below as she walked towards him her braless breasts showing through her red silk dress. He thanked her and she was excused from the office.

About an hour after the police raid, Monica was interviewed by WPC Mary Barker and satisfied that she did not know what Cross and his fellow directors were up to and certainly not having taken part in any wrong doings she was allowed to leave.

Monica quickly grabbed her handbag and made a hasty exit for the door and when she was out on the street, she hailed a cab to take her to Holland Park.

Cross sat annoyed and angry at the officers that were ransacking the other offices, taking hard drives and files away to a waiting police van, "What the fuck is this? What is going on? We are a legitimate business and charity, where is your search warrant?" Miller took the warrant from his pocket and smiled as he handed it over for Cross to examine, he then produced a set of handcuffs.

McVeigh stood in front of Cross with his arms folded. He looked at the man, the disgust on McVeigh's face evident to see.

"This is all a front is it not Cross?" McVeigh asked motioning with one arm around the office "The charity, the recruitment agency. You took homeless people off the street? Gave them accommodation, a job or did you recruit the right people to do your drug smuggling and supplying for you?"

Cross looked livid, his face red with anger, he stood up and started shouting at McVeigh "What the fuck you going on about? I'm going to make sure you are back walking the beat by the end of the week you fucking idiot!"

McVeigh smiled and then laughed out loud "Of course you will you moron", McVeigh threw the photograph of the five dead drug smugglers taken six years before, it landed on the desk in front of Cross. "These men were found dead on the property of a well-known Columbian drug cartel. The five men were all on the books of X-Service Recruitment and five weeks before their deaths, X-Service Recruitment transferred ten thousand pounds into each of their bank accounts."

Cross slumped forward his head on his crossed arms on the desk, he could not believe that this was happening.

McVeigh placed down a picture of a man in a tuxedo holding a champagne flute in one hand, "Do you know this man Mr Cross?" Cross glanced up and looked briefly and apparently uninterested in the photo, it was only after McVeigh repeated the question that Cross shook his head and uttered "No."

McVeigh placed another photo of the man in the tux down. This one showed the man and Cross also in a tuxedo, arms around each other's shoulder smiling broadly for the camera.

McVeigh looked down at Cross, "That is Frank Gosling, but you know that don't you, not only did you smuggle drugs for him, you laundered money through the agency for him too, add in to the mix that you were half-brothers, both sharing the same poor excuse of a father".

Enjoying seeing the defeated man in front of him McVeigh continued.

"Putting the accusation of the drugs aside, in nineteen ninety-two you were responsible for the deaths of Claudia Jones and her six-week-old daughter, you, along with your colleagues who are also fellow X-Service Recruitment directors, and the officer investigating the crash DCI Edward Phillips all covered up what really happened that day. For his part Edward Phillips was rewarded with a fifth share in this company I believe."

McVeigh was looking at Cross, he truly looked like a beaten man and had now slumped back in his chair not believing that he had been found out.

McVeigh was struggling not to smile but as a professional police officer he knew that he had to hide his delight in seeing Cross suffer. So it was in a professional manner that he read out the charges to Cross.

"William Cross you are under arrest for causing death by dangerous driving, being in possession of an illegal firearm, illegally importing and distributing banned substances and money laundering. You do not have to say anything but, it may harm your defense if you do not mention when questioned something which you later rely on in court. Anything you do say may be given in evidence. DC Miller, cuff this prick and get him out of my sight."

McVeigh chose to ignore Cross's continued rantings and instead summoned in officers to take away Cross's computer hard drive and search filing cabinets. Once he was alone in his office he sat in Cross's chair and wished that Monica Watson was under the desk.

CHAPTER THIRTY-SIX:

October 1971

Even at eight years of age William Cross knew that living in Shepherds Bush was not the life for him. He had never met or known his father and his rock in life was his mother, this despite the fact that she was addicted to drink, drugs and could barely look after herself let alone a young son.

William lay on his belly on the front room carpet playing with his three toy planes, just plastic toys, but to him they meant the world. As soon as he was old enough, he would join the RAF and become a pilot, of that he was certain.

When the front door bell rang for a second time in the high rise flat, he shared with his mother, despite it being two in the afternoon it was apparent that she was not going to raise from her bed to answer it.

He reluctantly left his prized possessions and barely being tall enough to reach the lock to answer the door he struggled, but eventually managed to prise the door open.

The man that stood on the doorstep was well dressed in a suit that looked to be of the highest quality and expensive, not your C&A or charity shop quality that you would associate with other men in this area.

Frank Gosling smiled broadly at the young boy before him. "Alright kid, your mother in?"

Frank was seated on the worn sofa in the front room waiting for the boys' mother to get herself out of bed and greet her visitor.

Frank looked at the boy, who in between running back and forth to the bedroom to wake his mother, was playing with his toy planes.

Frank could not believe how much the lad looked like him when he himself was that age, but as they both had the same father this was no surprise.

Frank Gosling had discovered this fact whilst going through paper work associated with his deceased parents that he had found in the flat in Poplar. A simple letter with a picture of William as a baby and a copy of a birth certificate clearly naming his own father, Gerald, as the child's father. After some investigation the mother and her son were tracked down to this address. It turned out the mother worked behind the bar of a pub his father used to frequent and a brief affair followed.

Frank Gosling, despite his tough guy character was not like his father, this boy William playing with his aeroplanes blissfully unaware of who this man was and who didn't know it yet, but Frank was going to take care of him and his mother, change their lives for the better.

Frank was getting increasingly annoyed about how long the mother was taking to emerge from her comatose sleep. So much so he contemplated going in to the bedroom and dragging her out of bed by her hair. He had heard that she was a junkie, a piss head and brass. Well, she had something coming to her for sure.

The boy's safety was paramount to Frank, she would be given two choices, clean up her act and accept the offer of the silver spoon he was offering or fuck off and Frank and Mandy would adopt the boy. Frank knew enough bent social workers and had lawyers on his payroll to make the latter happen.

Grace Cross eventually emerged from the bedroom after her son was relentless in his pursuit of rousing her from her bed. Frank could see the needle marks in her arms straight away, she looked like she had been dragged through a hedge backwards. Her dyed blonde hair matted and roots on show; her bones visible through the yellow, blue and black bruised skin that marked her body.

Frank knew that the woman before him was going to be a challenge to get cleaned up and to step up as a mother, but he owed her the chance to prove herself to him.

Grace Cross slumped down in to an armchair, it was even more worn than the sofa, she kept glancing over at Frank, but had yet to acknowledge him. She reached for her cigarettes and lighter off the coffee table and lit one up, coughing up her guts in the process.

William had manoeuvred across the floor so that he was now playing at his mother's feet. During her coughing fits and drawing on her cigarette she playfully ruffled the boy's hair, "Go and make mummy a cup of tea sweetheart, have you had your breakfast?" The boy jumped up instantly, "Ok mummy, yes I had cereal" and with that William went scurrying off to the kitchen.

Frank could see that despite her appearance and addiction's, Grace and William had a close bond.

With the boy out of the way and ear shot Frank leant forward on the sofa, "I am Frank Gosling, Mrs Cross."

Grace put the cigarette out in the ash tray and immediately lit another one, she drew deeply on the cigarette and exhaled the smoke loudly, "It is Miss Cross, I know who you are, you are the spitting image of your father, the bastard that knocked me up and left me high and dry, what I don't know is why you are here."

Frank smiled softly, "I am here to offer you a chance to turn your life around Miss Cross, that boy in there is my brother, well we have the same father, it's not his fault or mine who our father is or should I say was."

Grace was intrigued, the man before her, although the spitting image of his father at least appeared to have a heart, something his father never had.

It was Gerald who got her reliant on drugs and was also the one who had her out on the streets selling her body so she could keep using the drugs that she had become addicted too. "Go on, I am listening Mr Gosling."

William returned with her tea, she took it from him thankfully and asked him to go and have a wash. The boy did not question his mother but set to the request.

Frank could not help notice how unlike other children of his age how obedient and polite the boy was.

With William out of the way once more, Frank lit his own cigarette, "I want to be part of the boy's life, I am nothing like my father where it comes to family at least, William is blood, I want to see him regularly. I have an offer for you Miss Cross but you need to clean up your act."

Grace laughed out loud, and with anger in her voice "Clean up my act, it was your fucking father that got me addicted to drug's Mr Gosling, and pimped me out all over the smoke!"

Frank remained calm, he knew that what she said was true "And it will be me that gets you off them, and there will be no more walking the streets for you."

William returned after his wash and carried on playing with his planes as Frank Gosling talked at length to his mother.

Frank had spelt out to Grace that on the promise she could get off drugs and booze, she would be given his old flat in Poplar above the bookies to live rent free, it was fully furnished and decorated to the highest standard, Mandy had seen to that. In addition to that she was to work in the bookies, with an above average wage. Her hours would work around school times and even during school holidays, William would be in the flat above her so she could still work. He would also ensure that she received a weekly income of fifty pounds to help towards William's upkeep.

It took Grace less than one minute to give Frank an answer and a little over a week later she and William were moving in to the flat in Poplar.

Grace had attended her first of many counselling sessions for drink and drugs addiction, again paid for by Frank. She had not had any alcohol or taken any drugs since the day Frank paid her and William a visit.

Frank visited William every week without fail, each time armed with an air fix model of an aeroplane.

He would take him out for the day, sometimes Clacton or Southend but mainly because it was William's preferred destination of choice, it would be Duxford, the Imperial War Museum, or museums closer to home. William always had a desire and need to learn.

Grace had cleaned herself up as promised and now looked totally different from their first meeting, quite attractive in fact, she had acquired a long list of admirers who would come in to the shop on the pretence of having a bet just so they could chat her up but would also lose their hard-earned wages on a flutter.

As William grew older, he and Frank had developed a close bond, William enjoyed spending time with his brother along with Mandy and their children too.

At the age of seventeen he went off to join the RAF, despite Frank offering him a job in his firm, but from an early age the RAF was after all what he had wanted to do and Frank could not compete with the boy's dream of flying aeroplanes.

Frank, Mandy and Grace were at William's passing out parade, Frank as proud as any relative there. But then when William was posted abroad, he and Frank saw less and less of each other but this was only to be expected.

When William left the RAF, it was Frank that gave him the business unit at half of its market value for him and his colleagues to set up in business. It came at a cost of course.

Within weeks of setting up the agency Frank was getting William to use the best recruits to do drug runs. Europe initially, mainly Amsterdam, then further afield, Mexico, Columbia, etc.

Ex-servicemen were professional and less likely to panic in a situation where others might. Apart from one incident in Columbia where five men had gone missing the operation was a success and was run like clockwork.

The other side of the business enabled Frank to launder money through the firm which was undetectable.

Property was purchased to house the homeless and money was used to do up the properties, the dirty money was used to buy the properties and pay for builders etc at an exaggerated price. All in all, it was a very lucrative business.

CHAPTER THIRTY-SEVEN:

McVeigh opened his desk draw. He pulled out the manilla envelope that had been placed there all those months ago. It contained all the names and addresses of the places that Gosling was using for various crimes including money laundering.

He then placed his hand back in the draw and pulled out a white envelope which was unsealed, he pulled out the letter within. It was type written by Daniel Phillips and the envelope was addressed to the Editor of a leading London based newspaper.

The letter stated that following several police raids over the last few days on many various London businesses that were all associated with Frank Gosling, information had come to light that to secure a lighter sentence, Frank Gosling had done a deal with the Metropolitan Police and had become a police informant.

The letter was unsigned.

McVeigh sealed the envelope and placed it in his suit jacket ready to post in forty-eight hours after the police raids had started to take place.

He afforded himself a smile and whistled softly as he headed to the briefing room where over three hundred police officers were gathered to receive information of raids that were to take place all over London simultaneously at six o'clock the following two mornings.

***

Marcus Jones was restrained and led away by psychiatric nursing staff.

He had during the interview admitted to shooting Daniel Phillips but swore that it was a case of mistaken identity. It was dark and the car he was getting into was registered to the intended target Edward Phillips.

When the investigating officer sadistically told him during the interview that it was likely that Daniel Phillips was his son after the affair, he had had with his mother, Marcus Jones broke down. Once the information had sunk in, he then went absolutely berserk and it took six officers to hold him down and eventually restrain him.

Eventually, the on duty medical officer was called and was able to give him a sedative, he was then sectioned under the Mental Health Act.

Six weeks later Marcus Jones was found dead in his cell, he had hung himself with a sheet tying it to the bunk bed that was in his room.

A public enquiry took place four weeks after Marcus Jones death and details emerged that there should have only been a single bed in his room and that unfortunately he had not been put on suicide watch.

Measures were put in place to stop a similar incident happening again in the future.

***

Henry Cartwright and DC Johnny Miller sat in the prison investigation room, opposite them Frank Gosling sat with his brief.

The charges to be brought were read out by Henry Cartwright, Gosling was charged to stand trial for the killing of Natasha McVeigh and the injuries to her son by dangerous driving, arranging the murder of Emily, Jason and James McVeigh and also arranging the murder of Joe Whyte even though the body of Joe Whyte had yet been discovered, he was also to be charged with the murders of Joe's girlfriend Sandra and the taxi driver.

Cartwright took great pleasure in telling Gosling that he should expect to receive a full life term and that he was never going to see daylight outside of a prison ever again.

The screws led Gosling away, he remained emotionless but had the look of a man defeated, a man whose reign of causing terror into the hearts of thousands of Londoners had come to an end.

***

The cell door slammed shut behind William Cross, he threw the bundle of prison bedding and clothes onto the lower bunk bed, he slumped down on the edge of the bed, his head in his hands and cried.

In total he had received sentences amounting to thirty years to run concurrently, the judge ordered that he serve a minimum of twenty-five years. To add insult to injury his three fellow directors were all given suspended sentences for their part in the crash all those years ago.

The CPS did not have enough evidence to bring charges against them for the drug smuggling or money laundering.

They had all signed identical witness statements to say that Cross was the instigator and had managed to keep it from them by having two sets of accounts. One set of accounts being used for their benefit which were only produced at board meetings.

The remaining three directors were now free to run the business alone whilst he rotted in prison.

***

The evening of the day that McVeigh had seen Daniels father in the office with Barry Green, Edward Phillips had flown back to his villa to be with his wife.

After Daniel's funeral, Edward Phillips and his wife had gone to their villa abroad to mourn the death of their only son. Edward would fly back once a month to deal with personal matters and to get an update on the investigation in to his son's death.

They quickly returned back to the UK when Daniel's killers were arrested, yet little did they know what would be waiting for them.

From the moment Ex Deputy Chief Constable Edward Phillips walked through arrivals at Gatwick Airport to find Henry Cartwright and two armed offices waiting to arrest him, he had been planning for this moment.

It was the day of his trial, but like a Japanese warrior he had decided to die with dignity rather than face the shame of a trial.

His wife, in the months after the death of their son, had become a changed person rarely being in the same room as her husband and she withdrew into her own shell.

After the charges were brought against her husband, she snapped out of her depression and walked away from her husband and their marriage.

What hurt him the most was her telling him that his beloved son Daniel was not even his real son, he had never once suspected, it was like she had ripped his heart out with her bare hands.

He lay on the bed, the blood was pouring more quickly from the slash on each wrist now, it would only be a matter of time before unconsciousness overcame him, with that unconsciousness would come relief and he would no longer had to live the hell he had been doing.

The bottle of whiskey he had drunk along with the tablets he had swallowed for double security were helping with the pain.

Slowly but surely the room began to go darker as he slipped into unconsciousness.

Edward Phillips was found dead the next day by officers sent out to arrest him for not turning up in court.

A photograph of his son was found lying on his chest.

CHAPTER THIRTY-EIGHT:

Joe Whyte stood outside on the balcony of his flat in the Isle of Dogs smoking a cigarette and waiting patiently for the arrival of Sandra who had called to say that she was on her way in a cab.

He stubbed out the cigarette and was just about to go back inside when he noticed the two men stood beside a white van just outside the perimeter of the flat's car park.

Even from a distance he recognised them instantly as the Douglas brothers but Joe remained calm, cool and collected, he even allowed himself a smile.

Out of all the hit men that Goose could have sent to wipe him out he had chosen dumb and dumber! They had the muscle alright but were as thick as two short planks.

Eventually, Sandra in the black cab pulled up and he answered the intercom in a cheerful mood.

Just as he got in to the taxi the white van screeched in to the car park blocking the cabs exit, the Douglas brothers got out, machine guns in hand.

Joe pulled Sandra onto his lap and kissed her passionately, she expertly undid his flies and released his cock with one hand whilst moving her panties to one side with the other, he easily slipped into her, violence always gave Joe a hard on and Sandra, who loved cock, had no idea that Joe was using her as a human shield. It was then that the bullets had started to penetrate the cab, so at least Sandra had died happy.

When the firing stopped, the rear door of the cab was pulled open and the Douglas brothers grabbed what they thought was a dead Joe Whyte and hauled him across the flats car park before throwing him non to ceremonially into the back of the white van. They were under strict instructions from Frank Gosling to give him a half decent burial at least.

The journey to Epping Forest didn't take too long, Joe was shot once in his chest, Sandra and the taxi driver had taken the brunt of the bullets and luckily the bullet in Joe's chest had narrowly missed his vital organs. He would need treatment and soon before he bled to death, but he knew a doctor nearby who could help with that without too many questions being asked and for the right price.

Dumb and dumber had thrown their weapons into the back of the van in easy reach of Joes grasp.

As they drove along each bump in the road causing Joe excruciating pain, Joe quietly reloaded the guns with fresh magazines that luckily were also to hand.

When the van pulled to a stop, the back doors were opened and the look of bewilderment on the Douglas brother's faces was priceless, Joe, a gun in each hand, fired until the guns magazines ran out.

Joe left the dead Douglas brothers laying where they fell and drove the van at speed but in some discomfort back to the city.

After the doctor had treated his wound's and having a set of keys to Sandra's apartment in his possession, he holed up there as the flat car park in the Isle of Dogs was crawling with police investigating the shooting.

He was being nursed back to health and being waited on hand, foot and mouth by Meryl until he was well enough to head out to Europe then on to Columbia three weeks later.

As a parting gift to Meryl, Joe gave her the keys to Sandra's apartment along with the combination number to the safe. He knew that Sandra had no known relatives and as long as Meryl paid the bills that would come in Sandra's name, she should be able to live in comfort for some considerable time.

***

Monica Watson walked in to the trendy wine bar in Fulham just round the corner from where she lived.

As usual she felt every pair of eyes in the bar on her as she walked to a table.

She sat and the waiter came over and took her order, surprised that she only wanted an orange juice. She was one of the bars regulars and he had seen her down anything up to two bottles of wine in one session on more than one occasion.

With her drink in front of her Monica opened her bag and took out the photo and smiled at the image of the baby growing inside her. She hoped that it would be a boy, she needed it to be a boy. A daughter would be seen as a threat to her, Monica needed to be the centre of attention. A girl would give her to much competition especially if she was as beautiful as her mother.

The one thing Monica was certain of with this pregnancy was that the baby would not be kicked out of her like the last one. But as her father was now dead thanks to Monica extracting revenge, history would not be repeating itself.

***

Jamie Bennet walked into the shower room, he could not believe that he had waited so long for this moment and now it was here.

Bennet was a big muscular lad, at nineteen he had the brawn but not the brains, his father used to joke that he was a plastic toy short of a Happy Meal.

Bennet blamed Frank Gosling for the death of his father Peter, if Peter had not shot dead the undercover copper and fled abroad, he would have still carried on with the treatment for prostate cancer, would still be alive today. This and the fact that Gosling had belittled him in the restaurant that time was enough for him to be stood here now waiting for Gosling to emerge from the shower.

Gosling had lost face in prison over the past few months, the hit on McVeigh's wife and kids was seen as unnecessary, you did not go after innocents whatever the husband had done.

Rumours had circulated around the prison that Gosling was now a police informant this meant that it was not just Jamie that wanted Gosling dead.

Gosling's bodyguards were in on this too, which is why Jamie Bennet was allowed to walk into the shower room unchallenged.

Gosling walked from the shower cubicle drying his hair, he looked up and saw Jamie standing there, "Oh it's you, wondered when we might bump in to each other again Jamie, how you doing son? Sorry to hear about your dad, he was a good man Pete, one of the best"

It was then that Gosling clapped eyes on the make shift knife calved from a toothbrush in Jamie's hand and sniggered, "What you going to do with that son, pick the bits out my teeth? Walk away while you still can, one shout from me and my boys will be here in a flash and beat you to a pulp."

Jamie just stood and stared and then laughed, "Your boys? Not anymore Gosling, see we all think that you are a grass, that and a kid killer, oh and let us not forget me dear old dad, he is dead because he saved your fucking bacon, now you are going to pay."

Before Gosling had time to say or do anything Jamie quickly lunged forward, taking Gosling by surprise, the first movement of the make shift knife caught Gosling in the throat, the second in the chest.

Gosling, despite his own size but without the assistance of his guards, was no match for the brute strength of Bennet and was soon lying on the shower room floor, unable to defend himself as Bennet stabbed him over and over again

The sixth blow went through his heart, and even though he was long dead and the make shift knife had snapped in two, prison wardens pulled a blood splattered Jamie Bennet off him twenty minutes later as he was still stabbing, kicking and punching Gosling.

Gosling lying on the tiles of the shower room was unrecognisable as a human being.

EPILOGUE:

McVeigh sat in the restaurant opposite his son Robert, his face beaming with love and pride.

Robert had just told him that once the family home was repaired from the damage the explosion had caused, that he would move in with his father on a permanent basis.

If this was not enough news to make McVeigh smile, Robert had also said that he wanted to join the police force if he could get through the medical that was.

Through hard work and physio his arm was getting more and more back to one hundred percent of its full use.

He did tell his father though that if his application was successful that he wanted no favours in climbing the career ladder and through shear hard work and determination, would make his own rise through the ranks.

McVeigh had agreed but did not let on that he had no intention of giving his son a leg up in the first place.

***

Winston, the auxiliary nurse, and McVeigh met at a West Indian club in Hackney on a Friday night.

The rum was flowing and despite the fact that this would not normally be a place that McVeigh would frequent, he found that surprisingly he was enjoying himself.

Winston and his mates were great company and McVeigh felt he was able to laugh for the first time in months.

It had gotten a bit serious too when they had all related to him stories of how they had arrived from Jamaica on the boat all those years ago, hearing what they had left behind and what they had to endure over the years with racism and not having two pennies to rub together began to put life in to prospective for McVeigh.

Despite his own troubles and woe's that he had had to endure over the years, there were always other people to relate to who had been through hell as well.

At five o'clock the next morning and as promised all those months before, Winston and McVeigh sat on the back of a milk float heading in the direction of Winston's place with the promise of a spare room for McVeigh to sleep it off, that and the fact Winston had bragged that his wife made the biggest and best full English in London, he was right on that one as a stuffed McVeigh slumped down on the bed in Winston's spare bedroom and slept solidly for ten hours, it was the first time he had slept so well since he was a teenager.

THE END

A note from the author

A big thank you to all of you that have purchased my first novel "In Reverse Order"

I carried this book round in my head for over fifteen years eventually having the time to put pen to paper and write it.

The outline of the story in my head, stayed the same for most of the fifteen years but even I did not predict the twists and turns until I was actually writing it.

Please leave a review on the Amazon web-site good or bad (Preferably good).

I am in the process of setting up a website but in the meantime if you wish to contact me you can email me at bobbydavisonauthor@gmail.com.

I would like to hear your feedback on the novel and I will endeavour to reply to all emails.

I have summarised my next three novels and these can be found on the next pages.

Thank you once again

Bobby Davison

Coming next from Bobby Davison

Coincidence:

Coincidence tells the story of a boy growing up in Belfast. After seeing his twin brother killed at the age of eight accidentally by a British soldier, Sean Connor grows up despising the British Army and vowing revenge.

By the age of eighteen Sean has become a member of the IRA and works his way up through the ranks becoming one of their leading soldiers.

Sean is IRA through and through, but it soon becomes apparent however that not everyone within the IRA ranks is happy for him to be there.

To make matters worse after twelve years since it happened, the identity of the British soldier who killed his brother is revealed and Sean sets off to seek his revenge.

When he arrives at the house of the former soldier on the outskirts of Manchester, Sean discovers a catastrophic blood bath.

Sean starts to think that he has been set up.

Was it even the right soldier? And who got there before him and is trying to set him up for hideous crimes that he did not commit?

The Right-Hand Man (Joes Story):

A sequel to "In Reverse Order" The Right-Hand Man tells the story of Joe Whyte, Frank "Goose" Goslings best friend and right-hand man.

The story starts in Manchester where Joe grew up and gives insight in to his life and as to why he killed his brother and ended up in borstal where he meets Frank "Goose" Gosling.

The story reflects on time spent after borstal in Goslings gang and goes on to cover what happened to Joe after he fled abroad following the unsuccessful attempt on his life.

Just like "In reverse order" there will be many twists and turns before the end.

The Personal Assistant (Monica's Story):

The Personal Assistant is the third and final instalment of "In Reverse Order" and covers the life, from a young age of Monica Watson who first appeared in, "In Reverse Order" as William Cross's personal assistant.

Like "In Reverse Order" there are twists and turns as the reader discovers why Monica became the person that she did in a life full of abuse, deception and greed.

It portrays her life from the age of three leading up to the time she starting working at X Service Recruitment and what happened to her after Cross's imprisonment.

Printed in Great Britain
by Amazon

81762337R00183